Strawberries Are Free

W. T. O'Brien

This is a work of fiction. Names, characters, businesses, places, events and incidents are either the products of the author's imagination or used in a fictitious manner. Any resemblance to actual persons, living or dead, or actual events is purely coincidental.

DEDICATION

To Julia, who inspired me when I most needed inspiration.

And to Melinda, who inspired the letter that grew into this manuscript.

Prologue
i

Rachel, dressed in his judicial robes, sat strumming his fingers on the desk and periodically looking up at the clock on the far wall. When Strawberry came through the door he came to life, "Where the hell have you been, it's almost .."

"They won!" Strawberry was more excited than Rachel. "McNee — they won, seven to two, I've been reading the transcript, the Chief Justice rendered the majority opinion. He might as well have been directly quoting the arguments made by Spencer Dawes, Dawes was amazing. You know, almost all such cases are decided by the briefs submitted by petitioner and respondent, but without Dawes' oral arguments this one was a toss-up. He shredded the other side."

Rachel wanted to say something like "that's light years away from us, who the hell cares," but didn't want to damper Strawberry's high. "Okay, great Straw -- but how about getting back to matters at hand, you're due in court in five minutes, this is a capital case after all."

"Uh, yeah, but I can't do it, I can't .."

"What the hell !"

"You know I don't believe in the death penalty, how can .."

"Christ, not that again. Do you think your super hero Spencer Dawes believed all the crap he had to throw out to win his case, no way — but it was his job, now you have a job to do."

"I don't want my name appearing as a death penalty prosecutor."

"These are only preliminary motions today, I'll get you out of there in five minutes, someone has to present the state's case, and that would be you."

Tony rushed into the office, "Let's go guys, game time."

"Straw's trying to back out."

"Bullshit, let's go Straw." Tony casually walked around behind to usher him out, then forcefully "After over a year of federal and state negotiations, pardons, time and effort, there's no stopping this locomotive now. Let's go Straw!"

ii

On this bright summer afternoon Alec was leaning on the hood of his car looking down at a two-story building below, further down was a small lake. It was a serene setting, with ducklings toddling after mother through lily pads near the shore, and a few small boats interspersed and drifting around a lake surrounded by homes with yards of green grass sloping to the shore. Alec had never imagined living in such a docile environment, and questioned his own decision about doing so at this point in his life.

Another car, with a Manor Realty insignia stenciled on the side, pulled up and parked next to his car. An attractive middle-aged woman got out and approached Alec, "Admiring your view?"

"Yes, admiring and wondering."

"Only natural to be wavering about such a life-changing event, but I have no doubt you'll love it here."

She let it sink in, and when he didn't respond, "Shall we go down?"

"Sure."

Susan Seales had been a realtor for over ten years, she knew all the schmoozing was over, it was now time to close the deal. She marched down the walkway, briefcase in hand, to the two story condo, Alec in tow. There was a split set of stairs, ten steps down to the lower unit, she took the flight of ten stairs up to the door of the second unit. It was open, they strolled through the vacant condo to the kitchen where there was a pair of stools beneath an extended countertop. She opened her briefcase and cluttered the counter with a raft of documents with "sign here" tags stuck to them. Alec and she had been through them all with the realty lawyer two days before, but Alec was not quite ready then and had postponed the finalities. He was now committed and made quick work of it, only scanning the forms to refresh himself before affixing sixteen signatures, the last with a sigh of relief.

Susan looked over at him, preparing to say something, Alec seemed puzzled about it. "Well, just one last detail .."

"Oh, of course, be right back." He dashed out to his car and grabbed an envelope from the glovebox, then dashed back to the condo. He heard a pop as he reentered. Susan had produced a bottle of champagne from somewhere and was pouring into two plastic cups when he walked in and handed her a certified check. She looked at it and thanked him with a smile. "A toast to you and your new home."

Alec had never seen signs of humanity in Susan, she was all business from day one. Her appearance was manicured, even down to the designer streaks of light grey in her dark hair. They drank a couple of toasts and made trivial conversation, then she was off, promising to come by to see how he was doing after a few weeks, a promise both knew would not be fulfilled.

Alec nursed the last of the champagne as he blankly stared out the window overlooking the lake. He had spent the last four and a half years on a whirlwind tour around the country, testifying as an expert witness against mostly local communities trying to hang on to the status quo, and also being second fiddle to his lawyer Spencer Dawes at speaking engagements sponsored by upscale universities. But the cause célèbre from the Supreme Court decision was on the wane, and after the initial thrill of importance had gradually become stale he knew it was time to come back to earth. As of today he was a property owner, he was invested in the community. He knew he didn't want to return to his former life of investment in nothing.

He only wondered, "What now?"

iii

Strawberry was hard at work, researching a legal matter for Kammy Lee, the local barber. Except when seeing clients at his small office in the municipal building he worked from home, he had access to legal websites not available to most users. He thought he heard his doorbell ring, but knew he was mistaken until it rang a second time, it was the first time he could remember that happening. He went to the front door and was surprised to see Rachel waiting there for him, he invited him in.

"I don't think I've ever been here, this is nice and cozy."

"We don't get a lot of visitors."

"Oh .. so how are you and Terry D getting along."

Strawberry answered slowly, "Uh … fine."

"Are you working, did I disturb something?"

"Yeah, I was working."

"Something for Tony?"

"No, Kammy Lee has a problem."

"Oh, what's it about?"

Strawberry stared at Rachel, then "What's this all about Rach?"

Rachel took some time. "Did you know your time is up?"

"My time?"

"Yes, your time — Mayor Ben knows your time is up, he sent me here to fetch you."

"Oh."

"We're all worried about you Straw."

"Why, haven't I been doing my job?"

"Nobody's ever complained about your work, everyone appreciates what you do, that's why we're worried — we don't want to lose you. But to say you've been morose would be an understatement. Do you keep up with your monthly therapy sessions, have you talked to Tony or Betsy lately. Betsy is very good."

"I don't need .."

"You do need .. I'm okay with it, I'd wait for you to snap out of your funk, but Mayor Ben will not wait. You can't stonewall him Straw."

Ten minutes later they entered the office of Mayor Ben Whitlock. It was a large office, but with very little in it other than a lot of space. From over fifteen feet away the gruff voice of Ben echoed, "See you later Rachel."

Rachel took the cue and silently left, Strawberry sauntered in toward Ben's desk.

"Rachel told you why you're here." Strawberry nodded. "Good, have a seat and we'll have a little chat. So, have you made any plans for the future?"

"No, only what I've been doing."

"Well what have you been doing then — when I look at you all's I see is a miserable human being. Why are you so miserable?"

"I'm not."

"Well then why do you look so miserable. You've gone steadily downhill since the trial, that was what, four years ago."

"I didn't want to prosecute, everyone knew that, I .."

"Yeah, but I saw it coming even before the trial. I blame myself really, I thoroughly vet everyone I recruit, but I took you on after one quick interview — I needed a lawyer and .."

"You always say you needed a lawyer, I would think there'd be lots of lawyers in the system."

"Oh you bet, there are. I've interviewed more lawyers than any other brand, and a more mendacious lot could not be found, they were all a waste of time. And then there you were, virtuous in comparison. You fooled me Straw. You hid something from me that my antennae are honed to decipher. So, what is it, what's your big bugaboo."

"I don't know."

"Don't fucking continue with this bullshit boy!! .. Okay .. okay, don't talk to me, talk to someone else then. Otherwise you are gone in one week. Now get the hell out of here."

Strawberries Are Free

I

Alec sat in his 2012 Limited Edition Tesla Model S Sedan, acquired two years earlier and newly fitted with a battery and rail adapter. The fall clouds hung thick and threateningly low in the sky as he looked up at Max's house and reminisced on his two tours of residence there. They were college buddies when Max was endowed with a loan from his builder father to purchase the old two-story house in Miller Park, a dark neighborhood on the east side of Capitol Hill, one of the seven hills, like Rome, on which the city of Seattle is built.

Max Zastera was never a serious student. Both he and Alec recognized that this purchase was likely to be the beginning of a career move for Max, as indeed it turned out to be. The dilapidated stairs and porch, and the chipped and peeling paint on the outside walls were a standard for the area. The inside was old and drafty, and spacious, but the price was right for Max, the rent for Alec was cheap, and the relatively close proximity to the U-Dub was the closer.

Alec recalled his first encounter with a neighbor while sitting on that porch eating an apple on a sunny spring day some twenty years before. He had watched a tipsy, middle-aged, black man slowly saunter from down the street to the house and stumble his way up the stairs to knock on the front door, not noticing Alec only ten feet away. Alec ahemmed loudly to get the man's attention, but remained sitting as the man finally noticed and approached.

The man stammered rhetorically, "Youse prejdezed against black folks ain ya." Not waiting for or needing an answer he turned and walked to the other side of the porch and slowly peed off the ledge. He then descended the stairs and ambled back down the street. No other words were spent.

This recollection reminded Alec of a second, both of which projected negatively about other residents although there were never any serious episodes, mostly just avoidance. The people across the street, who were never actually seen as they must have used a rear entrance, had a fenced yard which was patrolled by a seriously large Doberman. It was young and menacing, but when it managed to leap the fence and come across the street, which once done was repeated daily, it turned out to be a playful lamb. Max and he became frolicsome buddies, the dog spent most of the day in and out of Max and Alec's house. But this didn't last long, as the Doberman was replaced by two large pit bulls, thankfully too heavy to negotiate the fence. These two were not about to be befriended by neighbors. It almost seemed cruel to stand close to their fence and watch these dogs bark themselves into a lather.

The stairs and porch Alec now ascended showed little resemblance to the original. Max had replaced the woodwork some years after occupation, everything was now smooth, neat and shinier than the well-used Custom Remodeling van parked in the driveway. Alec walked right in the unlocked front door and was greeted by a waft of warmth, and by an approaching mid-sized dog of mixed breeding that at first barked but quickly turned puckishly friendly.

It was a considerable living room with a leather sofa near the center facing a large t-v screen hanging from the north wall. There were two other stuffed chairs surrounding a table with a bronze iron lamp, the shade with Seahawk colors and logo. Off to the left against the wall was Max's office, with a desk and two filing cabinets next to the door to the kitchen, from which came a black man munching on a piece of toast. He looked to be in his thirties, a little shorter than Alec, with a thin frame and thin face that lit up pleasantly when he saw Alec coming into the room.

His voice belied his smallish physique as he boomed a friendly, "Hi, you must be here for the game .. I'm a neighbor, stopped to see Max, Sy," and extended his arm.

"Sihugo, uh Sy. Alec, yes, here for the Seahawks, is Max around?" Alec clumsily converted his open hand for the fist bump.

Sy was initially somewhat taken aback, but then quizzically "Do you know me man — what did you call me?"

"Oh ya, sorry, just a name from the past, Sihugo. Sihugo Green was an old NBA player. He had the distinction of being the first player picked in the 1958 draft, right before Bill Russell."

Sy was now even more perplexed. "Hey man, what are you doing to me man?"

Alec didn't know what to say. "I didn't mean nothing, just making noise, .. is there a problem?"

Max came in from the kitchen. "Alec, long time, how you doing Scuff?"

"Maximilian!" Alec and Max converged into a warm hug, while Sy slinked over to the door and the dog rubbed against Max.

Max saw Sy leaving. "Hey Sy, did you meet Alec?"

"Ya, we met .. I gotta go now," as he left the house.

Alec inquired, "What's Sy's last name?"

"Green, why?"

"You know his middle name?"

"Uh, ya, let's see .. um."

"Is it Hugo?"

"Ya, that's it. How did you know that?"

"Jesus."

They were interrupted by the entrance of Porter Nash as the weekly Sunday football party was renewed after a four year hiatus. Porter had taken those years to add two kids to the now family of five, which made it problematic that he would be a weekly attendee. He was a handsome and solidly built man, keeping in almost as good shape as when he was a high school linebacker. Porter knew everything to know about the wildly successful Seahawk teams of the past, and even the current crop which had drifted into mediocrity. He and his wife were both middle school teachers and were devout Christians, he had taken the family to Sunday services prior to the game. He and Alec had been teammates on an intramural U-Dub basketball team in their freshman year, and had become fast friends. Porter was good natured but extremely humorless, which made him the brunt of many a joke, most of which he didn't see coming or going.

Rick Kirby was a late arrival, getting there just before halftime. He, too, was a happily married man, which was no surprise to Alec. Rick was the intellectual of the group, purposeful and methodical. He got a job working for the city out of college, and was methodically working his way up the ladder. Tall with a rugged face that featured a slightly hooked nose, he married a well-to-do but modest sorority girl eight years his junior. No kids, but surely they were in the master plan. He had run for state senator the year before, and was the clear favorite, his upset in the end was instituted by a media blitz from his opponent.

They sat around and had one more beer celebrating a Seahawk win, not the revelers of the past but enjoying the moment more sedately.

Alec looked over at Porter. "So, Missnash, I hear your wife has hatched two more since I last saw you, up to seven kids now are ya?"

"Uh ha ha ha ha ha, I haven't heard that name in like forever." Max unleashed one of his patented guffaws, famous for their intensity and the unbridled joy he took in them, they were usually infectious to others too. Missnash was Alec's personal nickname for Porter whose achromatopsia subjected him to wearing a black, brown, green and purple combination on a double date. The girls were quite amused, and Alec, to Porter's chagrin, further amused them with his concocted appellation.

Porter was not to be allayed by Max. "Shit, hatched, you should have a little respect, Cici's not a hen for Christ sake."

"Hey Port, you shouldn't use such language right from church. I know Alec is famous, but he's not yet a god. Well, I could be wrong about that, maybe he has a few more miracles up his sleeve."

Alec felt some discomfiture starting with the gibe since he saw Porter so seldom. "Sorry Port, bad joke. So, anyway, how's the family, what is Colley, first grade now?"

"Try fourth. He's almost eleven and big for his age, going to be trying out for flag next week."

Alec wanted to say something like "chip off the old block," but decided not to stir up any more potential acrimony. He let the others talk on about family and stayed out of it. When there was a break he turned to Rick, but Rick beat him to the floor. "So, what you been up to since the big event, you really out there giving speeches bigshot?"

After a pause without an answer, Alec sidled into a pensive tone. "You know, I do have something new in mind, and you are the genesis. I've been thinking about your run at Olympia."

"It wasn't much of a run, more like slow motion — and that moron Robarts is turning into a total screw up."

Max could tell that Alec and Rick were about to get serious, and he wasn't about to wait. He had been bored many a time once they got going. "Port, you want to see some of Smokey's shots of the new buildup from inside Mt.

St. Helens? They're pretty amazing, even for a drone." He headed over to his desk computer. Porter followed, after a sneer at Alec.

Once they left the couch, Alec continued, "Didn't you tell me you were outspent by about ten to one. So, where did his money come from? No one who knew the prick would give him a cent, which brings me to the point, why not limit the monies that can be donated from sources outside the district a candidate represents?"

"Uh, great idea, but, well, it's a free speech issue, money being considered speech .. You certainly have evolved into a serious fuck?"

"Ya, I guess. After the flurry of the last few years I find I have little to do again. I don't want to drift back to the waste of time life that I was in before, so now I'm going to be a crusader for liberty and justice for all."

"Ya, right. You aren't still touring?"

"Very rarely, it got a little old, though the perks from it were nice .. So, who says money is speech?"

"Only the Supremes, I think it was the central theme of Baby Love."

"Oh no, Pink Floyd wasn't it?" Alec sang, "Mon-ee .. get away .. get a job with more pay."

"Are you serious about this. You trying to emulate Tom Piatt. He used to get initiatives on the ballot way back when, mostly about taxes. Got a few passed I think, though the Legislature blew them away for the most part. This altruism kick you're on must be habit forming?"

"Maybe I am developing a social conscience — can you believe I just said that. So, what you got going on now?"

"Hey, hey, you're not going to recruit me old man. I have all I need without whatever hair you have up your ass."

The party tired out not long after that. Everyone did seem to enjoy the reunion, and all promised to be back the next week. Porter and Rick left, leaving just Max and Alec.

"Your old room is still vacant," said in an invitational tone.

Alec wasn't sure Max was serious, but it didn't matter, they both knew that wasn't going to happen. Alec looked over near the desk where the dog lay curled up on its mat. "Looks like you have a roommate."

"Uh ha ha ha ha ha, Sikma, ya .. never thought I could take care of a pup, but he's pretty easy."

"So, tell me about Sy, his folks."

"Still lives with his mother and uncle up the street, never knew his father. What the hell was that all about anyway, did you piss him off or sump'n, he sure left in a hurry."

"Tell him I'm sorry."

"About what!"

"He can tell you if he wants, just tell him I'm sorry."

II

Alec had driven the eight miles from Max's to his condo on city streets rather than get on the freeway where the traffic was always bad, though less so on a Sunday evening. He had purchased the two bedroom condo on a dead-end private street well-camouflaged by large fir, maple and birch, that circled for five blocks around the east end of Haller Lake, a small lake in north Seattle. At age forty-two, this was his first piece of property and he was damn proud to own it. Twenty years earlier the builder had managed to re-zone in order to put up six condos, two each in three buildings, after buying and razing two homes that had deteriorated from old age. Alec had the top floor of building number one, noted for its high cathedral ceiling and deck that looked out over the lake. He slept in the back bedroom, but spent most of his time in the front one, more accurately his office/den, which had a window to look out of when he was at his desk and computer, as he was now. But, he found that he was a little too tired to get into anything this evening. The beer and rare sociality had taken its toll, it had been a good day.

For breakfast Alec rotated from Raisin Bran one day to scrambled eggs and sausage the next. Today it was coffee, Raisin Bran, and an English muffin with raspberry jam. He sat at the table in the kitchen nook and looked out. This was his favorite part of the year. The fall weather and moisture created an early morning fog that covered the lake making it invisible, primeval. He watched for half an hour as the fog slowly lifted off the water. At first the waterline was little distinguishable from the fog, but gradually the water became evident and seemed to turn more and more blue with time, until time revealed it all. Discrete houses surrounded the lake, built close to the shore, most with lawns and shrubbery running down to the water. Small docks, with kayaks and rowboats laying upside down on them, littered the water's edge, motorized vehicles were verboten . A transcendental and picturesque sight.

After showering and dressing, Alec was ready to attack the day. He perused some of the legal material he had accessed within the last week concerning political contributions, but he knew that a quick study would not prepare him for combat with seasoned professionals, the research was simply to try to avoid any obvious blunders. He got online and sent a skype invitation to Sig Ulrick. Sig was the financial backer who funded his legal run leading up to the Supreme Court victory in "McNee v State of Washington." Alec was always entertained by Sig's skyping, he did connect but never revealed himself, always projecting a blank wall instead.

And, in fact, did so now. "Alec my lad, good to see you, how do I rate the honor?"

"And nice to see you too, Sig, but it looks like you've put on a little weight, and what is that, snot drooling from your nose."

Sig was not amused by such drivel, he was all business. "What do we got?"

"I'm coming down to see you, be there in one hour."

"Uh, no, later, 2:00. I'll be free after that."

"Roger, see you at 3:00 then."

As Alec hung up, he received a phone call from a restricted number. He answered and heard from a male voice the terse enigmatic, "Tomorrow at 7:00, be there." He looked puzzled for a moment, and then smiled.

Sig had lived in an apartment in Denny Regrade, a community just north of downtown and south of Queen Anne Hill, for the last thirty years. He seldom left his apartment. Like many nowadays who rely on autobots, he didn't drive, had never driven, in fact. He also seldom let anyone into his apartment, but Alec had been there many times now, so that hurdle was long past. It was a rarity that they first met in a courtroom. Sig had seen Alec's initial court appearance, not there for Alec specifically, merely to find someone in Alec's predicament.

Alec punched in Sig's address on his Tesla, which gave him a recommended route, then he hit it a couple of more times for alternatives. There wasn't much difference among the top three, so Alec decided to take Aurora to 105th, over to Holman road and 15th NW, down into town via Elliot Way, then up the hill to Mercer, and take a right on Queen Anne Avenue to get to the Regrade. The estimated time was forty minutes. Alec considered this the least likely route to be cluttered with autobots. The bots were great riding the rail on the freeway, but cluttered up the city streets, always only going the speed limit. Sig had a parking spot for his apartment, he sometimes rented it out, but it was now available. That was a major boon for Alec who parked there forty-seven minutes later.

Sig was waiting at the door, the elevator had informed him Alec was on the way. He was a tall man, but with a pallid, tottery physique that made him appear much older than his sixty-six years. He had a round face and bulbous nose upon which routinely rested a pair of glasses that defied gravity as they rested on the very tip. His bearing was like Scrooge before the epiphany, his actions like those after. He led Alec to his den, the only room permitted, which had a fantastic view of Elliot Bay and all it had to offer. A bagel and cup of coffee were waiting on the table.

As was expected, Alec got right to the point. Disenchanted with the results of Rick Kirby's loss orchestrated by a massive money influx from questionable sources into his opponent's coffers, Alec felt strongly that the system was broken and had been for some time. His proposal was a simple one, limit contributions to candidates to only residents of the districts they represent. No corporate donations, it seemed inherently unfair for a stockholder in a company to have that company donate funds to a candidate to whom he had a strong aversion; the same for unions. So, mayoral candidates could only dun residents of their city, county elections only from county, state and federal representatives only from their districts, and senators only from their state. All donations would be open to public scrutiny and be closely monitored.

Sig was not impressed. "Alec my boy, after riding as a passenger on a great enterprise you now want to steer the ship, trying for another miracle. A noble idea, but not a practical one."

"I was thinking an initiative. Better and more difficult would be a referendum, but that takes the Legislature."

"And you're here hoping for money I presume. No, sorry, changing election law is not my cup of tea."

Alec wasn't expecting more. He knew he would sound like the neophyte he was, so he was not going to give up with just a few noes. "Do you know anyone who might be interested, even to help flake like me? .. Do you remember Tom Piatt?"

Sig was amused by this. "Ha ha, Tom the Pie man. Yes, we fought a few battles together. He's old as the hills now, older than me, no way he has the energy for another run, even if he liked the idea. You have no idea how much work it is, and as well-intentioned as you may be you don't have it in you. I'll tell you what though, I'll give you his number. See if he's still as wacky as he used to be."

They talked for another hour about the odyssey to the Supreme Court. Sig had taken Alec's simple traffic stop and rode it all the way. Alec was ready to pay the fine after the first failure in municipal court, but Sig was looking for a warrior to fight his cause, and he had found him in Alec. He told Alec he would pay all court fees, and hire a lawyer if Alec would be his horse to ride. It was a two year ride, through county court, then state, then federal district court, the Ninth Circuit Federal Court of Appeals, and then a year wait and on to the Supreme Court. Finally a win, and a landmark win at that. What a ride.

III

Later that evening and the next morning, Alec got online to find out all he could about Tom Piatt. Piatt had indeed been active, bringing over ten initiatives to the ballot some twenty years earlier, most to do with lowering taxes and fees. Half of those initiatives were passed by the voters, although the Legislature managed to find ways around most of those. Alec called the number Sig had given him. The first two times the connection was made but quickly terminated, the third allowed a message, so Alec dropped Sig's name and said he would call back. On the fourth call a creaky voice answered, and they introduced themselves.

Tom was reverential in his praise for the Supreme Court decision, and for Alec's tenacity in just getting there, he had obviously talked to Sig about it. After Alec assured him that all he was interested in was advice, they agreed to meet the following afternoon in La Connor, a quaint town to the north, at a restaurant where Tom assured him they would have some privacy.

The wind had been blustery for the last few days, and even though it was still very early in the fall, the trees, primarily the maples, had exuviated a sample size of what was to come throughout the season, a layer of leaves over the yard and walkways. The downstairs tenants were a very gracious elderly couple, Hugh and Joselyn Sparkman, who Alec nodded at but spoke to infrequently, other than at one of the six-family condo association meetings thrice a year. The association retained a management company which was responsive to minor issues, on call, and took care of the grounds on a schedule, but his neighbors below were frail and wary of the slick leaves on the cement.

It was an overcast but dry day, a good day to be out, so Alec procured the requisite tools from the community shed and went about some yard work. The contour off the grounds rose somewhat from the second building to Alec's, so that the entrances to his building were from a split-level stairway, unlike the other two buildings where the walkway was at a level with the lower units. The heavy outdoor broom had difficulty peeling the leaves off of the hard surface to which they clung, so he used a bamboo rake to flick them off. He limited this to the sidewalks of all three units, about thirty feet each, and ignored the parking areas, so the deed was accomplished in short order. The grounds were nicely landscaped, the well-defined planting areas around the buildings were home to a variety of shrubs. Yellow and green hydrangeas were still in bloom but fading. The rhododendra were flowerless but last year's buds were still withering on their stems. Alec set about snapping the truss of each of these buds to allow improved blooming for the following season, although implements such as gloves were too advanced for his expertise, so his hands became covered with sap not easily removed.

After cleaning up, Alec was again driving toward town along the city streets rather than the freeway. He went north to 130th, then across the freeway to 15th NE and headed south to Lake City Way, and then to Roosevelt Ave, all the way south on Roosevelt, across the University Bridge to a left on Boston Street, up to Boylston and right. This took him under the freeway, jammed as he expected, and turned into Lakeside Ave for a mile, then up Belmont Ave to Roy Street and up to Broadway, the main thoroughfare of Capitol Hill. Next, left to Aloha then right to 15th E, and another right four blocks to the Canterbury Ale House, a quiet restaurant that was at one time one of his primary dinner haunts.

Alec sat for a few minutes to relax, he was actually early

as he had allotted himself a little extra time. He wondered if anyone had ever taken that route before. He suspected not, it was a first for him. Normally, he would take 25th NE straight south, but that would take him past the U-Dub and through Montlake, a death trap at rush hour.

The restaurant was well-populated, but there was only one woman at the unattended bar as Alec approached and veered toward her. As the bartender, who was new to Alec, returned from the kitchen, Alec turned to him while motioning to the lady. "Why would you let an ancient slut whore like that into a place like this?"

The bartender blanched. It took him a bit to interpret the rudeness, then begin to get incensed, but the woman cut him off with "Well, if it ain't the rat bastard with the pencil dick looking for trouble."

Alec continued toward her and they both smiled and hugged. The bartender got the picture as Alec ordered a Mac and Jack.

"We have our regular table." Sandy had arrived early to secure it, and they proceeded arm in arm to a table in the back. .

"So, who was the pimp who set this one up?" Alec had not recognized the voice.

"Gene." Alec looked for more. "You know, Eugene Hoiberg, my husband?"

"Ah, of course, how could I have not known that. So, you finally told him he wasn't good enough." Alec had trouble holding back the smirk on his face.

Sandy was used to such banter, and took it in stride. "Gene has severe priapism, we have been forced to abandon our sex life. But he is very concerned about my happiness. I told him about you before we got married. The call he made was his idea, I didn't know about it until after, and I did not request it."

"Wow, what a guy .. but let's get back to that problem, prapisy?"

"I knew you'd want to dwell on that you bastard. Priapism — it's when a man gets an erection that he can't control, you know, it stays hard."

Now, Alec was really amused. "You mean like those old Viagra ads 'if it lasts over four hours, call the doctor.'"

"I assure you it is not funny, I wouldn't wish it on anyone, even you, oh, maybe on you. Yours might get gangrene and they'd have to whack it off, how would you like that." She said this with some venom, not amusement.

Alec waited awhile, biting his tongue, then changed the subject. "Where's the roast duck on this menu, it's a totally different menu."

"New ownership, new entrees, no roast duck. I was in a few months ago. It's good though, you can find something. They have very good lamb stew."

Prior to Sandy's marriage eight years earlier, before she cut him off, she and Alec had been lovers for about five years. It was totally carnal, sins of the flesh, and though they were fond of each other, neither wanted it to be serious. Sandy's permanent residence with Eugene was a ferry ride away on Bainbridge Island, so after their repast they retreated to her secondary residence, an apartment in a downtown high-rise. They enjoyed some lengthy, healthy sexual exercises before both settled down for a well-earned nap. Alec was now awake and was studying Sandy as she slept. She was a beautiful woman. Alec was a sucker for the exact shade of her natural reddish hair. She had put on a few pounds over the years, but was still very well-proportioned. Hers wasn't a perfect face, with thin lips and a somewhat pointed nose, but her brown eyes were alive and her intellect sharp.

She seemed to sense that he was awake, and slowly turned toward him and opened those eyes. "What are you doing?"

"Admiring the view." She smiled at that, and tucked herself into his arms. He gave her some time to awaken before he softly asked, "If you didn't know about him calling me, how did Gene get my number?"

"You don't know him well, but I can assure you he is a very resourceful guy."

"So, is he really okay with this, is this a one-timer or do I get more?"

Sandy ignored this entirely, then propped up on her elbow. "So tell me about it, how on earth did you of all people become such a hero?"

"Didn't you read the book?"

"No, I may be the only one in Seattle who didn't. I didn't want to learn the story in the abstract, I wanted to hear it from the jackass', uh, horse's mouth, so give."

Sig Ulrick had arranged to have the story published, co-authored by the lawyer, Spencer Dawes, and Alec, but embellished and ghostwritten by a professional. Sig was hoping it would provide a monetary resource for Alec for all the time he put in, and indeed it worked. The publication turned out to be a great success, mostly because of the felicitous subject matter. Alec became a popular expert witness for a variety of court cases, and was occasionally asked, along with Spencer, to lecture at some upscale universities about the whole process. These endeavors as a collective turned out to be very lucrative, allowing Alec to purchase his condo outright and pad his b-r for the future. Alec relayed his well-rehearsed tale of McNee v State of Washington to Sandy.

His weekly golf foursome had an 8:30 tee time at Jackson Park Golf Course, thus he was in a bit of a hurry to make the time as he drove from Max's down 23rd towards the Montlake Bridge and the freeway. Three weeks later, he received a citation from the Seattle Municipal Court for $236 for speeding through a twenty MPH school zone at twenty-eight at 8:01 am. At first, typically, he thought it was a mistake, even with the attached picture of his car and license plate number. What would he be doing driving around at

8:00 in the morning? Then, he realized it was on a Thursday, his golf day, and he connected the dots. Still, $236 was a formidable fine, so he requested, without professing innocence, to see a magistrate rather than pay the ticket.

Another three weeks later and he was before the magistrate whose job was to settle minor disputes without having to take them before a judge. Alec began with the argument that the magistrate had no doubt heard with every such appeal, that it was his car but you can't give a ticket to a car, only to a driver of the car, and that fact was not determined by the picture. The magistrate proceeded to load up his computer with a video that showed Alec's car approaching, the driver visible through the windshield wearing a baseball cap, and the car driving through the school zone, with blinking yellow lights flashing that stated such, at the time identified. Even so, the magistrate generously offered to reduce the fine to $120 and confirm that the ticket would not be put on Alec's driving record, thereby it would not affect his insurance. Alec should certainly have been satisfied with the offer, but no, not good enough. Alec had a buzz up his butt and foolishly was not to be placated, he wanted to have his say about the injustice of the system before a judge.

Two months later he was in traffic court. Before his turn, he watched appealed case after case ritualistically denied by the court. It was scary and ugly to watch, but it was speedy, and then it was Alec's turn. The other defendants were all nervous and intimidated, Alec also was nervous but was not about to be intimidated. When the judge asked if he was contesting the citation, he had his say about the injustice of the system, he rattled off the obvious pap akin to no to taxation without representation, and he did so confidently and forcefully. The judge listened, then told the prosecutor to proceed.

The prosecutor got to the point, asking if Alec had been driving the car at the time of the infraction. Alec asked the judge if he had to answer that question, and was told no by the judge, so he declined to answer. That produced a clamorous crack of the gavel on the sound block from the judge. "Pay the full fine. Next." Alec was stunned by the ineffectiveness of his eloquence.

As Alec sullenly made his way out of the court, lamenting that his foolish ego had cost him $116, a man in a row he was passing got his attention and waved him over. In a stupor, Alec went and sat when the man invited with "I've been looking for you, son." When he came to his senses he got up to leave, but the man, who turned out to be Sig Ulrick, cajoled Alec into hearing him out.

Sig asked Alec what his plans were for the citation. Alec looked over, then again started to his feet, but again Sig was determined to have his say. He told Alec to appeal. He said he would pay all court costs and even get a competent lawyer to take up the case. He went on to complain about Big Brother, about how currently there were cameras only at select locations working traffic violations, but eventually they would be on every corner watching everyone. He didn't want that day to ever come. He had been looking for a knight to carry the torch, and Alec fit the bill perfectly. Sig offered to buy dinner at the Georgian in the Olympic Hotel, and Alec accepted. In the end, Alec acquiesced and they made a pack. Sig would finance all the way and Alec promised never to settle.

The next venue was in King County Superior Court. Sig had already introduced Alec to his lawyer, Spencer Dawes, and they had gone over the case thoroughly at two separate meetings. This was now a real trial, but with few witnesses. Alec answered all questions truthfully except the most crucial one, "Were you driving the car?" to which he was coached to respond, "I do not admit to being the driver."

Alec was impressed by the multitude of iterations lawyers come up with to ask that same question, but they all elicited the same response. The only other witness was the original magistrate who brought along the video. Fortunately, Alec had not specifically admitted to the magistrate that he was the driver, although he didn't deny it either, at that time it was obvious, but not stated. He said that he could recognize Alec as the driver from the video until Spencer showed him photos similar to that in the video. They were of three different people in baseball caps, the magistrate could not distinguish between the three. The crux of the arguments had little to do with Alec. It was the question of whether law enforcement could use cameras to issue tickets to the owner of a car. They lost the case in Superior Court.

On to the Washington State Supreme Court six months later. Spencer Dawes turned out to be a near genius, which Sig already knew because he had written voluminous briefs for the court, and had all the precedents down pat. The state's lawyers were good, but no better prepared than Spencer. Again they lost, and it was on to the United States Court of Appeals for the Ninth Circuit in San Francisco a year later. They were prepared to fly down to the Court when the process was suddenly halted. The Ninth Circuit had already heard two similar cases in the last two years. The first was won by the plaintiffs and the second was lost. The Ninth Circuit had submitted this for potential action by the Supreme Court, and, lo and behold, they had taken it up. Such cases were being litigated across the country, and the Supreme Court decided to act. It was like winning the lottery for Sig.

"And the rest is history. The experience was fantastic. The proceedings were fascinating. Spencer Dawes was brilliant. The Justices were regal. There was no direct testimony, so I was only a spectator, the process was all about the submitted briefs of the lawyers and the defense of those briefs in oral arguments. Commentators and journalists are always talking about the politics of the Justices, to me, they were all apolitical in this litigation. And we were victorious, a seven to two decision. The Chief Justice wrote the majority opinion. McNee v State of Washington was hailed as a landmark decision because it had such a profound effect on ordinances in every state of the union. They all need to figure out if they can still be using traffic cameras, and many of the large cities were working with drones to monitor traffic and give out citations."

After this soliloquy, Alec finally looked down at Sandy. "I'm surprised you're still awake."

"The story was great, and the way you delivered it with barely a breath was amazing."

"That was the short version. I've given this hundreds of times, trials, lectures, you name it."

"Who'd a thunk it, the least ambitious person I ever met turns out to be famous."

Alec let it go for a bit, then queried, "So, I didn't get an answer to my last question." Nothing from Sandy. "Well, I'm getting ready to be even more famous, if you are .."

IV

Alec slept in until 10:00 the next morning after leaving Sandy's apartment well after 2:00. He was due in La Conner to meet Tom Piatt at 5:00 in the afternoon, and decided to go up early to tour the town beforehand. He was on the road just before 11:00 for the two hour ride north. He got on I-5 at 145th and had only a short wait to get on the rail. His Tesla had already passed the rigorous tests necessary to get clearance to ride the rail, and he had created a Bubble account a few weeks before. The traffic at this time of day was minimal and there were gaps on the rail, as usual in the city, so he had little wait to get on. About half of the vehicles on the rail were Bubblebots, the others were a mixture of more expensive autobots, and a variety of conversions of personal vehicles like Alec's.

Bubblebots were not so named because of their shape or design but because they were built by Bubble Automotive. The owner, Winston Bubble, was a visionary. He had owned a company that supplied automotive parts for the large automakers, and with his son, Gabriel, and daughter, Vanessa, had spent years working on a self-driving car, the Bubblebot. He wanted to build a somewhat smaller car with few advanced features, yet with a solid chassis that was aerodynamically state-of-the-art, to be priced cheaply for every-man, a modern day Model T. His Bubblebot was perfected a few years after the larger companies such as Tesla, Ford and Toyota had entered the autobot market, but it soon found its niche and sales were healthy after a few years.

Winston had bigger plans in mind. His factory was located in Skokie, Illinois where he had built up a good deal of influence. He bargained with local government to allow him to build, at his own expense, a half-mile lane on the shoulder of Lincoln Avenue, Highway 41, where he installed the first beta Bubblerail. His team redesigned the Bubblebot to add an arm beneath the bot which would connect to the electrified rail and thus provide power for the bots. This technology was routine compared with the more difficult task of controlling the autobots once connected to the rail. Software was created to allow one main computer to have access to each of the individual autobot built-in computers and control them on the rail through that master computer. This included monitoring all facets of the individual autobots through their computers, most importantly the tires and brakes. The course for the lanes of this new arterial consisted of three components, the rail down the middle, not unlike that of a train, and two tire tracks, each exactly two feet wide.

Originally, the tire tracks were made using common blacktop, but it became apparent very soon that blacktop would not hold up since all wheels were using the exact portion to the track, rapidly degrading it. Winston put together think tank with Allen Myers, an asphalt supplier, and Union Carbide, which eventually came up with a double asphalt composite mix that was a vast improvement. It was triple the expense, but the arterial used only about one tenth the surface area of most highways. He also made an arrangement with Goodyear to supply a hard rubber tire that had a six inch wide, flat surface. His own company rebuilt the wheel casings, adding enhanced bearings to lessen resistance.

After a year of testing, the Bubblebot rail debuted before a host of local businessmen and officials. There was a great deal of commuter traffic between Skokie and Chicago, mostly via I-90 and I-94. Winston sold the collective on the idea of building a ten mile rail on Highway 41 between Skokie and Chicago to ease the traffic burden. His company would supply the rail and the autobots, the consortium would deliver the arterial with tire tracks and handle any easement legal battles. A year later it all began, and was an instant success. Even more of a success once Winston added a new feature he had not envisioned until he saw the system in action. He attached two slightly magnetized six inch by two inch metal plates horizontally to the front and rear bumpers. This allowed bots driving at speeds around eighty mph to abut each other in transit creating, as Winston referred to it, a Bubblebot Bubbletrain. The Bubblerail went viral throughout the country. Two years later the first intercontinental link up, à la the 1869 Transcontinental Railroad, near Pierre, South Dakota, was completed.

Winston was a good businessman as well as an innovator. Although he had ten patents, and more pending, he did not want to fight off lawsuits from other envious automakers who would try to test those patents, so he gave linkage technology to the rail and any other expertise he could provide to qualified competitors. He only wanted to control the conductivity on the rail itself, which he did manage to monopolize.

Alec punched in his destination. The Bubblerail computer told him that the sixty mile trip to Mount Vernon would take forty-seven minutes, and his account would be billed. The billing was not only based on miles, but also for wear and tear on the rail. Alec's round, old fashioned Michelin tires, great for roads and tight turns, took more of a toll on the tire track than the more flattened tires on autobots designed for the rail. He lowered the car seat to a near vertical position and soon was napping. It seemed like he had just shut his eyes before the computer told him he was five minutes from his destination.

Alec exited the rail and was soon headed west for the

twenty miles to La Conner on Highway 20. Having four hours to kill, he decided to take a detour further west to Deception Pass, a narrow strait that separates Fidalgo Island on the north from Whidbey Island to the south, two of the main islands south of the San Juan Islands. Thirty minutes later his drive had taken him over Deception Pass Bridge. He was drinking coffee and munching on a tuna fish sandwich he had purchased on the way at Howard's Corner on Fidalgo, while taking in the breathtaking view of the Strait of Juan De Fuca and the San Juan Islands to the north from the state park at the north end of Whidbey.

There was a flyer littering the ground, he picked it up and happened to take a look before it hit the trash. On it was written the nefarious story of Ben Ure who, in the 1880s, was a smuggler of Chinese immigrants onto the mainland for generous sums of money. He was known for these activities, but had special knowledge of the tides around his home base near Deception Pass, and was mostly successful in avoiding capture. When he was trapped, before he could be apprehended, he would cast the booty who were tied up in gunny sacks overboard, attempting to avoid legal complications. The bodies were taken by the tides and many deposited on San Juan Island in what was to become known as Dead Man's Bay.

Alec lingered for about a half-hour, then headed back north, then east, then south towards La Conner. La Conner is on the eastern side of the Swinomish Channel, a ten mile long, three hundred foot wide, salt water slough that slices Fidalgo Island from the mainland. The channel is navigable for the most part, though it needs to be dredged at the southern end every few years to remove the sediment that builds up. La Conner is a quaint town of about one thousand souls. Originally a fishing village, it morphed into a tourist attraction with the aid of a vast array of artistic notables. It has a bustling main street with a variety of restaurants, art galleries and gift shops. Festivals such as the Tulip Festival, in nearby Skagit Valley, the largest tulip growing area in the world, seem to be a regular occurrence.

Alec was well aware of this history because he had lived only a little south of there in Stanwood when he was fifteen. He remembered seeing future Country Western Hall of Famer, Bonnie Raitt, perform at the 1980's Lounge in La Conner. He had many times walked down one side of Main Street stopping in all the shops, and then across and up the other side of the street, and he did so again this day to take in any changes. There were few. With this, he had managed to while away the day sufficiently so that it was now almost five.

Scheduled to meet at Ruby Sue's Tea and Treasures for dinner, Alec was surprised to see that it was not a restaurant. He wandered out to the deck which overlooked the channel and the Swinomish Reservation across the way. A few groups were there partaking of liquid refreshments. He leaned against the railing and looked back at Ruby Sue's. There was a somewhat smallish man staring at him, smiling. He had a round, ruddy, moustached face, beady eyes with layers of wrinkles beneath, and light thin hair. He reminded Alec of Teddy Roosevelt.

Alec wandered over and was greeted with a jovial, "Yeah, you look like a tin-horned city slicker."

"And you look like you should be panning gold in the Sierra Madres."

They had a robust laugh and handshake after which Tom motioned Alec to follow. They went into the gift shop and through to a door in the back which led down some stairs to a small private dining area below the deck. There was a pine table flanked by two benches with padded seats and backs under a window looking out at the same view as was seen from the deck. Tom went into the adjoining kitchen and pulled two Coronas from the refrigerator, opened them and brought them back to the table.

"That was sumpin' else, that trek you made all the way

back there to the Capitol .. sumpin' else, sumpin' else. I never had so much fun reading the paper before — golly damn that was great. Sig musta been in hog heavin. I wisht I coulda seen 'em when they give the verdic."

"Ya, it was a great. I was just there for the ride .. it was a great ride."

"Doin sell yurself short, boy, do'n do that. What ya did was brave boy, very brave, bet you wanned to giv up lots a time."

Alec nodded at that.

"Sig was the juice, Spence, that Spence is one great la'yer ain' he — Spence was the brains, but you, you were the man. They was workers and you were the man .. it's your name up there ain't it, McNee v, you neva needs do anythin again afta that, you did it boy."

Alec didn't know what to say to that, but he didn't have to when Ruby came down the stairs. "You ready for your dinner, Pie?" She bent down and gave Tom a full kiss on the lips, then gave Alec a peck on the cheek. "So who we got here?"

"He's the man, Rube, Alec, as in McNee v .."

"No, he's Mr. McNee? Well I'll be, and just a kid too. You're famous around here Alec. Pie didn't talk about much else the last couple of years. We gotta get Zinnie down here to give him a good time Pie. Is Zinnie around?"

Alec couldn't see himself, but had little doubt he'd ever been redder.

Ruby continued, "Well, look at you Alec. We gotta get Zinnie. You guys do your business, and I'll find Zinnie after I get your dinner. I got liver and onions Pie." Tom perked up at that, but Alec did not. "And I got a nice rib eye with trimmings, you look like a medium rare."

"Sounds good, thanks."

Alec and Tom settled down and drank their beers, Tom got them seconds and then Alec got current. He told Tom the same narrative he had told Sig the day before. When

Alec was finished, Tom mulled it over for a bit. "Sounds like a great idear, I'm all for it. My hole career was in tryin' to keep money outta the gov'ment. So, do it."

"Do it, do what? I have no idea what to do."

Tom thought some more. "I'm jus' a cun'try bumkin, but I ain' no cun'try bumkin. Six of my inits was passed by the peeple. Three were ov'turnd rye away by the legisla'er, the other three become law, but two years aft' they was as well as gone too. Soes, I say go for a constudinal amendment. They can' igore them."

"That requires the legislature."

"S'right, two thirs both and then to the peeple. Don' thin' we's ever ha' one yet. But this ain' a dem or pub issue, soes got a chance. You know Corey Rassmuss'n, sta' sen'tor from Pyalip. Good man, talk at him."

They had finished their second beer when Ruby brought in the food. Alec's steak was fabulous, as were the caramelized yams and the salad, a variety of which Alec had never before seen and didn't know the ingredients. They ate in comfort. Alec turned down a third beer, he could ride the rail from Mount Vernon but he had to get there first. They talked only slightly more about Alec's project, but Alec was somewhat in a hurry to leave before Ruby showed up with Zinnie. Alec was out of practice and Sandy had thoroughly worked him over the previous night. After a couple more "you're the man's" from Tom, he was on his way.

V

The next morning Alec called Sig, as he had promised, to tell him about the meet with Tom Piatt. Sig was loath to have lengthy remote conversations, but had already talked to Tom who gave a raving review about Alec. Tom also said Alec's project had great potential, he encouraged Sig to give a hand. Sig was still skeptical, but said he would give Spencer Dawes a call and broach the subject with him.

Corey Rasmusson held the state senate seat for the 25th District out of Puyallup as a democrat. Alec called the number Tom Piatt had given him, and wound his way through a maze of automated options until he was eventually able to leave a message for Corey, dropping in the name Tom Piatt. He much-doubted that this would lead to anything, and so tried online where he found a website dedicated to Corey. He left a similar email but was not confident that anything would come of that either. He decided to slow the pace and give it a few days.

That afternoon he wandered out to Drifty's, a poker room he frequented in down times, just north of the city limits where mild forms of gambling were permitted. There were three games going, one limit Omaha, one limit hold'em, and the third nolimit hold'em. He recognized and knew many of the players, and he recognized many others who wore different faces. Having gone there, he now wondered why he had done so, all of a sudden it was a very depressing place and all of the players were complete losers. Those who managed to beat the game, an impressive feat with the huge rake snagged from the pots, were losers because it allowed them to continue wasting their time and energy on nothing of value. Those who played because they enjoyed playing, win or lose, were compulsive and helpless, often very nice individuals with families and jobs which they short-changed. And then there were the lowlifes, guys who drooled over the game, over the idea of being able to beat the game, almost always broke and trying to drum up a stake however they could.

Alec often developed a soft spot for the later. Eddie came to mind. Eddie was a constant, basically a nice guy who was deeply flawed. He looked up to Alec, who was a regular winner, with puppy dog eyes waiting for a scrap from his master. Alec would occasionally offer up that scrap so Eddie could get in the game. Then, one day Alec tapped out at the same time Eddie was on a heater, splashing and having a great time. Busted but wanting to play some more, Alec swallowed his pride and asked Eddie, still at the table, for $50. Eddie, without looking up, said no, he never loaned out money to losers. When he saw Alec walking away he was beside himself, he quickly got up and apologized profusely. He had money in hand to give Alec, but Alec declined. He decided he would give it up for the day and left Eddie crestfallen, unable to help the hand that fed him.

As he was heading out he bumped into an old acquaintance, Judd Hemmings, a former poker player and U-Dub grad. "Hey Judd, how goes it, you still playing?"

"Ah, no, not for a long time. I came in to make a bet with Slimpy Ross. I think the Hawks are good this year, they're getting 3 this week at Minnehaha, I'm on 'em. Hey, I read all about you, amazing story Alec, great job. I always hated those fucking cameras too. You back here spinning cards?"

"No, just dropped in the take a look, a little depressing now."

"I'm with you there. I took up a more sophisticated game myself, bridge, been playing a little duplicate."

"Bridge .. I played a little back at the U, seemed a little

slow to me."

"Yeah, maybe, I'm into it though. Hey, there was a guy in here looking for you awhile back, said he was an old friend of your buddy Porter, didn't look like one though. He find you?"

"Uh, no, don't think so, what'd he look like?"

"Twitchy little guy, skinny, had a German name, Sch .."

"German, hunh, what'd you tell him?"

"Schmidt, ya, that's it — told him Porter taught at some high school, that right? I guess he found you then."

"I guess so .. hey, good to see you, Judd, I'm outta here."

"Later."

Central Market, about a mile away south on Aurora Avenue, was known for high quality and freshness. Alec was normally a two day shopper, get enough for dinner today and tomorrow, then back again. He seldom ate out alone because he preferred to prepare his own meat and potatoes. His purchase this day was a rotisserie chicken, pound of ground round, couple of large russet potatoes, Jewish rye, tapioca pudding, spaghetti sauce, eggs, sausage, six-pack, asparagus, Tillamook sharp cheddar, and a salad bar salad. As with almost everyone, he preferred the human touch, but had to admit that the speed of checkoutbot was agreeable.

He hadn't made up his mind as yet about dinner, either chicken and rice, meatloaf or spaghetti, he would decide at the last minute once he got home. It turned out later to be the chicken. He wasn't a great cook, but he had the advantage of not being a finicky eater either, so his own cooking was good enough for him. After dinner he broke into an old Michael Connelly, Harry Bosch, detective book he had been hoarding. That and a couple bottles of Beck's got him through the evening.

VI

Another Sunday football morning. Alec had taken the same route as the previous week and was again twenty minutes early as he sat in his Tesla in front of Max's, this time reminiscing about his second tour of residence there. He had worked part-time from senior year in high school all through college at Macy's downtown, beginning as a shipping clerk and then on to inside floors moving merchandise around and building displays, among other things. When he secured his degree in economics, Macy's management offered him a permanent job as floor manager of the fifth floor, beds, mattresses, furniture, rugs, linens, and bridal, primarily. It was storybook, from high school through retirement was the plan. He worked there for six years, moving to other floors at times so that he was eventually the maven of the store.

He had met Sydney two years before when she worked in the display department. She was gorgeous, vivacious and ambitious, none of which was one of Alec's attributes, but they became lovers, and she moved into Alec's Fremont apartment a year later. Then it suddenly came crashing down. Alec found out that Sydney was unscrupulous, not unfaithful to him, but to her genial boss whom she openly betrayed. Alec couldn't believe it and called her out, to which Sydney said fuck her and fuck you for taking her side. Alec had not seen Sydney since. He had quit the job and retired to the safety of Max's second bedroom.

By this time, Max was thoroughly ingratiated with his neighbors. Most of the houses on the block had been improved through Max's generosity with his carpenter skills. The area on the whole was going through a renaissance. New people were moving in and remodeling, while longtime owners took the advantage of greater home equity to refinance and make their own enhancements. Alec lived there for the next few years, shifting around, trying this and that, playing a lot of poker, had a fling at the fish business, and worked for Max when it suited him. Then, he got a speeding ticket and everything changed.

Alec was again the first one to arrive, and was again greeted by Sikma who didn't bark this time but was a bundle of energy wanting attention. Max was sitting on the couch watching an early game.

Alec went over and plopped down beside him. "No Sy today."

Max muted the t-v. "I'm glad you brought that up, what in the hell did you say to get him so spooked?"

"He said, 'Hi, I'm Sy,' and I said, 'Hi, Sihugo,' that's it." Max gave him an "and ...." look.

"You know how some names just stick with you. I read once that Sihugo Green was the first player picked in the 1958 NBA draft, right before Bill Russell. I told Sy that. That's it, that's all I know. So, now you talk, what's the big deal?"

"Sy's mother brought him to live with her brother when he was a baby. The uncle was good to Sy, but Sy always knew he was not his father. His mother never talked about the father, even now, but she did let slip the hospital where he was born in Trenton, New Jersey. From that, he tracked down his birth certificate. He has always been Sy Hugo Green, on his driver's license, Sy Hugo, but his birth certificate reads Sihugo Green Jr."

"Yowsa, what a freaking fluke — I guess I found out who his father was for him. Is he go'in looking?"

"He don't know what the hell to do about it. Works security at the downtown Sheraton, he can't just take off. He helps me out now and then too, a good man."

Rick wasn't the last to show up this time. Porter came in just before the end of the first quarter. He brought a friend, Lukas Schmidt, who grew up in Lakewood down the street from him, and who had recently returned from Montana after ten years. It was unusual to have a stranger there, but certainly not a problem for anyone. They sweated the Seahawks into another close win, this time over the Vikings, with some rowdy rooting. Maybe the Hawks would have a good year after all. They celebrated with a couple of extra beers.

Max and Porter then paired off. They had more in common than with the others as both were outdoorsmen. Alec oohed diplomatically when they foisted pictures of the two of them standing on a cliff somewhere looking down and out at a picturesque valley from the mountaintop, but, in truth, he was easily bored by them. They sensed that and they didn't push it too hard. Their mutual drone, Smokey, was the photographer.

Drones had freedom of travel in most rural areas, but had been banned over cities after a spate of air crashes which caused property damage and, in a few cases, personal injuries. And then there were the bozo hunters who made good sport of blowing drones out of the air, then bragging online about their scores. The death knell for personal drones in city traffic was from a Minneapolis crash where one hit a car that then veered into a pedestrian, causing a fatality.

Drones delivering items, usually purchased online, were allotted nighttime hours three days a week for that purpose, and the skies were cluttered. People came out to spectate, a modern version of the shooting star. Of course, drones for law enforcement were the norm. No more radar traps because drones were more efficient. They couldn't give tickets directly however, Alec had taken care of that, but they could radio patrol cars that could ticket without being an actual eyewitness.

Before retiring, Rick and Alec got together, Rick inquired about Alec's progress, and was impressed that Alec had already met with Tom Piatt and potentially with Corey Rasmusson, with whom Rick was acquainted. Impressed, but still not about to get personally involved. Lukas, on the other hand, had been listening in and took a lot of interest. It turned out that he was a lawyer, a public defender in Everett, and he offered to contribute legal advice if it was of use. He was diminutive and fragile looking, with a straight nose and thin cheeks, he said little but seemed to pay attention to everything. Alec thought his proffer odd, and was not comfortable yet with Lukas, so he let that go without comment.

VII

Through all of Monday Alec was expectant, but heard from no one. The wind was blowing and the leaves were flying, so it was fun to just stare out at nature. Haller Lake was stocked with trout and perch, along with a dabbling of native catfish, so there were always a few hardy souls out angling for them. Grounds-keeping day was Tuesday but he saw little need to rake more leaves, so he coasted through the day reading his book and mindlessly watching a football game in the evening.

The next morning he needed to talk to someone, so he called Sig Ulrick to find out if he'd contacted Spencer Dawes as yet. Sig had not. He had left a message but Spencer was not available until midweek. Sig knew nothing about Corey Rasmusson, so was no help there either. He told Alec to take a chill pill and don't call again until he warmed up.

In the late afternoon he received a surprise, a phone call from Tom Piatt. "Hey mah man, how's ya doin."

"Tom, hi .. good, nice to hear from you."

"Sig tell me you'a chompin' at the bit, tha's good boy, tha's good to hear. Can' get thru to Corey tho, eh. Tha's my faul, gave ya a bad num'er, here wri' this down, 'c-o-r-r-a-s-p-u-t-i-n at smg.com.' Ya got that."

"Yeah, corrasputin at smg.com."

"That'll get to 'em, tell 'em I sen' ya. Hey boyman, when ya comin' back to visit?"

"Well, I have been thinking about it."

"Sur ya has, I kno's why, tha' Ruby is fam'us fer her cookin' tha's fer sure, an she got some fam'us fren's too, thas fo real sure .. hav'n a good time tha's wha'ya thinkin' bout, ain't it?"

Alec stumbled a little. "Well, I .."

"Hey, neva min', jus memba, you always wel'com. Lemme know wa's happ'n, k. Yous' the man, Alec, yous' the man."

Alec was pretty sure Tom put on the hick jive talk just for him. He ratcheted it up with this call, but he could probably recite Shakespeare verbatim. Tom was right though, Alec had been thinking about Zinnie, wondering what that was like. He hadn't heard back from Sandy, but he wouldn't expect to this soon anyway, their liaisons had always been spaced out. He would like to be able to initiate, but that was not the historical arrangement, he would have to wait on her. He wasted no time in sending a message to Corey, asking to make contact and merely hinting at the subject matter of his concern.

Corey responded later that night with "Sorry to have missed your earlier messages, have heard good things about you from Tom, and will be available at home for a skype call Thursday evening, number 253-744-3453-5448. Let me know if that works for you. I'm looking forward to meeting you. Corey R."

Alec responded immediately, confirming his availability that time and day, and that he would make the call.

Thursday morning it was back on the phone to Sig. "What's this, I thought you were going to chill."

"I did chill, but now I'm hot again. I've been corresponding with Corey Rasmusson, we're going to meet via skype tonight. I need to know if I have anybody with me. Did you hear from Spencer perchance?"

"Yes, he's around now, I think he finished a case yesterday. But, you know, Spence is not just a paid mouthpiece, he'll listen but he will only come onboard if he thinks there's a chance."

"Christ, don't you think I know Spencer by now. I want

to hear his ideas, but he isn't the one who needs to be sold. You are Sig. I know you think it's a little wild, and I know you know I'm just a fucking amateur, but you've been helping, and then not helping. I need to know, Sig. I want to tell Corey we've got the same team going."

"You're getting a little big for your britches, son. Talk to Spence .. bullshit, Corey." Sig hung up abruptly.

Alec knew that he handled that conversation badly, he may have lost Sig permanently. He was quite disconsolate, he did need to cool down. He decided to hit the outdoors for awhile, stretch out, get some exercise. The condo association owned a small dock on the lake and one of the tenants supplied a dingy for community use. It was upside down and waiting on one side of the dock. He put on some boots, a mountain down jacket and ski cap. He even found a pair of gloves, and made for the dock.

Haller is a very small lake, a glorified pond really, about fifteen acres in total, almost circular, approximately a thousand feet across in any direction. The boat was a light craft that he had little difficulty flipping into the water. The oars had been under the boat. He slipped them into the oar locks, jumped into the dinghy and launched, with the cushion on his seat doubling as a life preserver. He rowed hard and with passion for about ten strokes, which was all it took to get him winded, then started to coast with light strokes. He kept near the shore, almost without saying considering the lake's size.

Many northwest lakes are clogged with lily pads, they are mild by comparison in Haller. There were two other boats on the water. In one a man and child were fishing, so Alec stayed clear of them, but rowed up in the vicinity of the other drifting along with an elderly couple. He and they nodded hello. He pulled two laps around the lake at a slow but steady pace, admiring the modest houses and their timeworn foliage and greenery, about twenty-five minutes in all, before replacing the skiff and going in.

An hour later Alec skyped Spencer Dawes. Spencer was not backwards like Sig and Tom. He did not mind being seen, though he was old-fashioned and natty, wearing a bow tie while at home in his private office. He was of medium height, solidly build with a square face highlighted by bushy dark eyebrows and full graying hair.

Alec felt awkward at first, but soon launched into the same spiel he delivered to Tom Piatt the previous week, even though he knew Spencer had heard it from Sig. In brief, limit political donations to individual residents of the district being represented. He took a breath and sighed, "Spencer, have you talked to Sig today. I think I really blew it, I got excited and got in his face — stupid, just stupid."

"Ahh, don't worry about Sig, he likes you, Alec. He's proud to see you doing this, although like me, he thinks the idea is dubious. You'll be bucking the money men, men like Sig, except they are not necessarily noble. Many legislators are honorable, and they would like to limit the whoring necessary to get elected, but their number one objective is just that, getting re-elected."

"I'll be talking to one tonight, Corey Rasmusson from Puyallup. Apparently he has some clout, and one of his issues is campaign reform."

"Even if a miracle happens and the Legislature puts the question to the people, and even if the people vote it in, not a given, there is still the elephant to deal with."

"Yes, I know, the feds."

"Numerous cases have taken pot shots at Citizen's United, none have succeeded, this amendment would be a direct hit not a pot shot."

"Yeah, well, about time, don't you think."

Spencer laughed, a rarity. "Yes. About time. But."

"So, Spencer, are you up for another miracle?"

"As Sig often says, I'm just a paid mouthpiece. If Sig goes, I'll go."

"Thanks, Spencer."

VIII

When Alec was working at Macy's he was regularly asked to golf by Cale Fazzio, the office personnel manager, and despite his limited exposure to the game he eventually agreed to play, one time. Alec had two siblings, a six years older brother, George, and a two years older sister, Pamela. Before moving to Ballard in Seattle, prior to his junior year in high school, the family had lived out north in Stanwood where there is a quality golf course, Kayak Point. George had worked there over the summers and had become a competent golfer over time. He had taken kid brother, Alec, out on a few occasions, but it never really stuck with Alec who became insecure about his abilities when he saw George pound the ball out a hundred yards farther than he could. Alec's parents waited until he got out of high school and divorced shortly thereafter. His mother moved back to Stanwood, his father disappeared for five years and reconnected from Arizona only by rumor. George married and moved to Portland where he provided Alec with a niece and nephew. Pamela remained in Seattle, but they were not a close family, he seldom saw her except on an occasional holiday with their mother in Stanwood.

Cale was not so intimidating as was his brother. He was an average to good golfer with a twelve handicap as a men's club member at West Seattle, one of three good golf courses maintained by the Seattle Parks Department. The other two were Jackson Park in the north and Jefferson Park on Beacon Hill. The one time game turned into a once a week game. Cale introduced Alec to quite a few other players, mostly from the men's club. Susan Carlson, an accountant from Boeing, and Hack Fulton, management at the Port of Seattle, eventually filled out a regular Thursday foursome. They played a friendly two dollar Nassau. The other three had established handicaps, they determined Alec's each week after much solicitous arbitration, depending on the partnerships. Early in the day golf, and a subsequent lunch, was the extent of their relationship, other than an occasional summer barbecue. This year's game took a hit when Hack was temporarily incapacitated with sciatica, and the weather was particularly severe. Although Hack and Cale were year-round players, Alec and Susan were strictly fair weather, thus it appeared it was going to be a short season.

Alec called Corey Rasmusson at the agreed time, but no answer. He skyped again fifteen minutes later and Corey had arrived, slightly out of breath. "Alec .. hi, sorry I'm a little late, give me a minute." He was a handsome man in his mid-thirties, well-groomed in a suit and tie, wearing glasses, which he now took off along with the tie, while unbuttoning the top two on his while tailored shirt. He left the screen for a minute, came back and sat down putting a newly opened beer on his desk. "So, hi again, it's Corey."

"Hi, Alec McNee."

"Alec, yes, I know a friend of yours, Rick Kirby. And I believe you know my sister, Angela."

"Angela, no .. what, from Macy's?"

"Yes, she uses our mother's maiden name, Nelton."

"Oh, that is a surprise. Well, anyway."

"Yes, Pie mentioned you have an interest in election reform. I read your book but saw no indication from it that you are an activist."

"I am the same doofus from the book, but it was ghostwritten. I had little to do with that, and I am a neophyte as an activist."

"Oh, I meant no disrespect."

"That's okay, no problem. So, should I give you what I have in mind?"

"Sure, go for it."

Alec recited again his ideas about limited campaign donations. It was simple but he expounded as best he could for emphasis.

"Whoa, that's certainly more than anything I was planning — that's one big sell. A lot of my contemporaries in both parties will balk at this. I'm pretty popular in an affluent district, but I still get most of my money from outside sources."

"My hope is to make politicians more receptive to their communities."

"Yes, yes, it will do that for sure. Constitutional amendments are rare and difficult to get since one party or even subsets of both parties can squash them easily. Don't get me wrong, I'm all for the concept, but it's naive of you to think you can get two-thirds of my colleagues to put their jobs at stake."

"There's no way I could do that. I was planning on letting you doing that."

Corey laughed at this, then, "So, what are you planning to do then. Is this just a whim because of what happened to Rick, regrettable as that was, or are you providing assistance other than counting on name recognition?"

"The exact nature of that is being worked out, and we thought we'd see what you have to say, whether you are interested in pursuing .."

"Let me think about it, talk to a few people. Of course, even if .."

"Yes, I know there will be an even larger obstacle ahead, even if."

"Well, good talking to you, Alec, quite a bit to think about. I'd love to see you down in Olympia sometime."

"Can we talk about this again?"

"Uh, sure, but give me at least a week or two to look into

it."

"Okay, Corey, thanks for the meet, later."

"You bet, nice to see you in the game anyway. Bye."

Alec waffled back and forth with himself about whether this was a positive or negative conversation. He thought about calling Sig the next morning to get his take on it, but decided against. He made up his mind to indeed chill out, no more until next week after some reflection over the weekend. He was pleasantly surprised later that evening when he got a phone call from a female voice he recognized. "7:00, tomorrow night, be there."

IX

Friday through Saturday evening Alec puttered around doing some yard work, but mostly browsing the internet, some sites out of curiosity and some for background material. The weather had abated so he went to the range at Jackson Park both days. On Friday, he hit a large bucket and did a little chipping and putting on the practice green. Saturday, he played nine holes, joining a threesome of two middle-aged Japanese men and a slightly built teenager who, with Alec, was a second walk-on. There was always something of interest in meeting random golfers, but this group less than most, although all were cordial. The two men hit it straight and short and mostly kept to each other's company. The youngster was very good, hitting it high and long. All Alec could get out of him was that he was a high school senior, number two stick at Roosevelt, trying to get a golf scholarship to the U-Dub. Alec felt challenged to at least poke one or two drives out with the kid, he had improved to about a ten handicap over the years. He made only one good connect for the nine, on the par five fifth where he got within fifteen yards or so of the green. Nevertheless, it felt good to get out and around.

Alec arrived at the restaurant rendezvous diplomatically five minutes late. Sandy was not at the bar. The place was packed so she had secured their table. There was no need to repeat salacious introductions as those from the previous week.

"It was nice to hear your voice yesterday. So, is Eugene still stuck up?"

"I've decided to allot you two slurs about Gene's condition before I smack you, knowing you can't help yourself, that is one down and one to go."

"I think I'll save the other till later, I'll probably need it. Anyway, you look lovely this evening, as usual. I'm glad you called, as it has been attempted that I be tempted by Zinnie, but I much prefer your company."

Since Sandy would always grill Alec about his activities, and get whatever of interest there was to get out of him, he decided to take the initiative. He described his La Conner trip, except for his reason for going, and she was duly amused. The waiter came and Sandy ordered a red wine, Alec decided to share a bottle with her. She ordered Tuna Nicoise, he had no idea what that was, he ordered the same lamb stew as the previous week. He had liked it and seldom gambled once he found something he liked.

"Eugene is really okay with this, and he doesn't mind that his wife is pounded senseless week after week after week?"

"Okay, that's it!"

"Wait a minute, wait a minute, that wasn't a slur on his condition, at least give me a real slur. How about:
'there once was a man with prapism
who bunked with a convict in prison
who tied up his cock
with suspender and sock
till the man was bloated with jism.'"

Sandy couldn't help but show amusement with her "You bastard, that's enough."

This time it was Sandy who awakened first. She lay comfortably in Alec's arms with her back to him. "Allie, what were you doing in La Conner."

"Ummm."

"You used to have some friends up there, didn't you?"

"Um .. can't you let anything slip?"

"Some guy, what was his name?"

He came awake, and told it all, with periodic prodding. After, she turned around and looked at him lovingly. "You really have changed, you do care, you're no longer just a body that fucks. I could almost fall in love with you now, almost. You know, Gene can help you, you should call him." She gave him a deep kiss and crawled on top.

X

Sunday football was a third straight win for the Seahawks, on the road against a playoff team from last year, the Raiders. Rick missed this one, but Lukas tagged along again with Porter, who now could name every player on the team and where they came from. Lukas endeared himself to Max who had a problem collecting from a wealthy client who, for no reason, simply refused to pay his bill.

"Rich people respect lawyers," Lukas iterated as he penned a lawsuit threat for Max. "I am now acting as your lawyer. This will get his attention."

The sense of urgency which had dominated Alec's thoughts was finally lifted. He didn't have a conversation with Sig or Spencer until Sig called him on Wednesday. It was an amicable call. Alec relayed as best he could how he thought Corey had reacted and what he might do, basically, he had no idea. It appeared to Alec from the tenor of the call that Sig was now in the fold.

That evening, a most surprising call came in from a man's voice. "Tomorrow, 8:00, on the phone, be there."

Thursday was a good day. The rains prevalent for the last weeks had subsided, and it was actually a sunny day in the fifties. Hack was better, and the foursome hit the links at Jefferson Park. The first two tee flips on the first tee pointed to Alec and Susan, and the stoke bickering began. In truth, all were glad that Alec didn't have a handicap, they enjoyed this.

"Cale shot a 79 last time, we need more," and "But,

Hack just got out of a hospital bed, we need at least two strokes," and such were the pleas this week, but there was something to complain about every time they played. Alec lost two bucks for the day, but he shot an 82, and he was happy with that.

The call came in at 8:00 on the dot. Alec answered on skype with "Hi, this is Alec."

"Alec, hi, Gene Hoiberg, nice to finally meet you."

Gene was very distinguished looking, at least ten years older than Sandy. He had a deep tan over only a few wrinkles around bright blue eyes. Despite what Alec knew, he looked very healthy, with a full head of light brown hair.

"Gene, hi — to tell the truth, I feel a little perplexed about this."

"No need. Sandy told me before we got married about your relationship, actually I already knew. I respect that you stopped it back then."

"Yeah, well, it's back, and .."

"I love her very much, she is a vibrant and physical woman, as you know. I can't satisfy her sexually, I know she told you about my problem, I'm just glad you're still available for her."

"For what it's worth, I know she loves you too. I knew it ten years ago and I know it is still the case now."

"Thanks, I appreciate that. But in truth, Sandy is not why I called. We don't have any secrets from each other, but I will assure you we do keep secrets. She told me about your current mission, and I might be able to help. If this is private, and you prefer to keep it that way, then that will be the end of it for me."

"Ah, well, I don't know what to say."

"I know Sig Ulrick quite well. He surely didn't tell you, but I assisted him slightly with your big win, though not with money. By the way, congratulations."

"This is a revelation to me — have you talked to him

lately?"

"I talk to him at intervals, he mentioned that he is looking into something startling that came out of nowhere, I suspect that would be you after what Sandy told me. I have to say, I am startled too, and very impressed. How did this come to you, of all people."

"That compliment sounds a little like an insult."

"No, no .. no offense, please. I simply never saw you as enlightened or political before."

"That's okay, I am willing to accept help from just about anyone. That probably sounds naive."

"Yes, it is."

"So, what did you have in mind then?"

"There are more of us in positions of influence than you might suspect who, in the end, have the best interests of the community in mind, although most do have secondary self-interests. I simply want to get your approval before I talk to anyone else, and then I'll work with Sig, you need not be privy to the particulars."

"Gene, if that's an offer of assistance, I accept. I actually didn't know if Sig thought favorably of this idea, I'm glad you have put me at ease on that score."

"Sig, no doubt like myself, was probably not convinced at first that you are the genesis. He no doubt suspected that you were being manipulated."

"Whoa, really, that didn't occur to me. I guess I am pretty naive."

"Stay that way. It's working for you. So, let's see what happens then. Thanks for the talk, and thanks again for taking good care of Sandy."

"Okay, Gene, bye, wonders never cease."

Alec was stoked again. At 8:00 sharp, right after his scrambled eggs, sausage, and English muffin, he called Sig. After introductions, "I got a call last night from a gentleman I believe you know, Eugene Hoiberg."

"Oh, and how did that happen?"

"Well, it turns out I have a connection, one that you wouldn't be aware of."

"I am aware."

"Aware of what?"

"Your connection to Gene."

"How could you be, what do you mean by that?"

"I'm going to do something that I never thought I'd have to do again before I died, I apologize to you, Alec. I didn't believe you. I thought someone got to you to get to me. So .."

"You checked me out — you had me followed, you son of a bitch."

Sig stayed quiet and let Alec vent, which he did some more with "I thought we had a relationship. I thought we were tight, ah, shit."

"I have to protect myself Alec. I ask for pardon once, I will not do it again."

Alec fumed to himself some more, then finally snapped out of it. "Okay, okay, I don't like it, I'm disappointed in you, but I'll get over it .. I am over it. Do you want to hear what he had to say?"

"Yes, very much. I don't suppose you know who Gene Hoiberg is, do you?"

"Let's not go there anymore, okay? He told me you are buddies, he has helped you from time to time, and he wants to help us now. He said he'd get in touch with you."

"Really? Oh, this is good news. I'm beginning to see some light. We should move now while we have some momentum. You need to get back to Rasmusson, give him another call, today if you can."

"I don't think I should call yet, he said he would call me back when he is ready, best to let him. I could send him an email reminder though"

"Perhaps you know best after all, who'da thunk it. You need to talk to Spence again too. I'll set that up."

Alec sent a terse email to Corey right after talking to Sig. "Hi Corey, wondering how it's going. We have our team in place, let me know. Alec."

He received a message back a few hours later. "Alec, good to hear from you and your team. I'm getting some good vibes down here too. We should get together again next week. Corey."

Sig called back to tell him that Spencer was free on Monday afternoon, all day after 2:00. Alec called Spencer and arranged to go see him at his Issaquah residence on Monday. Things were now moving along.

XI

The week went by quickly, Saturday no exception. The winds were back so there was no temptation to get out the clubs. Alec needed some more groceries. When he was leaving, he said hi to Joselyn and Hugh in the driveway and asked if they needed anything from Central Market. In fact, they did, cornbread, apparently Central Market's bakery was famous for their high-end cornbread. Alec would also get some for himself, to try it out.

When he returned he deposited the Sparkman's cornbread on their doorstep as arranged, and decided the leaves needed another raking off the walkways. He got out the bamboo rake and took care of all three units before returning to his condo. It was only a fifteen minute chore. For the rest of the afternoon he surfed the net and checked email, nothing new there. He had bought a rib eye steak for dinner, a rare treat, which he cooked to his liking, along with accompanying asparagus he enjoyed a full meal.

Alec was an old movie buff. He turned on Turner Classics in the evening, which was playing an old favorite, The Cider House Rules. He mentally thanked the neighbors, nuked cornbread with melting butter and beer was a great combination. The movie has two distinct locales, the first and fourth quarter in an orphanage, the center half in an apple orchard. Alec nodded off halfway through the apple orchard, but woke up and teared up as usual at the ending, when Homer replaced Dr. Larch in reading Dickens and saying goodnight to the princely orphans. He wondered if he was ruining the sentiment of the movie when he imagined Homer going back to his room and banging away at Mary Agnes, she had grown up and looked good.

When in his twenties Alec was a consummate movie goer. He didn't read the critics' reviews of movies prior to seeing them. He preferred spontaneity, to be able to decide for himself the merits. He did read reviews after seeing a movie, he reviewed the reviewers to find those who agreed with him. He found two he relied on, James Berardinelli and Peter Travers. Eventually, though, they both let him down.

Berardinelli wrote a brilliant review of The Cider House Rules, four stars and exactly as Alec had seen the movie, but he lost some cred when he gave the movie, Looper, an excellent review, three and a half out of four stars. It was basically a gangster movie where the plot revolved around the mob putting enemies in a time machine and sending them back in time where they would be eliminated by a hitman immediately on arrival. The highlight was when the hitman from the past killed his future self. Like, what else would you do with a time machine? It was a serious movie, not campy, and that plot was too ridiculous to warrant any stars.

Peter Travers was permanently ignored after the three and a half star review of the movie John Wick Chapter 2, which was even more perverse than Looper. Alec had not been privy to the Wick assassin prior to number two. The protagonist was equally the antagonist, after slaughtering off about a thousand bad guys in a two hour movie, many close-up head shots but with some more detailed gore, at the same time miraculously dodging an equal number of shots from his adversaries. Travers was enamored with the great martial arts features choreographed like ballet moves while our hero/villain dispatched two birds at once. The movie was like A Fistful of Dollars, from fifty years before, gone berserk, this reviewer needed help. Alec slowly faded away as a movie aficionado.

The Seahawks were away at Tampa Bay this Sunday for

the early morning game. Alec was pleasantly surprised to see Sy on the couch with Max when he barged in. He felt a little awkward nevertheless.

"Hey, Sy, good to see you again. You know, that was a total accident before, I had no idea."

"So Max says, but I was wond'rin 'bout it for a long time."

"Well, I don't blame you. I looked into it a bit more, you want to know about him?"

"I look too, but din' see much. Look like he's my dad a'right. Ma wouldn'd say so but I kin tell. Ya, I wanna know."

"He was All-American at Duquesne. They won the NIT in 1955 when it was the premier tournament in the land, more than even the NCAA. He was MVP of the tournament. Played nine years in the pros for a few different teams. Died in Philadelphia back in the 80s. Okay with this?"

"Ya, I'm okay. Been thinkin 'bout looking up kin back there, might have cousins or sumpin', maybe even a brother. Think I'd need to go back there tho."

"I could look further if you want, I'll let you know if I find out anything."

"Sure, okay, thanks."

"Is that okay with you too, Max?"

"Ha ha ha ha ha ha .. me, ha ha ha .. I didn't know I was even here."

Sy left right after the game started, whereas Rich had already showed up, early for him. Porter didn't make it, family, but Lukas came anyway. The Seahawks took their first loss, it was a close game decided by a last second field goal. After the game, when the conversation got somewhat serious, they all stayed to hear what Alec was up to. Even Max took an interest. Alec gave a quick rundown of the events to date, and added that he was to meet his lawyer tomorrow and Corey later in the week.

"Corey tells me you and he are friends, Rick."

"Acquaintances is more like it. His father was a mover and shaker, he raised his family in Puyallup, not far from us. Corey has a couple of sisters, one died I believe, and we picnicked with them a few times when I was a teenager."

Max jumped in with "What in the hell has gotten into you, what do you know about politics?"

"Now goddammit, not you too Max. I've been being told about what a worthless piece of shit I was by just about everybody now. Sig even had me followed 'cause he thought I was screwing him."

"Ha ha ha ha ha ha ha .. you are a worthless piece of shit."

It was hard to not appreciate Max's humorous laugh he enjoyed it so much himself, but Alec was not pleased here. Rick interceded, "For what it's worth, I never thought anything of the kind. I have always thought you would find something worthwhile to do. But I must confess, I am a little surprised by this particular avenue."

They all lightened up. "You and me both."

There was a little break before Lukas entered the ring. "You're going to see Spencer Dawes tomorrow. I'd love to tag along if I could."

"Uh. Thanks, but I'm not sure Spencer would be good with a stranger showing up."

"You wouldn't know, but I am actually quite conversant with this subject matter. Elections and donation reform is actually my area of expertise. Even so, I would never think to get in the way, just there to listen, but I would surely be able explain some of the ramifications to you afterwards."

Max was truly endeared to Lukas, the client had paid up after receiving Lukas's letter last week. "Let him in, Alec. We now have a lawyer in the family."

Alec looked to Rick. "What do you think?"

Rick took some time to ruminate. "I think it would be alright. Lawyers understand each other, and he might respect you for having your own man Alec. But Lukas, you have to be there as Alec's lawyer. I suggest a contract, and pay him a dollar Alec. It must be clear that to Lukas this is confidential and attorney client."

Lukas agreed. "That goes without saying, and a contract is certainly sensible, I will write one up."

So, it was decided.

XII

The weather had slackened over the weekend. Alec got up Monday morning at the crack of calm, he wanted take the morning to prepare for the meeting with Spencer later that afternoon. He had researched precedents as best he could, but knew Spencer would be way ahead of him with that. He began to realize how inadequate whatever he had to offer would seem. The concepts he had already enumerated were very straightforward and he knew they needed to be much more precise than whatever he could deliver. Nevertheless, he continued his homework.

At 10:00 he received a call from Olympia. "Alec, Corey."

"Hi, what's up?"

"The get-together planned for Friday, I want you to come down here, meet my team working on this. I have been surprised to find that the resistance is much more minimal than I could have ever expected. A poll recently showed that over eighty percent of both parties think that Citizen's United was wrongly decided. That's how I'm selling this, a direct assault on that decision, and it's getting great leverage. I actually think we have a great shot here. My guys are starting to write it up for legislation."

"Whoa, fantastic."

"It's our job to do this, but you got the ball rolling, so I want you to be appraised about what we're doing. It may not be exactly what you envisioned."

"Very kind of you, yes, we will want to see what you've come up with."

"So, then, who is your team, who'll be coming down

here?"

"The juice is Sig Ulrick, surely you know Sig, but he is unlikely to travel."

"Of course."

"I'll be down with Spencer Dawes, and perhaps one other lawyer, that remains to be seen. We're working on a written document this afternoon and will try to polish it for Friday."

"Great, perfect. See you Friday at 9:00."

"Ok, see ya."

Alec was more than just apprehensive about what he had promised. He didn't know if he could get Spencer to Olympia for one thing, and nothing had been written or even might be written at all, much less by Friday. This had the potential for great embarrassment, he might have to pull out altogether.

Alec picked up Lukas at the 135th entrance to I-5, he suspected that Lukas wanted to keep his domicile private. Alec pulled to the left lane then linked into the rail at Northgate for the trip, estimated at fifty-seven minutes by Bubblerail. Issaquah is a distant fourteen miles east suburb of Seattle, surrounded by a group of high hills or mountains with names like Tiger Mountain, Cougar Mountain, Squak Mountain, and Miller Hill. These are Issaquah Alps, on which are a small number of original dwellings and a much greater number of newer, modern homes. There is a large resort community further to the north, Trilogy, which hosts a manicured, private golf course. Around Issaquah the communities are more numerous, albeit smaller and more independent, as was Issaquah Ridge where Spencer resided.

On the drive Alec and Lukas exchanged minor pleasantries, then Lukas came clean. He knew Porter only slightly, but had found out he was friends with Alec and sought him out. He managed the invite to Sunday football with great cunning. He wanted to meet Alec because he was hoping to get an introduction to Spencer Dawes through him. That was his target, he was a great admirer of Spencer. He believed himself to be a first rate research lawyer, but Spencer was a court magician. Lukas had listened to the complete arguments in McNee v before the Supreme Court numerous times, and Spencer was brilliant on his feet. The seven to two decision sounded convincing, but the case could have gone either way by the briefs. Another lawyer might have prevailed, but Spencer was the difference in what was his fourth argument before the Court.

He was about to meet his personal superstar and he was excited. "But don't worry, I won't be a nuisance. I'll just listen and learn."

"That's quite a story — I'm not sure what to make of it. I'm tempted to haul your ass back and drop you off somewhere."

"No, please don't say that. I know I was surreptitious, but I mean no harm. And I have very much enjoyed the Sundays with you and Max and Rick and even Porter. I have been without a social life for a long time. I've done quite a bit on the case already. You might be surprised." He pulled a substantial document out of his briefcase. "Here's my brief so far, take a look at it."

Alec looked it over. Fifty-three pages, he was amazed. He recognized a few of the references but their context was unclear. "You've done this for my project, when did you do this?"

"I told you, I am a first rate researcher. I started after that second weekend, it looked like a worthwhile idea, and it is. I congratulate you."

There was no more talk about dropping Lukas off nor talk of any kind. Alec was delighted that he would have something in writing, even if Lukas wasn't proficient, though Alec suspected he was. His Tesla directed him to Spencer's residence without difficulty for the fifty-two minute trip. Spencer lived with his wife in an upscale condo complex on Sammamish Ridge north and east of Issaquah.

Until two years ago they lived in a house in Bellevue where they raised two sons, now both off to college.

Spencer met them at the front door. After seeing two bodies instead of one, he greeted them with "Well, what do we have here?"

Alec introduced them. "Spencer, this is Lukas Schmidt. Lukas is a friend and my lawyer."

"Your lawyer. Is Sig aware of your lawyer?"

"No, I don't believe so, unless he's having me watched again."

"You know this was to be a private confidential meeting."

"Spencer, Lukas is my lawyer, of course it's private and confidential. Last I checked this was my baby in the first place."

"It's more than you now, Alec. What kind of law do you practice, Lukas?"

"Mostly I've done research. Right now I'm a public defender in Everett, but I was both a prosecutor and defense attorney in my ten years in Montana before I came back to Washington."

"Well, okay, come on in. We'll go for it."

Spencer led them through a warm well-furnished house to the den in the back where there was a densely forested view looking out the wide back window. Cheese and crackers were offered, and liquid refreshments, but both declined and sat in lounge chairs facing Spencer at his desk.

"Let's see .."

Alec interrupted before Spencer started. He then related his conversation with Corey that morning.

Spencer let in sink in. "So, are you telling me that I'm going?"

"No, no, not at all." He wanted to say, "I have my own lawyer now," but thought better of it. Not the time for levity.

"Does Sig know about this?"

"No, Sig does not know about this, I haven't talked to

Sig today."

"Well, okay, let me think about it. Let's talk in general about our relationship with Olympia. Let's call these people in Olympia the Coreys. We can advise them, but we have nothing to say about the final legislative bill they produce. However, a second set of eyes to identify potential loopholes or lapses is always desirable. The bill that's produced, on the off chance it is passed by two thirds both House and Senate, will in almost its entirety be put before the public for a vote, we will have little to say about that, also. Where we can have some input is with any legal challenges to either activity before the fact, and, in particular, after potential passage when there are sure to be challenges. The Coreys will want legal opinions and possibly court appearances, and they will prefer that they don't have to foot the bill. Sig is receptive to that, at least he was earlier this morning. We need to convince them that we can help with that aspect if we want to be players. So far, I have taken a few notes, but need more than just a couple of days to write up a brief."

"Lukas has done some work."

"Let me see it." Spencer broke in immediately.

Lukas pulled out his brief and passed it over to Spencer, who studied it for about five minutes. "This is good, very good." He looked askance at Lukas.

Alec was out of the conversation for the next hour while Spencer and Lukas exchanged ideas about an argument in Vermont, or a judgment in Kentucky, or a ruling in Arkansas. Alec was left behind. From his perspective, the two seemed to be on equal footing. After their conversation Spencer seemed quite satisfied. Lukas's work was easing the way for both Alec and himself. Spencer reconsidered his original skepticism about the Olympia trip, and reclassified it as a maybe. As they were getting ready to leave, Spencer asked Lukas to let Alec have a private word with him. Lukas adjourned to the car.

"Where did you find this guy, Alec?"

"He's just a friend of a friend, I haven't known him long."

"His research is first rate, as is his knowledge of precedents, better than mine I suspect. He's also an excellent writer. I don't know where he came from, but he's a great find. Try to find out a little more about him for me."

Back in the Tesla, Lukas was ecstatic, jubilant, could hardly contain himself. Alec complimented him about his expertise and thanked him for his valued assistance. Then he took him to dinner. Lukas requested Mexican. Alec would pump him over cheese nachos.

XIII

It had been a relaxing dinner that Alec and Lukas shared the night before, they had had ample beers over dinner and the subsequent conversation. Lukas beamed when Alec related what Spencer had said about him. Alec had always thought Lukas secretive, he now realized that he was extremely timid, even childlike in many ways, although not intellectually. He learned little more about his past, what he was told was very generic, not much detail. Alec had warmed to him though, and not merely because of what he provided.

When they left the restaurant in Issaquah, Alec had to deal with Tesla the martinet. One of its features was blood alcohol testing. The Tesla pulled over and switched off a block out of the parking lot, telling Alec he was too physically impaired to drive. No argument would prevail, even though they were only a few blocks from the freeway and the rail. Alec opened the windows to clear the air, got out for a few minutes, then held his breath while he managed to drive a block and a half, then stopped, got out and repeated that procedure four times before they hooked onto the rail. He kept the window open the whole thirty-three minutes back to his freeway exit, and by that time, fortunately, Tesla the martinet found him fit to drive.

Alec was still in bed at 7:15 when Sig called. "What in the hell, boy, who is this other guy you brought to Spence's."

"That's Lukas Schmidt, my lawyer. I have to protect myself, Sig."

"Yeah, very cute. What was he doing there, where'd he come from, who the hell is he?"

"He's a friend, and a lawyer, a good one it appears."

"Well, how long have you known this friend?"

"Well, let's see now .... about three weeks, I guess."

"Three weeks, then you don't even really know him. This is no good. You don't know what his motives are, do you?"

"Motives, he has no nefarious motives. I trust him."

"You trust him, great. That's not good enough. I need to see him. No, better yet, Spence should vet him. Send him back to see Spence today, alone."

Alec knew that Lukas would jump at this, but, "Well, I don't know, he was just there yesterday, Spencer just saw him."

"He saw him, he didn't vet him, there's a huge difference. We have to know who he knows."

"Okay, I'll call him, but if he won't go I'll understand."

"I'll understand too. And why didn't you tell me about this Olympia trip. How did that happen?"

"Corey Rasmusson's idea, he wants to make sure I approve of what he's doing, he's looking for input from us. He believes that it may actually happen, they're starting to write up a legislative bill. It looks like Spencer and I and Lukas will be driving down on Friday."

"Holy smokes, the cart's now in front of the horse — slow down, we'll see what Spence has to say. You go, you may be going alone. Call your guy, get him over there." With that, Sig hung up.

Alec called Lukas to tell him Spencer wanted to have another talk. As expected, he was more than glad to go. Alec told him to order an autobot to pick him up and drive, and he gave him his Bubble card number and password, Alec would be paying the bills. Alec then called Spencer, lest Sig had not, to let him know Lukas was coming. Spencer wanted to know how Lukas was going to get the Issaquah. When

Alec told him, he suggested that Alec come later to pick him up, at about 7:30. They would likely be working until late, then he would have Martha cook up a nice dinner. It was agreed.

Although Alec's residence in his youthful years was rural, he had definitely developed into a city boy by this time. Fishing, camping, hiking, they didn't appeal to him, but he did enjoy an occasional drive through country back roads. He left for his appointment to see Spencer two hours early and drove himself, rather than hook onto the rail, past Issaquah to the Upper Preston exit off I-90. From there, it was a four mile drive on a parkway to Snoqualmie Falls, a tourist haven waterfall dropping almost three hundred feet onto the river of the same name.

Alec parked and walked the short distance from the gift shop parking lot to one of many sites that offered an unobstructed view of the falls. At times during the year the river is little more than a stream, but the rains earlier in the week were represented in the fullness of the waterfall. Alec absorbed the sight and observed the people for the requisite time, then got back onto Highway 202 for a five mile drive to the town of Fall City. Tall deciduous trees, maple, birch and alder, were prevalent along the way, but the area was not thick with the fir and pine of the Cascade Forest a little farther east. He stopped for a beer at the bar in the Fall City Saloon. Work was over and the place was starting to get rowdy, a live local band would get going in another half-hour. A young cowgirl, well, not too young, and maybe not a real cowgirl but dressed like one, sidled up next to him and struck up a conversation with the imaginative line, "I haven't seen you around here before, big boy."

That started Alec talking and buying a couple more beers, but when the band came in it was time to go. He kept his window open and head near the window when he got back in the Tesla, and punched in Spencer's address. The Tesla followed 202 and Duthie Hill Road back to the

Issaquah hills, arriving only a few minutes after 7:30.

Spencer's wife, Martha, who Alec had not met, answered the door and showed him in. He began the introduction, "Hello, I'm Alec."

"Alec, glad to finally meet you. I'm Martha. Please come in. I was just about to call the men in for dinner."

She was prim and proper as Alec would have suspected, with short light hair and a rather plain undistinguished face, until you looked at her eyes which were very alive. She excused herself, but was quickly back with Spencer and Lukas in tow. They were soon all at the dining room dinner table. Alec's eating habits were as those of a Neanderthal. He had an aversion to strong seasoning, into which most salad dressing fit, but for the second time of late he relished a salad, Martha's seemed unique. The entree was a pasta and seafood recipe that, again, Alec could not identify but which had the advantage that he was never able to get enough. It was an altogether culinary delight.

There had been some topical conversation during dinner, mostly about the meal, but no business had been discussed. At an appropriate time Alec looked at Spencer, which was perfectly interpreted. He invited Alec to his den for a talk, requesting that Lukas stay to entertain Martha.

Once seated in the den Alex inquired, "Well, what did you find out?"

"Find out, about what?"

"About what, about Lukas, where's he been, what's he doing here, you know?"

"Oh, well, there's no problem there. He's successfully vetted, I guess you'd say."

"Well, good then, and ....?"

"And nothing. Alec, did you forget that I'm a lawyer. Our conversation was confidential."

"You're not his lawyer, he's my lawyer. Don't I have a right to know who my lawyer is?"

"No. Sorry. Ask him, don't ask me. You know, Alec, I

had free assistance from a couple of legal experts with our victory in the Court, but all those lawyers were only helping to advance personal reputations. Lukas is different. He has no such thoughts. His motives are pure, you could say. Listen, we got some good work done here today, and he's going to check on some things and be back Thursday. Can you get him here? He had a little trouble in transit today."

"Oh, sure, Alec the chauffeur."

"Don't be an ass, for god's sake. You don't get it, do you? We are all working for you numbnuts. Lukas and me, and even Sig. I asked Sig if he thought we should include presidential elections in the out-of-state donations ban, he said, 'I don't know about that, ask Alec what he thinks.' I've never heard anything like that from him before. It's like Pie says, 'Alec, you're the man.' When and if we become a factor, and someone in the press asks me a question, I'm going to say, 'You'll have to ask Alec McNee about that.' And, by the way, Lukas and I will be ready by Friday. We're going with you."

All of this stunned Alec, he mumbled something back, but that was essentially all the discussion necessary. Shortly after this Lukas and Alec were saying cordial goodbyes and thanks, then were on their way.

They didn't have much to say. Alec let Lukas bathe in the success of his day with Spencer until they got to I-90 and on the rail. "I hear you had a problem getting to Spencer's house, what happened?"

"Oh, well, you told me to order an autobot and give him the card number you gave me. I did, but when it got there it wouldn't recognize the number. I didn't know what to do. I've never rented an autobot before. I tried the number four more times, then it finally told me to get out."

"You've never ordered an autobot. Really?"

"There was no such thing before I moved to Montana. I've ridden in them, but never rented one for myself."

"Was the one you called a Bubblebot?"

"Well, no, it said Ford on it. I couldn't get you, so I called Max. That's what he told me, to order a Bubblebot. Once I did that, it worked fine."

"Don't you have a bank card?"

"Oh, yeah, of course."

"You could have paid the Ford with your card."

"Yeah, Max told me. I didn't think of it. I thought I needed to use your number."

"Okay, here's how it works. There are lots of autobot rentals, including Ford, Tesla, Hertz. The rail is owned by Bubble. Any bot can ride the rail, they bill you for the ride and the rail, and then they need to reimburse Bubble for the rail usage. There is a fee for that which you pay. But if you rent a Bubblebot there's no extra fee since they own the rail."

"Okay, yeah, I get it now."

"So, where have you been that this is such a mystery? Apparently you told Spencer but he wouldn't tell me anything, confidential. How about you tell me?"

"I knew I had to tell Spencer about where I've been. I would have preferred not to. I think you might have a hard time with it. Give me a little more time, okay?"

"You are my lawyer. I will treat it as one hundred percent confidential, as if I am your lawyer."

"I'd still prefer to wait. It's pretty complicated."

"Okay, okay, but I hope you know I can keep a secret."

"I know, but .."

XIV

The next day Alec was on the road early. He had checked the Tesla for the best route to Sig's, but was overriding the directions to go south on Aurora because it was clogged with cars and autobots. The Aurora Bridge, a 3,000 foot long cantilever and truss bridge built in 1932, five years before the Golden Gate bridge, and at one time termed the suicide bridge because of all the leaps from it, connects Phinney Ridge to northern Queen Anne Hill and was down to one lane because of a recent fender bender. He turned off at 43rd and went west four blocks to Fremont, then south and over the Fremont Bridge, 150 feet almost directly below the Aurora Bridge, up Dexter Avenue, skirting the east edge of Queen Anne for two miles to Denny Ave. He pulled over and dialed Sig. When he answered, Alec said, "I'll be there in ten minutes," hung up and turned off his phone. He then turned west on Denny and drove the mile to the Regrade.

When Alec arrived Sig was waiting at the door, but was blocking the entry. "What's this all about, boy?"

"We need to talk, Sig."

Sig glared at him for a minute. "That is why you barged in here. We need to talk?"

"Yes, we need to talk. You going to let me in or not?"

Sig balked a little longer, then vacated the doorway and slowly retreat to his den. Alec entered, shut the door, followed him in, and sat is his usual chair facing Sig's desk. Sig sat waiting, deadpanned.

"Uh, did Spencer give you a report on Lukas Schmidt? You were apoplectic about him yesterday."

Sig was slow to respond, but did. "That is no longer an issue."

"Oh, good. Did Spencer say why, did he give any details?"

"No."

"Look Sig, you have always been great to me, I really appreciate all you've done, I don't mean to get uppity, but things seemed to have changed. Before, I was just along for the ride, but Spencer said something last night that really hit me. He used the same language as Tom Piatt, he said, 'Alec, you're the man now.'"

"Spencer said that!"

"Yes, then he said if someone asked a question he didn't want to answer he would say, 'You'll have talk to Alec McNee about that.' So, when we go down to Olympia, they're both going, what do I say to Corey or anyone else when they ask about 'our team'? I need to know a few things."

"Hmm, okay, go on."

"Like, money. I assume you are okay with taking care of Spencer." A subtle nod from Sig. "Is that all, when they ask for more support, are you amenable?"

"You'll have to duck that one for now."

"How about policy, if they ask about details can I make decisions for us? As an example, the topic of presidential contributions came up. It would be my idea to leave them alone. Can I make the call? Such things affect you, as in the time Spencer needs to put in, depending."

"Hmm."

"Corey said negotiations with other legislators have been almost painless, he's getting very little resistance. Do you know of others beside yourself exerting influence. I think you know where I'm coming from here. And back to money, Lukas needs to be compensated. He's already put in a lot of time, he had a fifty page brief written before we even met Spencer. Now he's spent two days over there and probably another full day tomorrow. If you won't do anything, I guess I'll have to, but it won't be easy for me."

"Well, let me talk to Spence about that, see what he thinks he's worth. I think that won't be an issue. You've made some good points, you're using your brain. Leave the money discussions alone — use your best judgment on policy and keep me informed. I'll back you, but we may need to change our minds about a thing or two down the road."

"But, yeah, I guess we might."

"Alec, my boy, I'm not the enemy. Please don't hijack me again, I don't like it."

"Yeah, I know, sorry. I get pretty nervous is all, scared actually, about this stuff, I don't know if I'm up to it."

"You'll be alright, just wing it. It's my money, all you can do is look stupid."

On Thursday, the foursome got in thirteen holes at West Seattle before the rains came and retired them to the 19th Hole for refreshments. Lukas was confident he could now get to Spencer's on the Bubblerail without a problem. Alec would retrieve Lukas in the late afternoon, after golf. When Alec picked him up at 5:30, they stopped for a teriyaki takeout meal before getting home. Lukas allowed Alec to drop him off at his Greenwood apartment. They were both home by 7:00. Tomorrow, they would be going south very early.

XV

Spencer drove his classic 1999 BMW 528i (M5) Sedan eight miles to the Issaquah Park-n-Ride, where Alec picked him up at 8:00 sharp, having already picked up Lukas on the way. Spencer wore his typical leprechaun wardrobe of a dark green checkered sports coat and yellow bow tie. Alec had picked out his number two outfit, a gray, herringbone, wool sports coat with blue dress shirt, no tie, and gray slacks. It was a little overcast and gloomy, but the clouds were not threatening rain and looked like they would dissipate by the afternoon. They picked up some coffee and donuts at an espresso stand near the freeway entrance for the seventy mile ride to Olympia, the eta was 9:15. The plan was to be in Corey's legislative office by 9:30 to meet with his staff, while Corey himself was to be in the Legislature conducting business. It would be breaking around eleven.

After Alec connected to the rail, he was presented with a seventy page document. To him, it didn't read much differently from that which Lukas had prepared earlier in the week, the detail the devil is so proud of. Spencer, in the front seat with Alec, went over some of the points of interest during the hour commute. Spencer itemized some of the topics not necessary to be documented, such as term limits, matching funds, and citizen challenges of other voters. In the document he showed references for topics which they had included, mandated registration and ID requirement, along with many others. Precedents in decided cases, such as Buckley v Valeo, Nixon v Missouri, Citizen's United v FEC, McCutcheon v FEC, were referenced thoroughly. The minutia of the document was written in lawyerese, covering as many loopholes as could be imagined. Alec was able to interpret very little of this.

"This is the blueprint for what we are agreeing to assist defending if it becomes necessary. It undoubtedly will be. Specifically, all state elections are included, with the exception of the presidential election. It is very unlikely that the legislators will touch on a lot of this, they have a different agenda, but we need them to be aware of our perspective." Spencer handed Alec a second document. "We did write up a rough draft of a potential bill they might be willing to submit. Lukas did a lot of research on this after reviewing a great deal of other legislation."

Alec perused this document. "It is an easier read than the brief, but I still need to digest it somewhat."

"Don't worry about it, they won't accept it as is, but it may give them some assistance."

They all took a break about halfway to Olympia, reflecting upon their own thoughts. They had already driven by Federal Way, Fife and were passing the Tacoma Dome, on the way to Lakewood which was just south of Tacoma, then past McChord Air Force base and the army's Fort Lewis, through the Nisqually Flats, and then up past Lacey and on to Olympia.

When the Tesla was directing Alec to his pre-approved parking space, he said, "You guys did a great job on short notice. Thanks for your hard work. I'm not going to be much use with the particulars. You have them well-covered. So, after the introductions I'll get out of the way. I'm not yet sure who all's going to be there, I think a lawyer of Corey's and his legislative assistant, possibly another legislator if I understood him correctly." Alec parked as they found the entry door. "Okay guys, let's go, fight, win!"

They were in the correct building and had no trouble finding room #223, which had Corey Rasmusson's name printed on the door. The room, once entered, was somewhat smaller than Alec would have expected. A middle-aged woman was seated at the only desk in the office, she had a plump face with short textured dark hair, her nameplate said Patsy Kincaid.

As Alec approached, Angela Nelton entered from an open door leading to a back office. She had always been fashionable and today was no different. She was wearing a light blue pantsuit with an egg-white, pleated, chiffon blouse. Her sandy brown hair that had before been long was now cut short, thick and well-styled. The way she looked and carried herself was what set her apart. Not beautiful but elegant in texture, her brown eyes beneath thick brown eyebrows were bright and alert.

Alec took this in instantly as they made intros. "Angela, hi."

"Alec, very good to see you, long time. Come on back."

He, Lukas and Spencer followed her into the inner office which was much larger. "Spencer, Lukas, this in Angela, Corey's .."

"Hi, I'm Angela Nelton, Senator's Rasmusson's office manager."

They all shook hands. Alec asked, "I was expecting a larger crew here, is anyone else coming, Angela?"

"Oh yes, we reserved the conference room across the hall. It's off season, but we found a few bodies floating around, most are already in there I believe. Shall we go over?"

"Ah, how many do you think? I have some documents but only two copies, perhaps you can make some more?" Spencer pulled out the brief and the legislative outline.

"Sure. Oh, quite thicker than I would have thought, but not a problem."

Angela brought the documents in to Patsy, gave her some instructions, and came back into the room.

They exited into the hall from a side door in the back of the office. She then led them down the hall to the conference room. It was a spacious, dominated by a large, oval, pine table that would seat about twenty. There were seven individuals in the conference room, four men and three women, all hovering around a refreshment table that supplied coffee, cheese and crackers.

They all were introduced to one another. Shabat Odbayo was a republican representative from Tacoma. He was a large athletic black man of about forty, very outward and well-spoken. Constance Ridgeway was a democratic senator from Walla Walla, on the opposite end of the spectrum, well over sixty, diminutive and reserved. Reese Daniels was Shabat's assistant, full-figured and about forty-five, no doubt a lawyer. Richard Ridgeway was Constance's assistant and son, a handsome thirtyish lawyer. James Woodway was Corey's assistant, young, bright and no doubt a competent lawyer. James Hardwick was the assistant of republican Representative Albie Short of Spokane. Terry Alger represented democratic Representative Storm Porcelli of Kennewick.

After a few minutes of mingling, Angela asked them to be seated. The seven had all staked out seats for themselves on one side of the oval. Spencer, Lukas and Alec sat across, and Angela stood at the point nearest the door. She began the meeting. "As you all know, I'm Angela Nelton representing Corey Rasmusson. I'd like to thank and welcome our neighbors from the north for coming down, and you locals for showing interest. I'll let you get to it. I'd now like to introduce Alec McNee."

To his surprise, Alec received some slight applause. "Hello, good to be here and meet you all. You are more than I had expected, but a welcome sight. As you surely know, I have been in communication with Corey for the last few weeks discussing some sweeping campaign finance legislation. We are not here to write legislation, but we do have some suggestions, as you will shortly see."

Right on cue Patsy arrived with a stack of documents,

delaying things slightly while they were dispensed.

"As I was saying, as you can see, our group expects that, should things go forward and a bill be passed, the explosive nature of the topic will make litigation an almost certainty. The large brief before you illuminates the nature of the arguments we will anticipate putting forward. Of course, it is not absolute since the legislation has yet to be written, but should give you an idea of what we would like to see and what we think we can defend. The second document, authored by Lukas Schmidt beside me, is simply an outline of potential legislation for your inspection. Included are suggestions which you are welcome to consider. I am not a lawyer and certainly not conversant enough to offer any valued opinions about the particulars, so I will leave it to you experts to hash it out. Thanks. Now, before I leave you, Spencer Dawes would like to say a few things. Spencer."

Spencer received more rigorous applause. "Hi, folks. The documents before you are our intellectual property, so, without meaning to be rude, I would ask that you return them to me before you leave. I will gladly make them available upon request, but will need a waiver from you for that. Thanks. Now, I'll give you some time to digest them, and then take questions."

Angela was still in the room. Alec edged over to her and they both sidled out into the hallway.

"You don't seem like the little boy I used to know who was still learning how to tie his shoes. How did you become a public speaker?"

"I've had a lot of practice in the last few years. By the way, you look great, it's good to see you."

"Thanks, you too. I never did thank you for what you did with Sydney, how you backed me up, albeit to no avail."

"I'm glad it happened. Who knows how long it would have taken me to wise up about her."

"Yeah, she surprised me too — the bitch."

Alec looked at her and smiled. "I never thought I hear

such words out of Ms. Sophisticated. You know, I would have hit on you, but you were way out of my league."

"Bullshit, Sydney was gorgeous. You were hopeless."

"I guess. So, where are you living now?"

"There's a coffee shop in the next building."

They went outside and across to the next building, and into the coffee shop. Alec had an orange juice only, Angela a cup of tea and a bran muffin.

"So, where are you living now?" Alec asked.

"My father died two years ago, Mother was disconsolate and out of it for a long time. I moved back home to Puyallup to take care of her and I've been there ever since."

"That's nice, and, are you still out of my league?"

She chuckled. "You are so suave and subtle, how did I miss that before? Didn't you forget how sophisticated I am?"

"With bitch and bullshit, you are now in my ballpark."

"Who's that Lukas guy, he looks familiar?"

"Oh, he's helping Spencer, and he's good. I don't know much about him."

"Well, I have to dump you anyway. A client is coming to see Corey, I have to go meet him. Can you find your way back?"

"Uh-huh, a likely story. Okay, I'll see you later then."

Alec stayed and read the paper while he finished the half of the muffin Angela had left. A group of four entered the shop, led by one who was espousing vigorously on the merits of something or other. He bought for the group, and was thanked by the attendant as Senator Purser. On the way to sit with the others he did a double take when he saw Alec.

"Hey, I know you, you're that McNee of McNee v. Well, what brings a man of your experience and intellectual might to the halls of Congress, more funding damage to deliver?"

Alec decided to play along. Purser and friends were having a good time with him. "Da damage."

"Da, da da da, damage, you amateur lightweight, like in

depleting monies from district coffers." He was chuckling and playing up to the others, also chuckling.

"I don't .."

"No, you dawdling dimwit, you do' do' don't."

The four picked up their takeout and departed with some more "da da das." Alec waited a bit, then followed. Two of the foursome veered off, Purser and one other continued into the same building as Corey's office, and up to the third floor where a stroke of luck sent Purser into a restroom alone. Alec followed. It was a narrow room. Alec stood between Purser at the urinal and the sink across the room as Purser finished and looked up to see Alec. He pretended ignorance, but when he moved to go by Alec moved into his way.

"Look, I don't want any trouble, fella."

"Fella? I thought I was a dawdling dimwit, have I come up in the world in only five minutes."

He blocked Purser again. Purser was afraid and did something stupid, he took a swing at Alec, but Alec ducked, spun him around and shoved him against the wall straddling a urinal. Alec put his hand over the electronic flush a couple of times, causing the urinal to flush and splash a little water on Purser pants.

"You know there are cameras almost everywhere now, but I read they are not allowed in restrooms. Good thing for you or I'd have you up on assault charges for swinging at me like that. I wasn't going to hurt you, I just wanted to continue our nice little chat, but I guess I scared you, why else act like such a coward? Well, anyway, it's been fun, I'll always remember you like this, you pompous pedantic pissant."

Alec made his way back to Corey's office. Patsy was still there manning her desk. He asked about Angela, then Corey. She had seen neither of late. She suggested he wait in the other office, which he did. Ten minutes later Corey arrived, keyed up. He was taller that Alec had envisioned, at least three inches taller than Alec at six three.

"Alec, hi, good to meet you in person. I understand they're meeting in the conference room. I have a couple of things to do, then I'll be right with you."

Alec indicated he could leave, but Corey waved it off. He went to his desk and shuffled some papers, then made a brief phone call. Alec ignored him as best he could. After a few minutes they walked to the conference room. Angela was there taking notes, and one more legislator had arrived, Representative Storm Porcelli. Alec conferred with Lukas and Spencer, Corey conferred with his confederates.

After about ten minutes, Corey took the lead. "Okay, good, it appears there was a lot said, and we are extremely impressed with the work you have put in already, thank you. But, as would be expected, there are a few things we need to iron out. Funding. Is your group willing to assist with money to sell the bill to the public? We definitely will have the people on our side, but the opposition will be fierce. We will need to combat their lobby."

Alec looked at Spencer, then, "Sorry, on that front it is too early to commit. However, I am confident that there will be ample donors on both sides of the issue."

"I wish I were that confident. Shabat, will you take it?"

Shabat was articulate, forceful and accurate in his speech, he was an imposing presence. "I'll talk about a couple of minor things first. Mayoral and city councilmen races. For many small towns, prominent members of the community do not live within city limits, farmers, ranchers, well-to-do businessmen. It would seem there must be a way for them to contribute to their communities."

Alec conferred with Spencer. "Yes, we agree. Do you have any suggestions?"

"Not as yet."

"Okay, we'll work on this and get back to you."

"Second, you suggest not only registration as a requisite, but also established residence for at least a year. We don't see this working. Currently, registration is all that is necessary to vote in any district, policing permanent residence would seem to be untenable."

"Difficult no doubt, but there are a lot of wealthy people nowadays who have little problem purchasing multiple residences. They can cherry-pick and register in whichever district they can be most effective, without actually ever having lived there."

"You have a point, but again, this would be difficult to enforce no matter the length of residence requirement. Third, out-of-state students. Many register twice, in their family districts and also in other states. This is tough to control, also."

"Yes, again difficult."

"Now, the serious differences. We believe that U.S. Senatorial races should not be mandated in this bill. We are mixed about U.S. Representatives. Some of us want all federal elections excluded, others see merit with representatives being included since they are affiliated with specific districts. But not senators. They work at a federal level."

Alec again conferred with Spencer and Lukas. He was their arbitrator and seemed to be the one making the decisions.

"Yes, but they are elected only by voters of their state. And, if you exclude senators, it seems most likely that after compromise in legislative negotiations representatives will also be gone on the same grounds that the senators were excluded."

Corey stepped in with "Yes, more than likely."

"Well, this takes the teeth completely out of the whole thing. I'm afraid we will not be able to agree to this, and we see little room for compromise, but, we will listen."

Corey jumped in again. "Let's not burn any bridges quite yet. This had been a great introduction, but no decisions need to be made today. Do you mind if we take some time off. I'd like to take a look at these data you provided."

Corey and Storm separated themselves, both started reading. The rest chatted among themselves for another forty minutes, then Alec called a halt to prepare to depart. Before they left, Corey took him aside to say privately that he agreed with Alec about senatorial races, so he would work on his colleagues. Spencer had amassed a huge stack of documents, he left half of them with Corey who guaranteed they would be protected. Alec was also able to orchestrate a goodbye chat with Angela. She presented him with a synopsis of the meeting, not all the minutes since she missed most of them, but all the participants, when they arrived, and what was said in the final segment when Alec and Corey had joined. She also gave him her private number in case he had additional questions. He promised to give her a call.

XVI

It was 2:00 when they departed, somewhat early for rush hour so traffic was light. Alec's morning prediction of clear in the afternoon was off the mark, the wind had kicked up, the skies were darkening, and rain looked to be imminent. Once he was hooked to the rail, he began to grill Lukas and Spencer.

He turned to the back seat. "Lukas, can you tell me your impressions of the other guys? I'm asking you first so I can get it unbiased, I'm afraid you would default to Spencer if he starts. I'm going to use last names, so let's start with Odbayo. What did you think of him?"

"Well, smart and imposing, but probably more of a follower than the leader. I think he's already onboard with Corey Rasmusson."

Spencer seemed to agree. "Our man in the back seat seems tiny and timid, but Odbayo would be no match for Lukas if push came to shove."

They all grinned at this, Lukas sheepishly. "How about Ridgeway?"

"She was mostly in the background but seemed negative to the whole process. She quietly led on the opinion to exclude senators and representatives, cited the right of the people to donate as they please. Not sure, but she may be against barring corporations and unions also."

Spencer commented, "I don't think that's quite accurate. It appeared to me that she may have known little about the focus of this meeting beforehand. She is one of the most senior members in the Legislature, twenty-six years I believe. I think Corey wants her support, he may think he needs her. Her questions and suggestions may have been more probative than opinionated."

Alec nodded. "Thanks, we may need to reach out to her ourselves. Porcelli?"

"I never talked to him. He came late, no opinion."

"Like Lukas, I didn't talk to him directly, but I believe from his history he is surely gung-ho in support."

"Good, I hope so. Okay, I assume Corey's man, Woodway, was representing Corey's opinions. I'm curious about them though, in particular the senator issue."

"He sort of played devil's advocate, I thought. He kept the topic front and center but didn't seem to express a strong opinion."

"Agreed."

Alec mused, "That's curious because before we left Corey told me privately that he was in agreement with us on that matter."

"Corey probably told him to be carefully diplomatic. Probably doesn't want his crew to confront anyone."

"Yeah, that's probably it. I suspect Hardwick and Alger were mostly spectators?" Alec asked.

Lukas shook his head. "Alger, yes, but not Hardwick. He was very vocal. It wasn't that he was totally against everything, only totally against our being there at all. He was obviously displeased with you Alec, and saw no reason to listen to anything from you. I suspect he was not a fan of the McNee v Washington decision."

"Yes, but I nevertheless think he's a buddy of Corey's, which seems to be the only reason he attended. He wasn't a fan of me either, I must say." Spencer shrugged.

Alec smiled back. "I think we know where Corey stands, I've talked to him at length. Anything else?"

"Well, sure, there's one other opinion to talk about."

"Oh, who's that?"

Spencer was enjoying this. "Angela, of course. How did

the two of you get along?"

"Oh, yeah. Well, we are old friends. Reminisced a little, that's about it. We didn't talk policy."

"Oh, come on, your headlights went to high beams the minute you saw her. She never asked you to turn them off, did she?"

"Okay, have your fun, but we're really only good friends."

"Right. You got her phone number, didn't you? How about her natural hair color? I'll bet you know that too."

This embarrassed Alec. He looked to the back seat for some moral support, but it was clear that Lukas didn't have a clue.

Alec called Sig when he got home. Sig had already talked to Spencer who had opined that the meeting went as expected, nothing conclusive. Alec echoed that sentiment. They agreed to get all together the following Tuesday for a strategy meeting. "And bring what's his name."

"What's whose name, who do you mean?"

"You know, your long lost friend."

"My long, oh, you meant Lukas, Lukas Schmidt. Why didn't you say so?"

The next morning at 9:00 Alec skyped Angela. She answered the phone but skype was turned off. "Good morning. Where are you? I can't see you."

"I'm not up yet. What are ..?"

"I couldn't sleep. I was thinking of you all night — I finally had to, well, you know."

"Oh god, that little brat is back."

"Now that you're no longer a sophistico, I thought we could get down and dirty. I'll pick you up at 7:00."

"What? Give me a break, no way tonight."

"Well, at least not no way. Anyway, seriously, can we get together, maybe next week sometime?"

After a long pause, "Let me think about it. But I don't

expect the next call to be like this one."

"I'll call you Monday, and be on my best behavior."

"Is that possible? Okay, bye."

Almost before he hung up, her brother skyped. "Alec, morning, old man."

"So, big brother calls immediately. What, am I not good enough or something?"

"What are you talking about?"

"I just called Angela, asked her for a date. Are you calling to protect her from me?"

This garnered a big laugh from Corey. "Well, well, a budding romance. It never occurred to me, I'm not sure what to think. She's been hibernating far too long, but, well, take your best shot. If you screw her over though, remember I am her younger but bigger brother."

"Forewarned, Dad. So, if that ain't it, what's up then?"

"I've just finished reading the legislative proposal you gave us. Did Spencer write this?"

"He edited it, but it was written mostly by Lukas."

"Lukas, the nerdy looking kid."

"If a forty-year-old is a kid, yes."

"Well, it's good. I'd like to use it, at least much of it, but Spencer said something about intellectual property."

"No, that was about the larger brief. The bill was meant as a suggestion, for your use, all or in part. You might want to give Lukas Schmidt credit as coauthor though."

"Can't do that. Referencing a lobbyist in a legislative proposal is not done, for obvious reasons."

"Lobbyist. I guess I'm still pretty green, but this is the first time that word has come up."

"Get used to it. Anyway, even if I use this document as a template, you probably wouldn't recognize it next January after four months of revisions."

"Did you get a chance to read the brief, which is the bible for our participation in this project, and we're hoping it won't be drastically affected by events?"

"Yes, I scanned it. The brief was good, but I'm not a lawyer, and it was a little tough to digest."

"I'm with you there. Say, we had a talk about your colleagues on the way home yesterday. Mind if I ask about them?"

"Sure, shoot."

"Briefly, last names, Odbayo is in the fold, Porcelli is in the fold, Hardwick sees us as useless, and Ridgeway is up in the air. You are courting her?"

"Short but sweet, and right on. You have some fine lawyers working for you."

"Anything we can do to help with Ridgeway? Our group, Sig, Spencer, Lukas and I, is going to meet on Tuesday, we can look into it."

"Hmm, can't think of anything offhand, except money, of course. Everybody will be running again this time next year."

"Ah, no money as yet."

"I'll think about Ridgeway. You're right though, if I can get Constance she'll bring in other votes, that may be all we need. So, let me ask you, were you and Angela involved back in the Macy's days? Is this your second chance?"

"No, I was in a relationship with her best friend at the time, Sydney. It all went south when Sydney went sour. Didn't she ever talk about it?"

"No, not really, I know she was pretty bitter for a long time though. So, that wasn't from you, right?"

"Not at all, we were friends, and we parted as friends."

"She needs another friend, so don't .."

"We're good then. I'm off. I'll get back to you after next Tuesday."

"Okay, later."

Alec putzed around the condo for the next hour, he wasn't mister neat and tidy but shower scum and garbage smells under the kitchen sink needed to be dealt with. He was just finishing hosing down the shower when he was again skyped, and was surprised to see Judd Hemmings on the line.

"Hi, Judd, how the hell did you find me?"

"Random dialing, and presto, there you are."

"Okay, okay, so what's up then?"

"I need a bridge partner tonight, duplicate at North Seattle Bridge. You interested?"

"Bridge, ah, why would I possibly be interested?"

"Because you should be, you need to be there."

"Really, you have a reason for that?"

"Let's just say it wasn't my idea. I was approached."

"Look, I don't know how to play bridge. I've played maybe three times in my life and I didn't understand it then, so tell whoever to find someone else, okay?"

"They asked for you specifically. Look, you know me, right. Would I screw you over?"

"That's a tough question now, it might have been easier twenty minutes ago."

"I don't know what's going on, but I do know these people. They tell me you would go if you knew why they're asking. I believe them, so I'm asking. At 7:30, corner of 165th and 5th N.E.."

"Jesus, why would, okay, okay .. for you, I'll be there. I don't believe this."

"You might like it. Get there a little early, we need to talk about our system."

"Our what?" but Judd had disconnected.

The drive to 175th and 5th N.E. was a very simple one from Alec's condo, up to 130th, east to 5th N.E., and north two miles on 5th. Alec tried his best to remember the game, all that came to him was Ace = four, King = three, Queen = two, Jack = one, and Spades, Hearts, Diamonds, Clubs, valued in that descending order. He knew there was something about bidding, but that was about it. He arrived at the bridge club at 7:15, Judd was there waiting. It was an ordinary office building, not a particularly large room. It could have been a beauty parlor or small cafe as easily as a bridge club. There were about sixteen bridge tables scattered around the room. Judd rushed him over to an empty table to give some instructions.

"This is a novice game, so these are all new players who don't have much on you. So, when you get a hand the first thing you do is count high card points. You know how to do that, right?"

Alec nodded and Judd continued, "Then the bidding starts. The dealer is first to bid. He either passes or opens the bidding with something, the bidding moves clockwise and the next player either bids or passes. To open the bidding, you need at least 13 HPCs (high card points), to overcall, or bid after someone has already opened, you need 10 HCPs, to respond after your partner has opened, you need only six HCPs. You always have to bid at a greater level than whatever the last bid was, one spade in higher than one heart, for instance. Always bid your longest suit first, not the suit with the most points, the longest suit. Okay, let's play a practice hand." Judd looked down at the table.

"If you expect me to remember all that, forget it."

"Don't worry about it, today we just want to get you to function, and you'll get a good idea what you need to work on before next time."

Alec sprung out of his chair. "Next time? What the hell are you talking about next time?"

Judd nudged him back down. "Now, look at this hand."

"What hand? I don't see any cards anywhere."

"Look at the table. There aren't any cards. Your hand is shown on the screen."

"You're kidding, right, no cards."

There were four computer displays on the table, one in front of each seat, with a flap between them so a player in one seat could only see one display.

"No cards, look at the screen, that's your hand. Over on the right is the bidding box, use the mouse to click on the number, and then the suit of your bid. Like this." Judd clicked the one and then the heart. The screen displayed 1H as the bid in the upper left of the screen.

The director running the event called game time, and everyone sat down at a table. Seven tables had players.

"We didn't get to the play of the hand, but you're a card player, you'll pick it up."

They played twenty-four total hands. Alec stumbled and bumbled his way through most of them, but toward the end he was getting the hang of it. Some of the opponents got testy, but most were patient. They remembered their own start. After the last hand, Judd went over to the director's desk and pick up three sheets of paper, he brought one back to Alec and studied one of the others.

"Hmm 42 percent, not bad for the first time. We beat two other pairs."

"We beat someone else, impossible."

"This is a hand record, all the hands we played tonight. You can study it, see what I did wrong."

"I'd have to know what was right before I would know what was wrong."

"Come on, there's a bar across the street. I'll buy you a beer."

It was a small local bar that wouldn't house more than about sixty people, but it had character. Pictures of early Seattle, logging and 1800s city landscapes were the dominant theme. There were about seven other groups of patronage. The lady bartender delivered their drinks, Alec's Beck's and Judd's bourbon and water, and they picked a table as two other pairs of bridge players arrived, carrying and discussing hand records.

"God, that was exhausting. I thought it'd never end."

"It'll be a lot easier next week."

"That again, hate to disappoint you, but I'd rather stay home and pick my nose."

"There's a regional tournament in Lynnwood all of next week, it's a big event. The two guys will be there, they're many time national champions, the best there is around here. For whatever reason, they want to meet you. You got the hard part out of the way tonight. Surely you're curious by now."

"Curious, yes, masochistic, no."

"Hey, come on, you have talent, a couple of those hands you played brilliantly. Remember, four spades making four, a top board."

"No, I don't remember four spades making four, nor any other hand for that matter. Some of those people were awful, all quiet while the hand's played, and then bip, bip, bip, bip, you shoulda made another trick .... bip, bip, bip, why didn't you bid hearts, we shoulda been in hearts, bip, bip, bip."

"Yeah, that's the way a lot of people are, I've been there, and you may get there too."

"Fat chance. Okay, next Wednesday. You're right, I am most curious."

"Lynnwood Convention Center, 7:00, next Wednesday. Take the hand record, and here, take this convention card. Study up."

XVII

It was a 10:00 starting time for the Seahawks against the Chicago Bears, losers of last year's Super Bowl, but favored to get back there this year. The Hawks were home team underdogs in this, the biggest game of the young season. The city was starting to buzz twelfth man themes as in the heyday of past Super Bowl years. Porter sported his old twelves sweatshirt, and chided the burly Max, who looked even more burly after donning his old sweatshirt, now two sizes too small. The whole crew was in attendance, even Sy stuck around for the first time. Porter ticked off the names and stats of all the players while the game played out, even most of those on the opposing team. He literally gleamed when the new Seattle running back, acquired this week in a trade, had a banner day, powering the Hawks to victory and a four and one record, leading their division.

Sy left the party at the end of the game. Porter was still high. He crowed and gloated for another half-hour before he ran out of steam and departed, he was late getting home as it was.

Rick inquired and Alec expounded on the progress with the potential legislation. "You know, that little shitbird over there is the hero here," indicating Lukas, who didn't get at first that this was a complement. "There was no way Dawes was going forward so quickly, until Lukeluke sprung this fifty page masterpiece of analysis on him. Here's to the German lackey. Tell 'em how ya did it Luke." Alec raised a beer in toast, not his first.

Lukas was embarrassed by the attention. "Well, it was

just interesting is all."

They drank to Lukas, and then Rick changed the subject to the persons in attendance. He inquired "Who was at the big meeting, the legislature wasn't in session. I'm surprised anyone was there."

"Well, let's see, a big jig named Shabat, seemed like a good guy."

"Shabat Odbayo, not far from me in Tacoma."

"Then, the wench Rasmusson, was after, Ridgeway .. Constance Ridgeway. An old bat of at least sixty" Alec added.

Rick was slightly hunched over with his neck pronated slightly upward, reminiscent of a vulture, not an abnormal posture for him when engaged. "She's from eastern Washington, Yakima maybe, has a lot of clout I believe. I had a solo with her last year, she's very savvy."

"Walli Walli. There were bunch of other grunt lawyers, and a couple of legislators who came late, Porcelli and Short. Short had no use for us, did he Luke?"

"Ah, no, Mr. Hardwick representing him was very rude, very. I didn't talk to Mr. Short though."

Alec was grinning now. "They had a hard time with that brief you gave 'em Luke. They were pouring over it but I'm not sure even the lawyers among them had any more of a clue than I did."

"Well, it was pretty logical really."

"For you maybe, not for a normal human being."

Max hadn't said anything until now, but the topic had definitely become a fascination. "Hey Alec, take it easy on Lukas there, okay?"

"Didn't mean nothing, Luke, didn't mean nothing okay?"

Rick now hit Lukas, and Alec, with a jibe. "Say, Lukas, I hear that Angela, Corey's sister, is quite a looker. Did you pick up any vibes from her?"

Lukas turned white, they all noticed immediately, he

was greatly agitated, unable to respond.

"Lukas, hey, just kidding there — sorry, you okay?"

Alec jumped in to relieve him. "What in hell do you know about Angela?"

"I know you went apeshit over her is all."

"You ... I didn't ... what are you talking about."

"I have my sources, you called her the next day didn't you. I don't hear any denials."

"So, how about those Seahawks, huh?"

"Uh, ha ha ha ha ha ha," Max was quite amused as was Rick. Lukas was still recovering.

Alec decided to wait until evening to call Angela, which was difficult for him. After eggs and sausage, he decided to take a walk to Central Market, about two miles. It was an overcast day, not cold, with possibly a light rain in the offing, but unlikely anything heavy. He walked to 128th, then over to Meridian, and north across the arterial at 130th to Roosevelt Avenue. Many years ago Roosevelt had been a central thoroughfare in north Seattle, but with the building of the freeway and streets leading to it, Roosevelt had become idle and had fallen into disrepair. Much of the housing along the route was middle class and in a not dissimilar state of repair. It was an angle street though, which made it a shortcut for walkers from 130th and 1st NE to 143rd and Aurora.

The seven hills in Seattle all have avenues with precipitous rises. From Ballard up Market Street to 46th and Phinney on Phinney Ridge, possibly the steepest is Dravus Street up to the top of Magnolia, from the Space Needle around Seattle Center up Queen Anne Avenue, from Harbor Island up Admiral Way in West Seattle, from the industrial area of Spokane Street up Columbia Way to Jefferson Golf Course on Beacon Hill, from Alaska Way on the Seattle Waterfront up through the city on James Street to Boren Avenue on First Hill, and from Fairview Ave under the freeway and eventually up Roy Street to Broadway Ave on Capitol Hill.

So, it is hard to visualize that this spot on 143rd and Aurora, with very little grade in any direction, is among the highest points of elevation in the city. Alec continued north on Aurora past the city limit at 145th. He passed a couple of gambling parlors, out of the city where they are legal. Walking down the mild decline toward 155th, there are an abundance of small businesses, from insurance branches to carpet stores, a variety of fast food, and a couple of sit down franchise restaurants.

Approaching Central Market a few blocks west on 155th, he loitered through a dollar store. He usually always bought something, here it was a box of incense which would no doubt be put in a drawer never to be used. He glanced in on a sports barbershop, four chairs with barberbots ready to serve at three of them and a youthful Asian woman at the fourth, the only one working. Colorful paraphernalia blanketed the walls between four t-v's blaring away with replays of weekend events, notably Seahawk game highlights. Although Alec's target was Central Market, once there he had little interest in shopping. A delibot built him a ham and cheese sandwich. It was receptive to Alec's particular choice of garnishments, lettuce, mayo and Dijon mustard. He sat and ate slowly, idly eyeballing other shoppers and pretending not to.

After shopping he took a different route home, east on 155th to Meridian, and then south somewhat uphill almost all the way home. He had encountered very few other pedestrians either going or coming, except the occasional unreliable with his hand out, until passing 145th again and then the esteemed private high school of Lakeside, whose graduates included the Microsoft team of Bill Gates and Paul Allen, which had on display scores of students sprinting around the outside facilities. He sat for a while on a fire hydrant, skillfully decorated to look like the lion mascot, and enjoyed their exuberance. He was not particularly tired after returning home from the two hour trek, but when he plunked down in his most comfortable chair to read up on Harry Bosch's latest exploits he soon dozed off.

When he called Angela at 7:30, she answered on skype this time, as elegant as ever. "Hi Alec."

Alec was excited. "Wow, you look hot!"

Her look told him this was a mistake. "I look hot."

"Wait, wait, I was at a football party last night, my tongue is stuck in jock talk. Let me switch over — oh man, you really, really look hot — wait, wait, that was chick shtick." He put both hands around his head and twisted his neck with them. "There, I think I have it now, debonair flair. Hi Angela, it's very nice to see you, you look pretty with your hair like that."

She was still not amused. "If you think this schizoid thing works, forget it."

"Well, just stay on the line, I'll try every approach I can think off, let me know if anything works. I talked to your brother the other day. I told him I was asking you out."

"You did. When was that?"

"Saturday, right after we talked. He called me actually."

"Why did you do that, what did he say?"

"I wanted to know if you were attached, he said he didn't think so. He had no objections, but he wanted to know if I had caused you the grief that ended Macy's for you."

"Oh."

"Are you home?"

"Yes, I only drive down on Tuesdays in off season, or for a planned meeting."

"Well, that's okay, I'm busy tomorrow too. How about Wednesday then, I'll be in the neighborhood around 6:30."

"In the neighborhood?"

"Angela, what I told you last week was true, if I thought

I had a chance eight years ago, but we both know I had none. I know you're way too good for me, but I'm going to try to fool you anyway."

"Why don't you call me again Wednesday. Debonair flair is better, but try one of your other personalities next time, maybe you can fool me then."

"I'm trying real hard right now. Look, I'm smitten, you have me in the palm of your hand. Be kind to me."

This schmaltz seemed to be well-received. "Good night Alec."

El Gaucho, once the most highly rated restaurant in the city, had lost some of its popularity but none of its elegance and high standards. Alec had picked up Lukas at his 91st and Greenwood apartment, and drove straight south on Greenwood to Phinney, to Fremont, and up Dexter to Denny, then west to Sig's. Although it was only seven blocks to the restaurant, a nice walking distance, Sig ventured out in public with others almost never, so Alec picked up Sig and Spencer for the short drive.

The ambiance of El Gaucho, even at noon, was haunting; dimly lit with tables of every size and shape perched on different layers of flooring. The foursome was escorted to one of many private rooms, this one no doubt Sig's regular, by a tall, long-legged, lithe, African hostess. Once seated, and after preliminary drinks were delivered, they would be left on their own until they decided to order. Sig began with a toast with no words, a simple raising of his whiskey tumbler. The others reciprocated, Alec with his beer, Lukas ice tea, and Spencer with his martini.

"Let me first welcome the newest member of my team. Lukas my boy, you do not exude confidence and it took a lot of convincing by Spencer, but convinced I am that you are worth the price of admission. Are you satisfied with your remuneration?"

Sig was a big, burly intimidating presence, and Lukas

was suitably cowed. "Yes, I am only too pleased."

"You're paying Luke, Sig? I .."

"Didn't I tell you I'd see to it, you think me not a man of my word."

"No, of cou .."

"Enough of that. Alec my boy, I am feeling jubilant, let's keep it that way. I can tell you point-blank that I never thought you had it in you. When you came to me with this cocky idea of election finance reform I thought it complete poppycock, not because I am against such reform, on the contrary, I simply thought it was preposterously impossible. It takes an idealist not to be dissuaded from the start, and by god that's what you've been. You have a special rabbit's foot it appears."

"Well, I .."

"Let me finish. Now, talking money, Spencer and Lukas are lawyers, I can pay them as such. You, my boy, are not, and I am not in the employee business. If we keep going with this, there will be little to do until and if the Legislature acts. You will need to become a registered lobbyist, I can then recompense you as a lobbyist."

"Hmm. Do I really need to do that. How is that accomplished anyway, can anyone ..?"

"Yes, anyone can. Talk to Spence about it later. And, yes you need to do it, you need to be paid for your time. I can tell you boy, as unlikely as I would have thought when we first met, you have a knack for it, and it can be a noble profession. This project need not be your last obsession. Now, let's talk about the future. I've had my feelers out, and it looks like this constitutional amendment has much less opposition than I would have believed, it has a very good chance. So, assuming it does pass the Legislature, the legal contests begin. It is surely not a given that we will subsequently be involved, it will flop into the State Attorney General's lap. But, he will need help. We have a more than good shot at becoming an advisor to the AG for a couple of reasons. The work Alec has done with the legislators will not go unnoticed by them. Plus I know a few people to talk to. And best of all, we have Spencer, everyone knows Spencer, his work speaks for itself. Take a bow, Spence." Spencer barely reacted. "And, apparently we now have the best legal researcher in the business, in Lukas Schmidt, take a bow, Luke." Lukas only looked embarrassed. "Okay, good, now I'd like to hear what you have to say. Is there anything you know that we need to do. Spence?"

"Yes, there is more we need to look at, but we have plenty of time. Of course, the sooner we get to see the legislation the better."

Alec spoke up, "There's a legislator that we should talk to, a Constance Ridgeway in Walla Walla, she .."

"Don't worry about her, she won't be a problem."

"Have you talked to her then Sig?"

"No, no, I don't know her, but, well, we need not get into that. This whole thing has been kept pretty quiet. There is one guy out there making a fuss though, a senator, Walt Pu .."

"Purser."

"Purser, ya, right. So you know him then."

"We've met."

"Well, what's the story, how do you know him?"

"Yeah, we met once, we didn't get along."

"Alec boy, no time for secrets now."

"Hey, I'm getting hungry, anyone else." Alec looked at the menu.

Sig gave Alec the long stare, then let it go.

Alec called Angela again that night. She answered the phone but not on skype. "Again."

"Wow, you look hot!"

"Christ!"

"Oh, sorry, I'll get serious then. I can't make it tonight after all, and I can't make it tomorrow as it turns out, so we'll have to do it Thursday then."

"No, Thursday's out. So, why not tomorrow."

"Oh, tomorrow then, okay, I can cancel."

"No, not tomorrow, just wondering if you're just playing around."

"No more playing around, all serious from now on. I have plans but it's something I don't need to do."

"Sure, what?"

"Bridge, I'm playing tournament bridge tomorrow night."

"You play bridge, I didn't know that. My mother played all her life, even still plays once in a while. When did you start."

"I didn't start, and I don't really play. Let's say a guy asked me to play, so I'm playing, once. This is not a hobby. What's wrong with Thursday?"

"How about Saturday, I'm .."

"Saturday, perfect, I was just going to suggest Saturday. I'll be there at, say, 6:30. We can eat then go to one of those new movie things, you know, the ones where the audience gets involved, I've never been to one."

"Virtualart. Okay, Saturday, 7:00, no virtualart, just dinner."

"Yeah, good thinking, then we'll have a lot more time to ourselves."

"See you Saturday."

XVIII

The meeting with Sig the previous day was enlightening to Alec. He spent the morning and afternoon mulling over much that was said. That he could be a professional lobbyist had never occurred to him. He decided to ruminate on the matter for a few days before getting further advice from Spencer. The current election finance project was in limbo for a few months at least, the Legislature was not even in session until then, and it was possibly completely out of his hands in any event, no matter what transpired. He scoured the internet for other ideas that might turn into passion, but nothing really hit him.

He emerged from his condo looking to find something to do outside since it was a pleasant day, the sun had even managed to come out for a visit. The yard man would be coming the next day so he saw little need in raking leaves. Instead, he took another casual turn around the lake in the dinghy before returning to the condo to work on the weekly Sunday crossword puzzle, to finish it normally took the week.

Judd called to arrange a joint trip to the Lynnwood bridge event. Though they were ostensibly friends neither wanted the other invited to their residence, so they decided to meet in Northgate at 6:00 and drive from there. On the way, Judd needed to talk over bridge conventions. Alec was more interested in finding out the nature of the meeting after bridge, but Judd didn't budge on that.

"So, last week we're playing and all the other pairs were like ghosts who never say boo."

Judd smiled at that. "Look, this isn't poker where ninety-five percent of the time you're just sitting, waiting for the next hand, and only when you do get into a hand is idle conversation out. In bridge you are involved in every hand, that's what they're there for, not to make new friends. When the hand is over most of the time they're still thinking about it, wondering if they or their partner could have done anything differently."

"Hand, what hand, there are no cards, a card game without cards."

"There was a rash of cheating at high levels a few years ago, using screens is an attempt to make the game pure, to avoid even the appearance of cheating. The first thing they tried was bidding boxes, cards with bids to avoid voice inflections that could be interpreted on purpose or intuitively as couples played endlessly together. But the unscrupulous overcame this by the way they placed the bidding cards on the table, or when defending, how they placed the playing cards, whether sideways or at an angle, to give partner illicit information. Now the screens would seem to solve some of these problems. You probably didn't notice, but the computer even throws in random pauses so players can't figure out if partner has a problem or not."

"Jesus, it's just a damn stupid game."

"To you."

The traffic from Northgate to Lynnwood was moderately heavy but not stop and go, they made it to the convention center by 6:30. Alec drove, but since they weren't pressed for time he stayed off the rail. Judd did talk bidding conventions, some Alec was familiar with, others he simply nodded and immediately forgot. The convention center had ample parking within a couple of blocks of the bridge event, they parked between both cars and autobots. Other autobots lined the entrance as they deposited bridge players, most were lol, little-old-ladies, an acronym that much pre-dated the now more common interpretation.

The main room at the convention center was immense, with hundreds of bridge tables and chairs carefully laid out in rows throughout the venue. Men and women, and a smattering of youngsters, which in bridge circles was anyone under forty, some dressed to the teeth but most in casual clothes of various designs, were mingling and sitting throughout the room. Judd led Alec through the crowd to the far side of the room where the entry forms were sold, he had explained on the ride that they were playing in a one-session side game, not dissimilar in quality of play to the previous week's club game. The serious players would be starting the second of two daily sessions where the combined scoring determined that day's winners. Judd bought an entry, led Alec through the maze to their starting table, then went off looking for someone or other. Alec sat in his east seat, feeling very out of place, with hundreds of people swirling around of which he knew none.

An elderly pair, though clearly not a couple, sat north and south. The woman was dressed to the nines, Japanese with high cheekbones, raised eyes and eyebrows, wearing an elegant yellow and green scarf with matching wardrobe, expensive jewelry including a big stone on her left ring finger and a pearl necklace, and a haughty look without the matching personality. He was about the same age but very different in tone, eyes surrounded by wrinkles etched by his smile with a rough pockmarked face, old man clothes but not too disheveled.

There was some time before the start, so Alec decided to become the conversationalist, turning to the lady. "Hi, I'm Alec. How are you this evening?"

To his surprise, she flashed a courteous smile and introduced herself in Japanese-English. "Helwo, I'm Tan Sherwy, hees Pike."

"Hi, Pike Vanerick. Don't think I've seen you before, are you a local?"

"Yeah, Seattle, but I don't play much."

"Good time to start, who's your partner?"

Judd answered that question when he returned and sat. "Hi, Pike, and demoiselle Sherry."

The public address butted in as the tournament director made some announcements and the screens lit up with the first hand in play, they were off.

At the break after the fourth round, Judd motioned for Alec to follow. They exited to a hall leading to the restrooms, but veered off into a small sitting lounge. Alec was led to two men standing by the window actively engaged in their own conversation.

"Hey guys, how goes it, still leading the event?"

"I doubt it, we just bid a seventy-five percent slam, one of two finesses, down, of course."

"You could have end-played him and made it .. I know, hindsighting again."

Judd introduced Alec to Luftar Koleka, the former speaker, and Calvin Coors. Luftar's name belied his Anglo bearing, five foot ten with a bland, nicely proportioned yet attractive face, and the grey well-groomed hair of the sixty-year-old he was. Calvin was a little taller, although his round hunched shoulders made him look shorter, with a thick dark mustache over thin lips and dark brown hair receding from his forehead, giving it the impression he wore toupee. The conversation quickly changed from bridge hands.

Calvin began, "The famous Alec McNee, nice to meet you at last."

"So, when were we scheduled to meet then."

"Oh, just an expression, no,"

"It's just that we've been looking forward to it," Luftar broke in.

"Yes, so I've been told, and I've been most curious as to why."

"Well, we're anxious to tell you, but we have to get back to the game, not much time. Do you suppose you could visit with us afterwards, come up to our hotel room." Luftar invited.

"How about a drink in the bar instead?"

"Please, that won't work for us, and there is a reason. We have a mutual friend, we need to keep it private," Luftar explained.

"We'll meet you back here after the game, we can talk about it then if that's okay Alec?" Calvin had to clear his mustache from the corner of his mouth as he talked, he was being as obsequious as possible.

"Alright, see you here later, I'll give it some thought."

"Okay, good." Luftar started to leave, then to Judd, "Are we okay now?"

"Yeah we're good, see ya."

As they headed back to the event, Alec raised his eyebrows. "So, what was that, are you pimping me out, Judd!"

"They wanted to meet you, again, I don't know why and they aren't telling me. Believe me, these are honorable guys, absolutely nothing to worry about."

"Uh hunh, and ...."

"Okay, they offered and I accepted. It wasn't much and I was not soliciting .. You're going to tell me later what they want, aren't you? I'm as curious as you are."

"I doubt it, and I doubt it."

They finally finished the last hand to the Alec's relief, Judd was able to get results of their game immediately from the computer screen, "So, 48 percent, not too bad, almost average."

"Well whoop-de-do."

"You know, you could be a really good player with some work, your declare play is already sound."

"Not likely, that will be it for me."

After a pause, "You want me to go with you?"

"No, I want you to fucking go away." This was said bluntly but without rancor.

"Okay, good luck with whatever."

Alec ambled back to the lounge. Neither Calvin nor Luftar had arrived, but they did so within a few minutes.

Alec was upbeat with "Did you win?"

Calvin answered, "No, second, but over a board back, so one hand wouldn't have done it."

"What did you do on hand sixteen, Judd went for a number on that one."

They quickly picked up that Alec was woofing. "Sixteen, oh yeah, the one where you have a six-bagger to the king/queen in hearts?"

Alec discontinued the ruse. "Okay, let's go to your room, find out what Lukas has done now."

Their Best Western Hotel was only a short walk during which Calvin and Luftar talked bridge hands, Alec ignored them. Once in the room, Calvin pulled three beers from the mini-fridge, Alec picked a lounge chair, and they sat on the couch facing him.

"This is about Lukas, isn't it?" as he took a swig from his beer.

Luftar took the lead. "What do you know about him?"

"He's a weird twitch, worst sense of humor I've ever seen. But, before we talk about Lukas, let's talk about the two of you, who are you and where do you come from?"

"We're from the same place Lukas has lived for the last ten years, Chance, Montana."

Alec whipped out has Phantom 4000 and said into it, "Chance, Montana?" His handheld responded quickly. "Ferry crossing on the Yellowstone River, post office closed in 1928 with .." Alec stopped the message and look at the two. "Is that the best Chance you've got?"

"Actually, it's Last Chance." Alec opened his Phantom but Luftar stopped him. "I would suggest that you don't ask about Last Chance."

"And why is that?"

"Your inquiry will not get you anything, and it might

draw some attention you don't need."

"What are you talking about?"

Luftar pulled out his handheld and asked, "Tell me about Last Chance, Montana."

The written response was "Classified Information, do you have clearance?"

"I do have clearance so there won't be repercussions, whereas you don't."

Alec reflected, "So, a military base. No, I don't see Lukas as military, what then — a nuthouse?"

"Close, but not quite. But, it really doesn't matter, we can't get into this. Why don't you let us ask some questions?"

"So you're not going to tell me who you are."

"My name is Luftar Koleka, I am a county judge in Last Chance, Montana. This is Calvin Coors."

"Yeah, the jury, I suppose."

"Ombudsman. Lukas has been both public defender and prosecutor there until a few months ago. We want him back, for us and for his own safety. We want you to tell him that we know everything, and he can come back anytime. Will you do that for us?"

"You may know everything, but I know nothing. Why don't you tell him yourself?"

"We are not allowed to talk to him."

"Not allowed by who? Oh, of course, you are not allowed to tell me." Alec wasn't too sarcastic.

Luftar let it go. "Do you know why Lukas came to you?"

"Yeah, he told me he wanted to meet Spencer Dawes."

"And did he, did you introduce him to Mr. Dawes?"

"You don't know, I thought you knew everything."

"The last contact we've had is a letter he sent over a month ago. He told us he was looking to meet Mr. Dawes, and he found you through talking to someone at a poker parlor. We knew Judd played poker and asked him if he knew you. That's it, that's all we know."

Calvin piped in, "You know Lukas pretty well by now, right, can't you see he's not your average Joe; do you even like him?"

Alec looked them over intently, then paused to think for a bit before continuing. "Okay, I wish I knew what this is all about, but I can see you aren't going to budge. I guess I trust you though. So, I'll tell you a few things. It took awhile but I can say now that I do like Luke, quite a bit. Luke was working as a public defender in Everett when I met him. I introduced him to Spencer, and they hit it off. The three of us, and others, have been working on a project to get a constitutional amendment added to the state constitution, Lukas is apparently a brilliant research lawyer, Spencer swears by him. This was all within the last month, we are now waiting for the Legislature to act, if indeed they do."

Luftar and Calvin stared at each other, quite surprised at this turn of events, Calvin fidgeting with his mustache. "It appears you see Lukas often then, even socially."

"Well, yes, we've been to a half dozen business meetings, drove down to Olympia and met with some legislators last week, and he comes over to my buddy Max's house Sunday mornings to watch Seahawk football with the boys, that would seem to be often."

"Lukas watches football!"

"I don't think he really watches the game, but he seems to enjoy coming over. He helped Max with a minor legal problem, he's made a lifelong friend there, Max calls him the family lawyer. He was talking to another friend, Sy, last week about something or other."

"Do you ..?"

"That's it. I've told you a lot more already than I expected to, more than you've told me. You are smart guys, Lukas is a smart guy, but you are just as clueless as he is. I can believe the three of you were cloistered together on some island in Montana. Now I'm outta here, thanks for the beer."

"Are you going to tell Lukas what we told you?"

"Unless you're willing to tell me what's going on, I guess you'll never know."

Alec left them grumbling.

Right after his Raisin Bran breakfast the next morning, Alec skyped Spencer, ostensibly for advice about registering as a lobbyist, but Alec had other things in mind. Spencer directed him to the proper website, and told him which forms among many were necessary.

"I advise you to deliver them in person to the Senate Office of Public Records you see listed on the screen. Stick your nose in their face, if you simply mail them in, who knows when or if the right people will get to them."

"Okay, will do, thanks. Do you happen to know a couple of gentlemen, one named Luftar, the other Calvin?"

Spencer delayed in responding. "What now, what are you talking about now. No, never heard of them."

"I had a visit from Luftar and Calvin last night. They had great interest in your new mole, Lukas, lots of questions and a lot of concern, they're worried about him."

"I see."

"They say they've been working with him most of the last ten years. Luftar is a judge in Last Chance, Montana. Ever heard of it?"

"No, I haven't. I take it you are inquiring further about what he has told me in confidence?"

"Not just me, them. They want him back, they say all is forgiven, for his own good. Doesn't this interest you, you know what this is about don't you — aren't you a little curious at least?"

"I don't know. I could speculate but I won't, you need to talk to Lukas."

"That's what they want me to do, talk to Luke, but, I want to know what the fuck I'm talking about when I do."

"Okay, go get him, bring him over here, I'll try to get

him to open up. That's the best I can do. By the way, have you talked to him today, he was supposed to have something for me and I haven't heard from him."

"I'll get him tomorrow, bring him to your place around noon, will that work?"

"Yeah, good."

XIX

Roscoe Romar was a forty-eight-year-old black man, small at five foot nine and slightly built. He had been a Seattle police detective for the past twelve years, and was affectionately called Special, short for Special Case, because he was known to crack the most difficult cases that came to the department.

Years ago, when still a beat cop, he took a bad spill over a garbage can while chasing a perp. He wrenched his back badly and, against medical advice, let it heal on its own. This left him with a permanent hitch in his step from his right leg. The hitch became part of him and morphed into the rest of his personality so that a hitch also became part of his speech when there was none before. It was not a stutter because he could recite M.L. King's "I have a dream" speech without a stammer, it was an affectation that was transparent to any intentions. He was sitting at his desk, one of six crammed into the drab and cluttered room #415 on the 4th floor of the North Precinct, musing over two slips of paper laying there.

"What the hell?" He picked them up and sauntered to the open door of Lieutenant Graham "Grumpy" Martin's office. "What's this shit boss, just 'cause nobody's home?"

Graham was the opposite of grumpy, probably why the nickname stuck, massively obese but good natured nonetheless. "Check it out, Rosc."

"Check it uh out, the blueboys already did, twice, and uh nobody's home."

"They didn't wanna break in the door, landlord wasn't home. His number's there, you gotta look inside. Take

Muscles with ya."

"I'm uh still working the Rosberg case."

Graham chuckled as was his want. "Sure you are Rosc. Take Muscles."

Roscoe and Detective Beverly "Muscles" Koenig were to meet the manager at his #102 apartment at 1:00, but he had not answered when they buzzed his apartment. They didn't have to wait long until a well-dressed man exited, allowing them access. The man turned to say something until he saw Muscles, then let it go. It was an aging three-floor closed building with eighteen tired units, clean hallways, but poorly lit, noticeable on this overcast day. They went upstairs and knocked on #206, but no one answered. They then tried some other units on the same floor, but nobody was home today it appeared. They went up to the third floor and finally found success at #306, directly above the unit of interest. The tenant responded quickly to their knock, but took quite some time getting the door open. She was a middle-aged woman in a wheelchair, who, no matter how old she was, looked older than her years, with pallid coloring and graying motley hair. They were not invited in, they conducted the interview from the doorway.

She appeared to be Spanish. After getting a "No" to his "Hablas ingles?" Roscoe knew he was in trouble. Spanish was required for a detective, and he had taken the requisite classes, but conversation with a native was a different ballgame.

He managed to get her name, then tried "Ruido" and pointed downstairs. He took some time interpreting the "Estrepeto ayer" response to indicate a crash, then after "dile a quien sea," received a long series of wheezed, "No, senor" for that and all other inquiries over the next five minutes.

"Didn't you find that a little odd?" Roscoe asked Bev after they left her, and got the full "Yes!" for an answer. Both were tuned in to the oddity of a wheelchair-bound person living on the third floor.

When they got back downstairs the apartment manager was home. He showed some irritation at having to wait for them, but when he was quickly put in his place he became very cooperative. He had heard nothing from the tenant, and had met him only twice, both times to collect rent. He described him as best he could, then let them into #206. It was a lightly furnished apartment. The manager indicated that there was nothing he could see that had been added except a two drawer filing cabinet next to the desk in the living room which housed a modern laptop and printer. He was thanked and dismissed.

It was a small one bedroom. The living room on the right had somewhat new light-green deep-pile carpet, a quilted Chesterfield sofa against the back wall, and a dark cotton Bilsby lounge chair facing the television mounted on the wall to the right. The flooring for the rest of the unit was laminate bamboo, including the kitchen on the left where the cabinets and sink were old but in good condition. There was a rectangular cane kitchen table with four chairs positioned in the "L" made by the countertop. The bedroom was back and to the left, the bathroom straight towards the back of the unit.

"You smell anything, I think I uh smell gunpowder."

"Maybe. We need to get a dog in here."

Roscoe motioned for Beverly to take the bedroom while he checked out the bathroom. They reconvened five minutes later in the kitchen. "How's the bedroom?"

"Only a few clothes in the closet and drawers, no pictures, nothing else personal, the pictures on the wall are permanent fixtures." This was a mouthful for Beverly.

"Same in the uh bathroom, neat and tidy, except for one prescription we'll uh need to check, essentials only. This here's the uh only thing wrong with this picture."

Roscoe was looking at an upturned bowl on the kitchen table, cereal spilled and milk that had dripped to and dried on the floor. "Whadda ya think of that?"

"Grapenuts."

Roscoe gave her a pained look. "Looks like he uh left before he had a chance to clean up, uh not like our guy."

They studied the kitchen, and looked in the refrigerator, the milk carton had been returned. Then they moved over to the living room and the laptop, it was security protected. "We need to uh get a tech in here."

They crawled all over the place for another fifteen minutes, then gave it up and headed for the door, Roscoe's look at her as they departed was really a question, she volunteered an answer. "I'm convinced .... foul play."

They stopped by the manager's unit before leaving, to tell him that room #206 was now a crime scene, no one in or out, unless the tenant miraculously reappeared. Roscoe inquired about the nature of the tenant in #306, they were told that not all units are rented out, that one was not. He didn't bother to correct him.

Back on the street in their unmarked Ford Fission, while penning some notes before heading back, an old Tesla pulled up and an athletic man got out and headed to the apartment entrance. He stopped to look at the listing of names for the units, then buzzed one of them.

Roscoe asked Beverly in the driver's seat, "binos?" She pointed to the glovebox where he found a pair of binoculars, he peered over in an attempt to see the number being pushed. "Uh, yeah, that's us."

The man soon returned to his car and drove off. "Let's see where he going." They followed.

Traffic was light as the car drove north on Greenwood, turned east on 105th, across Aurora to Meridian towards Northgate, then left and north until 122nd, around and then east again on 125th and into Haller Lake residentials. They watched him park in front of a newer two-story house and enter the upper unit. They looked at each other with a "what now?" expression, then simultaneously opened their doors.

When they rang, Alec was exiting the bathroom after a liquid deposit, and soon was at and opened the door.

Roscoe presented his badge. "Good afternoon, I'm Detective Romar, this is Detective Koenig, could ..?"

"Holy Jesus, look at you, Detective Koenig!"

She was at least two inches taller than Alec, shoulders like those of a football lineman, leg muscles perceptible in her pleated blue pants suit. She was not unattractive, dark brown hair with a rather solid bland face that gave away nothing, even with Alec's outburst. Alec made it a habit to be inconspicuous and respective to law enforcement, but he broke that habit here.

"Wow, what an Amazon, So, Detective Romar, you try to talk me into a confession and if you fail Koenig beats it out of me, is that it?"

They were not amused. "Sorry, sorry. You want to come in, guys?"

"Sure, thank you. And who are you sir?"

"Oh, yes. Alec, Alec McNee, come in."

He shook hands with both detectives as they all entered, then he guided them to the kitchen table and chairs. Alec and Roscoe stared for a bit, then Alec sat in a kitchen chair and Roscoe followed suit.

Beverly remained standing, and asked, "Do you mind if I look around Mr. McNee?"

"Alec, Alec works fine, and do you have a first name, Detective?"

She remained stoic and said nothing.

"You know, I had a friend once, way back when, who was a bodybuilder aka Arnold, you remind me a lot of him. His nickname was Muscles — anyone ever call you that?" Still no reaction. "Sorry, sorry again, I am just so impressed, seriously, it is an honor to meet you, Detective Koenig. You are a force of nature. Yes, go ahead and look around if you like, but please don't be reading any documents or look at my computer."

Roscoe waited patiently until Alec's attention turned back to him. "So, Mr. McNee, Alec, do you know a Lukas Schmidt?"

Alec looked askance, not intending to lie about anything, but unsure what to give, not knowing the reasons for the visit.

"Look, Mr., uh Alec, we're not here to trick you, we aren't trying to hide anything. There have been two 911 calls in the last two days claiming that Mr. Schmidt has being taken, we are looking for him. So please, do you know him?"

"Yes, I know him. How long has he been missing?"

"We don't know that as yet, this is a new case starting this morning."

"How did you know my name then."

"We just followed you from his apartment."

"Oh, of course. Who called 911?"

"Mr. Schmidt left two messages, we're not sure how that was done, possibly it was pre-programmed."

"Yes, he would."

"Any more questions before you answer some of mine, like when was the last time you saw him?"

"Well, I haven't really seen him all week, since last Sunday I guess. I know an acquaintance talked to him on Monday I believe, but he apparently missed an appointment after that."

"This acquaintance, who might that be?"

"Well, uh .."

"Do you need some legal advice, perhaps you want to make a call before continuing."

"That's the thing, he is a lawyer, both mine and Lukas' lawyer for that matter, we've been working on a project together."

"Okay, look, talk to your lawyer and have him get back to me, quickly if possible." Roscoe presented Alec with his card. "So, I'll wait on that then. Can you tell me how long you've known Mr. Schmidt?"

"Not long really, a couple of months. He's only been around here for that long, prior to that he spent the last ten years in Montana, or so he told me."

"Montana. Where in Montana?"

Alec took some time, then checked at the card. "Look Detective Romar."

"Roscoe."

"Roscoe, I really want to help you find Lukas, I didn't know him long, he quickly became a friend, but .."

Beverly returned and hovered over them.

Roscoe nodded. "Yes, I understand, I think we're good for now, but we'll be back, I hope to know a little more then."

They all rose and walked to the front door, Roscoe limped noticeably.

As he shook hands with Roscoe, Alec asked, "You okay?"

"Sure, just an old war wound."

"Detective Koenig, sorry I was such an ass."

She was as stoic as ever, but shook his hand.

Roscoe was obviously keyed up when they returned to the squad room. "Bev, get uh ahold of Brownie, we need him to crack uh that 'puter.' I'll get a K-9 down there. Let's uh get on this one."

"Brownie isn't in today, don't know who's on tech duty today."

"We uh need Brownie, need someone who speaks Spanish."

"Kelso has a dog."

"Kels, yeah, good. You uh get a tech, I'll call Kels."

Someone from across the room yelled, "Got a Special call on line 3."

Roscoe pulled out his handheld as he went to his desk.

"Yeah ... Dawes ... uh hunh ... do you ... Last Chance ... I see … okay, thanks for the call, I'll get back at you later then."

He got online with his laptop and searched around for about ten minutes, then bolted up and hitched his way to Lieutenant Martin's office, he shut the door and plopped down into a chair. "Are you ready for this, boss?"

Graham was suitable impressed, it was rare that anyone shut the door, he pivoted his bulk to face Roscoe, toweling off sweat from his forehead and neck. "Go!"

"Out of curiosity, Muscles and I uh followed this mope, Alec McNee, from our m-i-a's to his uh place out at Haller Lake. He knows the m-i-a, wants to help, calls his lawyer uh who also knows the m-i-a, is his lawyer in fact, Spencer Dawes. He uh just called me."

"Spencer Dawes, The Spencer Dawes?"

"Yes, that Dawes. And, uh, just looked up Alec McNee, ring a bell?"

"Ah .."

"As in McNee v State of Washington."

"Oh my, that McNee, oh. So who is this m-i-a, what's his name?"

"Lukas Schmidt, can't find anything uh about him anywhere. Dawes tells uh me he's from Last Chance, Montana, so I look that uh up, here, take a look." Roscoe shows Graham the "Classified Information, do you have clearance" message. "You uh know anything about this?"

"No, never heard of it. Okay Rosc, great work. Let's keep this quiet though, okay. Find out who this guy is. I'll see what this Last Chance deal is all about. You got any ideas there Rosc?"

"No, uh not a clue. I thought I smelled uh gunshot in the apartment, going to get uh a dog in there. We need to look at his uh computer, there may be something else going uh on in the building too, probably no connection though."

"What's that?"

"Let me check it out."

At 3:30 that afternoon a team of five descended on the Crown Hill Apartments, Roscoe and Beverly, Kelso Waits with his German Shepherd Loki, and River Thorne, their premier IT man. Forensic specialist Jake Heifer had cleared them to come, he had completed dusting for prints and collecting items for DNA testing. The entry door was propped open, Roscoe went directly to the manager's unit and knocked. The manager was at the door, waiting alertly. Roscoe didn't want the manager upstairs, so asked for a key to unit #206, the manager handed him the key, but told Roscoe he needed it back because it was the pass key to all units. Roscoe got what he wanted without having to ask.

There were chemical odors throughout the apartment, but Loki took no notice. He immediately went to the kitchen chair parked in front of the spilt cereal, minus the bowl, and barked. It had been explained to Roscoe one time that a dog's olfactory senses worked similarly to a human's vision, a woman in a dress shop can quite easily find the only green dress, just as does a dog identify the exact smell trained to be found.

The shepherd looked up, Kelso followed his gaze. "There's a bullet hole in the ceiling Rosc."

Roscoe identified the hole. "Bev, can you uh get that slug for us, have the manager find us a ladder." River by this time had found the laptop and was working away.

Roscoe took Kelso with him up to the third floor. He knocked on the door of #306 but no one answered. He tried a couple more times, then opened the door using the pass key. The unit was identical to the one below, including furnishings that varied only a little. The place was neat and clean, no one appeared to be living there. They left the unit and Roscoe examined the hallway floor where he traced the hint of wheelchair tire tracks down two units to #304, he knocked there. There was no answer here either, initially, but Roscoe knew from the manager that this unit was rented so he knocked again, louder. They heard shuffling through the door and finally a young woman, with an infant hiding behind her colorful dress, opened the door.

"Hola, viniendo dentro." They brushed past the women into the unit. The old woman in the wheelchair was in the living room along with two other children, both under the age of ten, and one other woman was stirring a pot in the kitchen. Roscoe didn't bother with any more broken Spanish, he had Kelso do the talking from that point on, which was about another twenty minutes.

They represented three families from El Salvador who had been working the fields at Mattawa in Eastern Washington since the spring. When picking dried up, they headed to Seattle where the men were out looking for day jobs with mixed success, one apparently had secured a three week job at a construction site. Roscoe was expecting such a finding. They thanked the women and left them in peace. Since the debacle of sanctuary city arbitration years earlier, it had become the policy for local law enforcement to communicate with ICE about any illegal activity by apparent undocumented immigrants, they were not required to investigate themselves unless action was necessary.

"So, uh whadda ya think Kels, we need to pursue this?" Kelso wavered, Roscoe answered for him, "No, I uh don't think so neither, but we better make uh sure they don't get in the way of this bis'ness below."

XX

After the unexpected visit from the police, Alec immediately called Sig. He told him about the visit and asked if he had seen or talked to Lukas lately. Sig denied any contact with Lukas, "why would he". Alec then called Spencer who also had not seen or heard from Lukas since a Monday phone conversation. Lukas was to do some research this week and have a report ready for Thursday, nothing was forthcoming. Alec gave Spencer an account of the visit by the two detectives and gave him Roscoe's number, Roscoe would want a call since Spencer was the last known person known to have contact with Lukas.

Alec was bewildered by the apparent lack of concern shown by both Sig and Spencer. He himself was quite grieved by Lukas's disappearance. He stewed about it all day, wondering if the surprise visit of Luftar and Calvin was more than just a coincidence. Spencer knew of these two, and had no doubt talked to Sig about them, but neither brought them up in their conversations. He realized how idiotic it was that he didn't get a contact number for those two. He considered calling Judd for one, but thought better of it. He also considered calling Porter to find out more about Lukas's history, but rejected that idea as well. Better to give it a day or two, maybe Lukas would turn up.

The next morning he was still keyed up, but he at least realized how foolish he had been to expect Sig or Spencer to display any reaction. These two spent their careers camouflaging emotions. He had an inclination to drive back to Lukas' apartment to see if he had showed up, but decided that his decision the previous evening to give it a rest was best. He did get out of the house, down the hill of 125th to his barber in Lake City. Well, not exactly his barber, but to a barber shop run by mostly young Asian women, Vietnamese he believed, who appeared interchangeable. After his haircut, he stopped by Tonto's Flowers to look at floral bouquets, wondering if this might be a little over the top, but then again, Angela was a female, so ..

Alec had again put on his number two herringbone sports coat that he had worn it to Olympia, with a white striped shirt with dark grey pants. By 5:30 he was ready to drive to the 7:00 date with Angela. He checked all routes and decided on I-5 to Southcenter, east on I-405 to Renton, then south on Highway 167 down to Puyallup. The eta was 6:28. He preferred being early, he could always dally away some time. He got on the freeway at 130th and jumped onto the rail at Northgate, it would take him to Renton, driving after that. He felt particular trepidation about this date. Angela was not some bimbo like the one-timers he had hit on during his tours. She was quality, he had liked her years ago and he really liked her now, and if she actually somehow foolishly took a fancy to him, that was it, he was hooked. He wondered if this qualified as a catch 22, where you get what you want, but do you really want all that you'll be getting? He wanted to rope her, but did he want to get roped back? Any number of such frivolous analogies crossed his mind on the trip, the final conclusion being "that's just the way it is."

He arrived a good half-hour early, and dallied away some time in a local mall's used bookstore. He was stuck on Michael Connelly and found an old Harry Bosch he hadn't read. Once aboard again, his Tesla directed him to Angela's residence. Alec knew her father was very prosperous, but his preconceived notion that she lived in his palace was misplaced, it was a large albeit unpretentious two-story house, well-kept and nicely landscaped at the end of an upper class cul-de-sac, with a turn-around drive in front of a three car garage. He parked in the driveway, walked to the front door, and rang the bell. He could hear her steps in the hallway, when Angela opened the door all the negativity he had experienced on the drive was immediately dispelled and forgotten. She was radiant, he had to check himself from telling her she looked hot, but he couldn't help thinking it. She was wearing an orange, ruffle sleeved dress that highlighted her hair which had taken on an auburn hue as it swirled down slightly covering her left eye, a provocative look.

Alec handed her the wrapped flower bouquet with a tempered "Hi, you look nice."

She leaned out and gave him a light kiss on the cheek, "Thanks, come on in." She turned into the house, he followed through the entry hall, past rooms to the right and left, and a stairway going up, through to the kitchen.

"Let me put these in something. You want something to drink?"

"Uh, a beer would work."

"Help yourself, I think Corey left some the other night."

Alec grabbed a Budweiser from the fridge, and wandered over near a back patio door. The patio was finished smooth concrete, beyond which was a lush lawn going back about thirty feet and then apparently dropping down. There was a summer house closed for the winter off to the right but no other dwellings visible in back. He sat on a bar stool he pulled from under the kitchen counter, the convenient place for breakfast he assumed. She had, by now, arranged the flowers in an appropriate vase and set it on that same counter, she then sat on an adjacent stool. They chatted about nothing of consequence for a bit, her mother was upstairs resting so they had the place to themselves. He trying to look and act natural, she succeeding in doing that.

The topic turned to dinner, he acquiesced to a selection from her, in her backyard after all. "I was thinking maybe Daniel's Broiler, there's one down on Pioneer Avenue, pretty close."

"Yes, sounds good." Alec was relieved since there were a couple of entrees at Daniel's that he appreciated, he had been worried she would pick someplace fancy where he would have to gamble on the menu, he preferred to know.

"I am hoping to make this simple, dinner and maybe a drink, then home, is that okay with you?"

"Sure, that's fine, home early and then to bed." He was trying not to be flip, but it was difficult. She took it with an amused smile.

They enjoyed a very good dinner, she the lobster club salad and he Australian lamb chops. Daniel's always provided excellent ambiance with private tables. They were on the last glass of an after dinner bottle of Cabernet. Alec had been much more pensive than she would have suspected, she asked him about it. "You seem a little distracted tonight, I expected to have to fight you off."

"That comes a little later. Well, I have tried not to bring it up, but I can't keep my mind off it." He went on to describe the events of the last two days concerning the police and the disappearance.

"Lukas, that's the little lawyer you brought down,"

"Yes, he did most of the writing in the documents we left for you."

She showed equitable compassion and the topic gradually and thankfully played out with Alec feigning resolution.

Alec opened the door for her when they arrived back at the house, and walked her slowly to her front door. She turned toward him as he moved in for the kiss they both anticipated. One led to a second more extended kiss, he continued it and let her eventually break it off. She took some time to recover.

"I'm going in now, you are not."

"What, I was in there already, it's like a second home to

me now."

"Thanks for the evening, you were very nice, but we can't be doing anything here."

"Yes, okay. Can I get you to come to Seattle next time, like next week?"

"Ah, well, maybe. When did .."

"How about Saturday again. We can make it simple, a good dinner and a couple of drinks, then home early and to bed."

She laughed, and he kissed her again, she was receptive, this time it was he who broke it off. He said goodnight and she went inside.

XXI

Roscoe didn't like working weekends, and rarely did so anymore. He was a family man, a rare happily married police detective, who preferred his family especially on Sundays. His wife, Rosalie, took his two kids, Roscoe junior sixteen, and Mahalia twelve, and occasionally himself to Catholic mass. They owned a four bedroom rambler on three acres in rural Duvall, a forty minute drive on a good day back into the city. Rosalie taught third grade at Woodinville Elementary, not far from their place. It was a mutual decision to move there ten years ago. Roscoe wanted the kids raised out of the city, he was a city boy and had had many difficult times when a teenager. The kids were good, though they often complained about going to mass, their friends never had to, but they had yet to openly rebel, they still went.

On this Sunday morning, Roscoe and Beverly were sitting in their car listening to the final quarter of the Seahawks at the Baltimore Ravens. The Hawks were down three points and used their last timeout with thirty-seven seconds left in the game, fourth down and three.

"You uh like football, Bev?"

"Tried out at Idaho, linebacker."

"They had a high school girls uh team in Idaho?"

She looked at him like he was an idiot. "Idaho State, I made the team, may have even started since the coach liked me, but our first game was at Weber State, they couldn't handle it, no locker room available. I wouldn't use the men's locker, I didn't mind seeing them but didn't like them staring at me."

Roscoe had never heard her give out anything personal, and felt badly that he had botched this opportunity, so he tried to recover from his faux pas. "Did you get along uh with the other players?"

"At first I had a little trouble, but when they found out I could hold my own they were great, they began to root for me."

"Long gone are uh the transgender days."

"Good they're gone. Anyway, I didn't want the attention so I just dropped out. I was only doing it to see if I could, I found out that I could."

Timeout over, the Seahawks were lined up for a field goal that would tie the score. But no, the holder, a backup quarterback, took the ball, sprinted to his right, and threw to a backup receiver on the right flat who streaked down the sideline and was knocked out at the two yard line. Still with twenty-five seconds to go, two runs up the middle produced the winning touchdown, and the Hawks were now six and one on the season.

They got out of the car and walked up the steps to Max's front door where Roscoe could hear revelry inside, so he knocked loudly. Max came and opened, the rest of the crew couldn't see through the front door from the living room couch.

Roscoe held out his badge. "Mr. Zastera, I'm Detective Romar, this is Detective Koenig, is Alec McNee available please."

Max balked.

"Mr. Zastera."

"Call me Max."

"Max, we know Mr. McNee is here, can you ask him to come out please?"

"Alec." Max looked in, his inflection made Alec come to attention. He quickly walked over and saw the two detectives.

"Well okay, couldn't you just come back to the house?"

"We wanted to talk to all of you. May we come in Max?"

"Look, I got here when the game started, I was going to talk to everyone after the game, which is now."

"Well, we can all talk about it then."

"It's okay Max, let 'em in."

They all walked in to a surprised group that included Rick, Sy, and Porter, but no Lukas. Roscoe took charge immediately. "Hello guys, I'm Detective Romar, this is Detective Koenig. Sorry to break up your fun, great game though hunh?"

The group looked up, stupefied. Beverly received the benefit of most of the stares.

"We're here to investigate the disappearance of Lukas Schmidt. Alec has been .."

"I was going to tell you guys after the game. It's true, Luke is gone, no one knows what happened to him."

There was a little grumbling, but only a little, Roscoe let it die down.

"Okay now, nobody here is under suspicion of any kind, we're only looking for ideas as to what might have happened." He pointed at the three in front of the t-v and got them all right. "Sy, Porter, Rick, hi. Sy, if you could go over and have a chat with Detective Koenig I would appreciate it."

"Me? I don' know nuthin, I har'ly even talked at 'em."

"Now Sy, as I understand it you had a nice chat with Lukas last Sunday. Just tell her what it was about, nothing to worry about."

"Wern't nuthin, jus .."

"Please, let's make this easy, okay?"

Sy got up and walked over to Beverly near Max's desk.

"Good. Max, why don't you sit on the couch with Rick and Porter where we can brainstorm there."

The conversations produced little of use. Rick pretty much opted out, the only time he had ever seen Lukas was at the Sunday games, and he almost never talked to him then. He did relate the one joke he directed at Lukas, and how affected he had become. Max praised Lukas for helping him collect a debt, but he too had seen him only on Sundays. Porter had a connection, they both grew up in the same neighborhood, but he didn't ever remember seeing him there. He had run into Lukas by accident at his school, and asked him to the game only out of compassion since he was new to Seattle. He, too, had seen him only on Sundays since that first meeting.

Beverly had a little more success with Sy. Sy had asked Lukas to help locate information about his deceased father. Sy wanted to find out about other relatives and the circumstances surrounding his death twenty-five years earlier. No one in Philadelphia would release anything to Sy, he thought having a lawyer probe might get him somewhere. He hadn't talked to Lukas since last Sunday, so didn't know if he had made any progress, he was hoping to find out today.

Roscoe turned his attention to Alec. "So I hear you're a bridge player, play tournaments and all."

"Now who, oh, of course. Well I did play last Wednesday, I guess you know that."

"Yes, we do, and we'd like to hear about it and maybe about some of the other players. We have talked twice now with Mr. Dawes. We have an appointment to meet him in one hour from now, I thought you might like to come along. You will find it quite educational."

"Is this simply an invitation?" Roscoe waited him out. "Okay, yes, I'd be delighted."

The detectives mingled a little longer, hoping to uncover another tidbit, but nothing was forthcoming. They gave out cards and collected addresses, and were soon off.

They followed as Alec led them to Spencer's house in Issaquah. Spencer preferred that to having to travel into

Seattle, they arrived right on time. Spencer invited them in to his den, he added a fourth chair from his dining room.

Again, Roscoe took charge, after thanking and showing great deference to Spencer. "Okay, I'm going to update you on some of what we've learned, then I want to hear from you, then we'll get to the whole story.

"So, we searched and dusted the apartment on Friday, we came up with nothing. When we got into the computer though, we came up with quite a bit. Lukas kept a journal, it began three months ago when he moved to Seattle from Montana. In it he explains some of the problems he faced, such as difficulty getting a driver's license, he never did get one you probably didn't know, and obtaining other identification needed to get work as a public defender in Everett. This was because he had his name changed after his arrest in Missoula eleven years ago."

Roscoe paused to let this sink in. "It turns out that he was fascinated by the legal process, in particular with McNee v Washington, which he had followed closely. He was a huge fan of yours, Mr. Dawes, as, by the way, are we all. He had a burning desire to meet you, no doubt as a fan but also looking to impress you I suspect. He was aware through the media of Alec's history, in particular your penchant for playing poker, and eventually found someone at Drifty's poker room with a connection, Judd Hemmings, who comes up again later. Judd gave him the name of your friend, Porter Nash, Lukas remembered the Nashes as neighbors growing up and was able to locate the school where Porter taught. Somehow, not quite sure, he managed to get himself invited to your Sunday festivities, and that got him eventually to Mr. Dawes. He mentions going to Olympia for some reason or other, but from that point on the journal becomes less exact. For instance, he never says what it is you guys were up to, perhaps you can enlighten us. There is an aspect to this journal that needs to be emphasized, Lukas was extremely paranoid about his safety.

He rigged his computer to make the 911 calls, they were to be sent automatically if he failed to log on to his computer at least once every three days. He feared being kidnapped and murdered, but he was never specific about who he was afraid of. Do either of you know anything about that?"

Both Alec and Spencer acted innocent, they gave him a blank stare.

"Okay then .. Ah, Detective Koenig, anything you want to add?"

"The note." She handed him her notebook to look at.

"Oh, yes, the note. On a piece of paper in a pocket of his laptop case we found this message. 'To whom it may concern, my lawyer's name is Spencer Dawes. I confer my power of attorney to Alec McNee. I authorize Mr. Dawes to consider Mr. McNee's concerns to be my own and function accordingly.' This was signed and notarized. That ties the two of you in nicely, wouldn't you say. So, now, let's hear what you have to say, we can start easy with you Mr. Dawes, if you will be so kind."

Spencer was nonplussed. "Fine, but let's take a break first. Would you like some refreshments?"

Spencer left the room and returned with coffee, tea and cheese and crackers, then left again for five minutes, Alec suspected he was calling Sig. He tried to make conversation with Muscles Koenig, but without success. Roscoe limped out of the office for a while, presumably to the bathroom. They were all back in conversation ten minutes later, Spencer had the floor.

"I do represent Lukas Schmidt. I know nothing about his disappearance, so can be of no help to you there. As his lawyer, I cannot repeat what he has told me in confidence, so can be of no help to you there, either. I will honor Mr. Schmidt's request to rely on Mr. McNee for his concerns. However, since, to date, I have not discussed any such matters with Mr. McNee, I have nothing else to add at the present time. When Mr. McNee does instruct me, I will follow those instructions, but we will need private time and he will need my council before any such revelations are made public. It will not happen today. With that, I pass the baton." Spencer sat back.

"Mr. Dawes, I would have expected no less from you, but I needed to hear it. So, Alec, you take the baton, there is much you can tell and I will be only too happy to supply some material. Since I think we have a good idea of his movements prior to beginning this project of yours, let's start there. What are you working on, who is involved, and who is it you met in Olympia?"

Alec balked. "I need to talk to Spencer about this."

"Go ahead."

Alec pulled his chair over to Spencer's side of the desk and conferred. He then turned back to Roscoe. "Spencer will talk to you about the project, then I will answer the rest, Spencer."

"The exact nature of our activities seems not pertinent to your investigation so we shall keep them private for the time being. If it becomes evident that this is no longer the case, we will become more transparent. We will, however, let you know about any of the principals Mr. Schmidt has in any way contacted."

"Mr. Dawes, for the purposes of this meeting, we will honor your esteemed judgment, however that will not be the case going forward. Alec, please continue."

"Well, okay, the principals, the people involved here in Seattle are merely the three of us you know, and Sig Ulrick, I will get you his address. In Olympia, we met primarily with Senator Corey Rasmusson of Puyallup. Also, other legislators and assistants. Angela Nelton, the senator's office manager, took notes and would be the one to talk to about other participants and the time and place of those meetings."

"Very good, thank you. She'll tell me who Lukas met with, okay. Did you meet with anyone else?"

"No, not really," Alec answered.

"That sounds like a yes, who then?"

"I bumped into another guy, don't know him, Senator Purser."

"And ....?"

"And nothing, that's it, that's all there is."

"Okay, okay, let's move forward then to the interesting duo of Luftar Koleka and Calvin Coors. Tell me about them."

"This is kinda strange. They came looking for me, through Judd, as you no doubt know by now."

"Yes, we interviewed Judd alright. He told us who, but not why. Why?"

"They told me they were worried about Lukas, asked me if I'd met him, asked if Spencer had met him. They told me to tell Lukas that they know everything and that he can come back to Montana, that they want him to come back."

"And what is it they knew?"

"How the hell do I know! They wouldn't tell me what the hell they were talking about. That was it." Roscoe waited for more, but got only "I told them to fuck off."

"Where in Montana are they from?"

"They called it Last Chance, they looked it up for me online and got some warning message. They told me I might get in trouble if I got too nosy."

"So you don't know anything about Last Chance?"

"No, nothing. Are you going to tell us about it?"

"Why didn't you mention those two characters on Friday?"

"I don't know, it was so — I didn't really think about it."

"He disappears and the day before two weird guys are asking about him. So what, you thought it was a coincidence?"

"I, umm .. They didn't seem that way, one of them was a judge for Christ's sake. Anyway, it really didn't occur to me until later."

"You had my card .. Okay, okay. And you haven't seen

them other than that one time?"

"No, never before, never after, I hope never again."

"Bev?"

"Last Chance?"

"Uh, no, let's wait on that, we assumed they already knew but I guess they don't."

"Wait a minute, no, let's talk about it now, Jesus! And what was he arrested for eleven years ago." Alec demanded.

"We thought you knew that, too."

"Was he in jail? Is Last Chance a penitentiary? What kind of jail do you get invited back to?"

"No no, sorry, we're done for now. Counselor, Mr. Dawes, I expect you to have a long talk with your client. We have things we'll want done in Mr. Schmidt's stead."

Roscoe and Beverly got up and said their goodbyes, thanking Spencer for his hospitality, and departed.

Alec sat staring into space for a while, then focused on Spencer. "So, can you tell me what Luke told you in private now?"

"Yes, it appears so. He didn't say a lot, some of it you just heard. He was arrested for the sexual assault of an under-age girl and sent to a federal penitentiary for ten years, he didn't tell me where. He had been a lawyer before he went in, and spent most of that time doing legal research in prison, apparently he had access to whatever he needed. He didn't describe the prison itself but said the time served was not difficult for him."

"Shit, a little twerp like Luke would seem to be easy prey in jail. A convicted felon can't keep his law license can he?"

"No, that is puzzling. When I asked, he said he wasn't permitted to explain. When I asked if he ever actually practiced law, he gave me a strange look and said he once prosecuted a man for rape who was subsequently executed. I looked that up, there hasn't been an execution for rape in any state since 2008."

"So, come on, Spence, what's going on here, you must have some idea?"

"Alec, I consider myself a good lawyer. I understand and use facts, but I am not good at speculation. I leave that for more imaginative minds such as yours.

Sunday evening, after their meeting at Spencer's, Alec skyped Angela. She answered on the phone only, "So soon."

"Why are you hiding, covered with that white facial cream that keeps you so beautiful?"

"No, I'm naked."

"You're supposed to leave the wisecracks to me darling."

"No wisecrack, I'm naked, or I should say dressed in a towel. Sunday night bath."

"You take a bath on Sunday night?"

"I do."

"I can hardly wait! Hey, I called to tell you to expect a visit from the gendarmes. Spencer Dawes and I were questioned at length about the Lukas Schmidt disappearance this afternoon by the SPD. They wanted names of all persons he had talked to, thus, you and your brother came up. I doubt there will be much to it, but .."

"Oh damn, we didn't .."

"Sorry, nothing we can do about it. So, we still on next Saturday?"

"I'm still thinking about it."

"Good, later then."

XXII

Graham "Grumpy" Martin reserved the second floor conference room for a high profile meeting at 10:00 on Monday morning. Along with his detectives would be the Seattle Police Commissioner Sharon Beardsley, Seattle City Attorney Goren Golanski, North Precinct Police Superintendent Trish Smith, and whoever these notables might bring with them.

It was now 8:50 and the thread that would bind the meeting together was still absent, Detectives Romar and Koenig's case report. Graham seldom got out of his chair once in it, yelling out was a more common occurrence, but it was usually done with some diplomacy by not using monikers, unlike now. "Special, Muscles, get the lead out, let's go out there, it needs to be out by 9:00 at the latest, let's go guys!"

Roscoe and Beverly were working on it together, he the brains deciding what was important to include, she the brawn refining and writing it with clarity. At the last minute, he decided and she agreed that they better include a reference to the itinerants on the third floor, he didn't want anything coming back to haunt him should other investigators get involved and be overly scrupulous. They would leave out the trespass, if no crime could be attributed then not notifying ICE was not a problem. They had both arrived in the squad at 6:30, and now, just before 9:00, they completed the report and brought it in to Graham.

Graham started the meeting at 10:15, shortly after the Commissioner arrived. Along with those expected, Graham had a stenographer to take notes and recordings, Commissioner Beardsley brought her Special Assistant, Attorney Golanski brought two other attorneys, and Superintendent Smith brought the North Precinct General Attorney.

Grumpy began, "Hello everyone, good you could attend on such short notice. We invited the Federal Bureau of Prisons to send a representative, but they are not yet prepared to do so. Hopefully, you have all read the report by Detectives Romar and Koenig. We are not going to read the report, but, to start, the detectives are willing to answer questions any of you might have about it. Commissioner, is there anything you want to clear up?"

There followed some posturing, but less than normal, some very inane questions, and some pertinent ones. Golanski's number two asked about following up on Sy's request that Lukas contact people back east to locate some of Sy's lineage. It was suggested that perhaps that had precipitated the kidnapping which, in turn, would obfuscate the need to confront the Federal Bureau of Prisons. Roscoe told him they were checking it out, but doubted any such action from back east would take place so expeditiously. Questions about the farm workers were inevitable, and mostly dismissed. Roscoe fielded most of the questions, but a few were directed at Beverly and she handled them tersely and well.

Goren Golanski made the most cogent statement, and asked the most appropriate question. "It appears that you have concluded that the only pertinent leads are these two penitentiary denizens, Koleka and Coors." Roscoe answered in the affirmative. "So, why is it you don't send someone to Montana to interview these persons?"

Superintendent Smith interrupted, "Let me break in here. We have been talking since early this morning with Warden Ben Whitlock, he prefers to be called Mayor. He obstinately refuses to allow anyone in law enforcement into

Last Chance to interview any of his inmates, or citizens, for any reason, ever. So far the Bureau of Prisons has backed him up but we have yet to meet with anyone there, we will pursue this until we get a favorable outcome."

There was then a discussion between the agency heads about protocol and obstruction and the like, most of which Roscoe considered a distraction.

Commissioner Beardsley finally got back to the point. "This Alec McNee, obviously we know who he is, but do you believe him Detective, that he didn't know Koleka and Coors before this week?"

"So he says, and yes, I believe him. His thinking is not consistent with these two kidnapping and taking Mr. Schmidt back with them to Montana. He claims they showed sincere concern for Schmidt. We did check them out though, Luftar Koleka is listed as a Montana State judge in District 16, Calvin Coors is the District 16 ombudsman. They both have criminal records that are currently sealed. They were scheduled to play in this bridge tournament for a two day event beginning on Thursday, but they canceled and, instead, returned to Last Chance. This is very suspicious and leads us to believe they may have been playing McNee."

Golanski's number one assistant counted with "That seems impossible, that a district judge has a criminal record, and what would a state judge be doing in a federal penitentiary, something's very wrong here." Others chattered along in the same vein.

Graham Martin had been simply letting anyone jump in, now he did so. "It appears that Last Chance, Montana is a big black hole where nothing comes out. We certainly need to get someone in there, to interview Koleka and Coors at a minimum, and to find Schmidt as the goal. We at our level are stymied by the feds, we need you guys to get us in there."

This started more chatter, and some finger pointing, but ended any fruitful discussions, the meeting continued, but

Roscoe and Beverly were dismissed.

Roscoe decided it was time to take another look at the apartment. "Hey Bev, lunch?" She shrugged a yes. "How about Ivar's, then another look at the scene?" It was agreed.

Ivar Haglund's fish and chips restaurants and takeout counters were a Seattle staple. He opened Ivar's Acres of Clams in the mid-nineteen hundreds, on Pier 54 of the Seattle Waterfront. The restaurant did well, the fish and chips counter did even better. Patrons would crowd up ten deep and yell their orders to waiters writing on small pads, "Two fish, two small chowder," and the waiter would yell back a random number "59" which he would add to the pad. Orders were paid for and picked up on the left side of the overflow crowds. Most would eat right there on the waterfront, flinging chips to hundreds of swirling seagulls that plucked the chips out of the air, despite the "Don't feed the Gulls" signs.

Ivar taped his own commercials for local television, playing a ukulele and singing arcane "Keep clam" songs. Roscoe could always distinguish a non-native Seattleite by their pronunciation of Ivar as in "-ar," instead of the actual Ivar as in "-er." Ivar eventually opened two more restaurants and a multitude of takeouts, including the one Beverly was driving to on 135th and Aurora, the best fish and chips in town.

Roscoe ordered his usual fish and chips, and a cup of white chowder, while Beverly tried coleslaw and the salmon chowder.

"That was uh quite a circus they put on today, nothing like uh getting a bushel of bureaucrats together in the same room. Looks like we may uh need 'em this time, for a change."

"I don't think he's in there."

"Who, oh, Schmidt. Not in Montana. Why not, where is he then?"

"That diary stuff about being scared, the shot, think might all be a scam."

"A scam. who's to uh scam?"

"Wants to disappear, so those guys from Montana give it up."

"Hmm, never uh entered my mind. Maybe."

The apartment was unchanged from the previous Friday, with the exception that the computer had been removed, the spilled milk had not been cleaned up. The slug from the ceiling was your basic 22 caliber, no match had been found. The prescription drug found in the bathroom medicine cabinet was Cyproterone, a sexual drive inhibitor. Speculation was he wanted to avoid the temptation to commit another sexual indiscretion with a minor. They felt somewhat useless since nothing in the apartment jumped out at them as sometimes happened.

They both went up to the third floor to see if the migrants had been scared away, they had not. The same group was there, less one of the women, but plus one man who was sleeping. They woke him up. Being that they were cops, he was no doubt scared into cooperating. Fortunately, his English was better than their Spanish.

He and his brother had been out on the patio in the back smoking. He had heard what could have been a shot that the wheelchair lady had mistaken as a crash to the floor. Five minutes later, two men carried something heavy out of the rear exit and into a car parked at the back of the building. It was late, they had worked all day and were tired just before they were going to bed, about eleven. No, he couldn't tell if it was a person being carried; no, he didn't get a make on the car; and no, he couldn't possible identify the two men. When he got all that he thought could be gotten, Roscoe thanked him, Ricon, and let him go back to bed.

Roscoe was tempted to take him in for a full statement, but decided it would be better to come back in the evening when both brothers were around. In truth though, he suspected they might never see Ricon again.

"You better come up with a new theory Bev. Can you come back here tonight with Kelso and get a signed statement from these two brothers?"

"Will do."

One word more than he expected.

The squad room was bustling on Tuesday morning, or at least Graham Martin certainly was. He arrived at nine wearing his uniform blues, no one had seen that except for the rare funeral. Indeed, no one would have believed he could find a uniform to fit into. His normal attire was a white shirt and tie, with a sweater or casual jacket as cover. He lumbered out at 9:30 for a meeting at the Downtown Headquarters, was back at 11:00, then went downstairs for a meeting with North Precinct dignitaries. At 1:00 it was back downtown meeting with Federal Justice officials.

Roscoe spent most of the morning at his desk. He went over the statements of Ricon and Domen, the Ortega brothers, that Beverly and Kelso had manage to obtain. Nothing new there, except Domen was sure one of the men threw something in the dumpster, he said he heard it clang. Roscoe called sanitation to see when that dumpster would be emptied, tonight before 9:00. He also made a lot of other calls and received a call from his cohort detectives, Todd Wallace and Steffi Sanchez, who were enlisted to drive to Puyallup for personal interviews with Corey Rasmusson and Angela Nelton. The feedback was the "nothing new" they expected, but phone numbers for the other contacts Lukas had made in Olympia were provided by Angela, all avenues would be explored. Beverly and Roscoe covered them, learning the expected "nothing new."

"Interested in uh climbing through the garbage?" Beverly knew it was coming, she got up and grabbed her coat.

"I'm uh going with you."

It turned out that Roscoe did the climbing. Before going to the apartment building they stopped by sanitation in the north end at 69th and Roosevelt to get protective overalls. Unfortunately for Roscoe, even the largest of those available were not big enough to fit Beverly, it was her long muscular legs that caused the problem. Roscoe regretted having tagged along. But the regret and unpleasantness were rewarded, a 22 caliber handgun had nestled to the bottom of the dumpster, retrieved after much cursing and complaining by Roscoe. They bagged it and sent it downtown to forensics to get a match with the bullet also sent there.

Graham came huffing back at 3:30, he went straight to his office and closed the door. Roscoe gave him ten minutes, then he and Beverly looked in. Grumpy was fast asleep, his bulk balanced in his chair in a miraculous way that kept him from tumbling to the floor. A light tap on the door did not disturb him, so they took the tactful approach of shutting the door and yelling "hey, Grump" through it just before reopening. The ploy worked, Graham had come to, albeit still groggy.

"Hey Grump, thought you uh might like to know that we found a gun, in uh the dumpster behind the building."

"Gun, really. It match the bullet?"

"22, like the uh bullet. Been fired, one bullet missing. An uh upstairs neighbor saw two men uh carry Schmidt out and dump the gun on the way."

"Seems strange, don't you think?"

"Yeah, unless it uh wasn't their gun. We think it was probably uh Schmidt's, they wouldn't want to keep his, doesn't seem like the uh type to be carrying though."

"What time was this?"

"Estimated at about uh 11:00. McNee said he uh left the primes at 10:30, perfect chrono."

"A little more ammunition for tomorrow, we'll be

having another conference downstairs. Should clear up a few things for us, the DOJ is sending someone."

Roscoe arrived in the squad room punctually at 8:00 each morning. He would get an eta online and depart from home accordingly, on the way he could often give Rosalie a ride to school, sometimes one or both of the kids as well. This Wednesday, after taste testing the coffee from the first floor stand, it was usually palatable, he checked incoming calls. The old days of texting were long gone, Seattle Police were banned from texting when on duty because hacking had come so prevalent. Officials and celebrities who relished privacy were the first to voluntarily give it up, even many regular folks got fed up with everyone knowing their business, texts were transparent to all.

Roscoe had never seen a live airing of the old Mission Impossible t-v series, but had seen clips of the intro where the protagonist received a confidential tape which self-destructed after playing. He thought it ironic that such a mechanism was now standard operating procedure. Even the common man used audio apps that self-erased recordings after they were played. Others could still spy and steal the messages, but the user would have a record of the call and know he had been hacked when the recording was blank. Hacking an audio became an illegal activity though they were seldom investigated, with the exception police messages, these they vigorously protected.

Roscoe checked his messages on the handheld from his desk, most of the numbers he recognized, but he took interest in the one that came in at 4:00 in the morning with "restricted access" as the origin. He switched on his record-audio disk, an off-line stand-alone unit that would re-record messages, "R-A on," and clicked the message. "To Detective Romar, I will call this number tomorrow at exactly noon. Have Alec McNee available to receive, only he, end of message." Roscoe called Beverly over to listen.

"Luftar Koleka."

"Yeah, uh maybe."

"I wasn't asking." Roscoe looked at her and waited for more. "I found a video of him accepting a trophy on the ACBL website, same voice."

"On where?"

"ACBL, American Contract Bridge League."

"Oh sure, where else."

The gathering at 11:00 began on time. Other than the North Precinct's Trish Smith, none of the other top brass were present, but Golanski's number one, Sherry Orlanski, and number two, Thom Molder, returned as did Beardsley's assistant, Reggie Jackson. The new man was from the DOJ Bureau of Prisons division, Earnest Bagnoll. Graham Martin introduced everyone, then gave a brief outline of the purpose of the meeting before turning it over to Bagnoll of DOJ. Bagnoll began with the default dictum that everything said would be confidential, he emphasized this sufficiently so that everyone eventually thought it would be best to believe him. He got to the point quickly after this start and began a long monolog.

"The town of Last Chance was built by the federal government fourteen years ago in a remote area of eastern Montana. It was incorporated as a Montana city ten years later. Comfortable modern apartments were built for an original population of 2,000 residents, the current population is 5,673. All the essential entities of a normal city are present. A municipal building housing a courthouse, police department and utilities department, and a community center are all functioning. A mayor is elected every four years, a district judge resides appointed by the state of Montana, a city council appoints a sheriff, etc. There is one major employer for the city, an automotive parts company specializing in computer electronics. It employs about half of the citizens, and a healthy construction company is growing with the population. Wages are commensurate with industry standards.

"Originally, the state of Montana, with support from the federal government, controlled most of the commerce, restaurants, grocery, pharmacy, and such, but capitalism has thrived, personal property is honored and residents have bought out most the restaurants and other small businesses. They have improved those services for the most part, also have started other enterprises, and they build their own houses.

"In addition to being an incorporated city, Last Chance is also a federal penitentiary, with no bars and few guards. All residents in the city are male, and all, with the exception of the mayor aka warden, are convicted felons, and all are felons convicted for a sexual offense."

He paused just long enough to let that sink in, but did not look for a reaction. "You will remember twenty years ago when the prison population was at its highest, the Congress and the Judiciary finally got to work and released about half of the inmates convicted of non-violent drug offenses, they found other ways to punish these individuals. Your current President, then a senator, was instrumental in getting this done and it was a great success.

"Five years later, still as a senator, he looked more closely at the penitentiary problems, and a second set of convicts, sexual offenders. He came to the conclusion that few of these inmates were hardened criminals in the sense that they were looking for personal gain by their crimes, they were for the most part crimes of passion. Their actions were caused by a sickness not criminality, although many were brutal in the extreme. Many of these offenders were normal looking citizens from all walks of life committing multiple offenses before finally getting into the big house. Recidivism rates were high, and even those not found re-offending may merely have found ways to hide their acts, prison is a good school for scoundrels. He concluded that many belonged in an asylum, not prison, but that was not a practical solution. He and some of his cronies wrote up some legislation authorizing a revolutionary incarceration technique, the building of a penitentiary exclusively for sexual offenders. His bill was a pork barrel earmark attached to a farming subsidy bill, and received little to no notice.

"This facility has miraculously remained under the radar for fifteen years now, and it has proved to be very successful. Creating Last Chance was quite expensive, but it now almost pays for itself. The town has 100 percent employment. The citizens or inmates pay taxes, and pay for their own apartments, homes, food and all other amenities. The state of Montana has an incentive to keep the profile quiet, money. They spend little to nothing of state funds, there are no public roads in or out of the town, yet the state is the recipient of sales tax and other state taxes. Nevertheless, it has been a longstanding concern that despite all the benefits, an outcry from many do-gooding quarters comparing the system to a Mengelean experiment might create too much scrutiny to keep the city functioning as is.

"One other thing for now, the success of Last Chance is primarily due to the management of its warden, Ben Whitlock. Convicts from every prison in the country are interviewed as potential residents. Of utmost importance is selecting the right blend of potential non-violent offenders who can contribute to the success of the city. With few exceptions, Ben has been masterful at doing this, he personally approves every person admitted. So, that's my pitch, let me take a break and then I'll answer some questions."

Bagnoll left the podium and walked down to a refreshment table set up in the back. The audience, limited as it was, was greatly animated by this presentation, as was Roscoe who grunted to Beverly, "Whoa, uh never saw anything like that coming."

"No."

Graham approached Bagnoll but their conversation was casual, no one in the group pursued with questions until Mr. Bagnoll returned to the podium.

Thom Molder began the inquiries. "How can this work, it can't be both a city and a penitentiary. Either it's state or federal, who owns the property?"

"You must be a lawyer. Well, this is one good reason not to rock the boat. I cannot answer that question, but so far everyone is happy."

"What happens when ..?"

"Your question was clearly brought up when the city incorporated. No doubt some arrangement was made by state and federal, but I am not privy to that. And surely whatever arrangement that was made would face serious legal challenges once exposed, another of many good reasons to keep in the shadows."

Molder persisted, "In this day and age, how can this facility possibly be clandestine, satellite imagery can spot a penny on the pavement."

"Yes, that is correct, but you may not be as familiar with the enhanced satellite camouflage technology that effectively shields visuals except from the most sophisticated spying, and who would want to be looking that closely at some remote area in Montana."

"There are no bars, so what's to stop someone from just walking away?"

"Okay, I need to mention some logistics. The only way into the city is by railroad, only once has a helicopter landed there. Every day the train brings in supplies and takes out automotive parts and possibly some other products. The only guard in the city watches over the railroad entrance which is very well secured. Inmates have voluntarily been fitted with a chip, which is monitored only if an inmate wanders five miles or more outside the city. The trip to anywhere habitable outside of Last Chance is much greater than five miles, it would take little effort to track that individual."

Roscoe rose with a question. "I would hope you are familiar with our current investigation. We need to interview two individuals residing in Last Chance, Luftar Koleka and Calvin Coors. Do you know when we might be able get in there to do that?"

"Yes, I can give you an unequivocal answer to that, never. No outside law enforcement person has ever set foot in Last Chance, Ben Whitlock will not allow it. In the few instances where an inmate was required to be interviewed for other legal proceedings, such as to testify at another trial, that individual was taken out of Last Chance after he agreed to do so. Ben doesn't even honor subpoenas.

"Let me make something clear. As I mentioned, there have been three mayoral races at Last Chance, in all Ben Whitlock ran unopposed, there has only been one vote against him when a citizen humorously voted for himself. The general sentiment of inmates at Last Chance is that they were taken out of hell and delivered to heaven by Ben Whitlock."

This put a hush over the audience, but they recovered and continued peppering Earnest Bagnoll for another hour. He finished his presentation with one more plea for discretion. "I think you all get the picture now. The challenges to retaining the anonymity of Last Chance have been ongoing ever since its inception. This is a unique situation, but we are hopeful we can solve your problems and still avoid exposure. Please keep in touch and let us know what you plan to do, we will assist as best we can."

They broke for a late lunch for which Roscoe invited Graham to join him and Beverly, it was not uncommon that they ate together, but Graham begged off saying he needed to consult with the brass from the precinct.

"How uh about Beth's?"

"Sure."

Beth's cafe was a greasy spoon on 73rd and Aurora that specialized in all night breakfast, providing a multitude of hashbrowns and generous strips of bacon. The lunch menu had been improved of late, and included an excellent chili favored by Roscoe, and vegetarian chili equally liked by Beverly, along with their freshly baked rye bread. It was a favored eatery.

Before leaving for the day, they managed to get Graham alone. Roscoe played the anonymous message which Beverly had managed to un-anonymize.

"Are you sure that's Koleka?"

"Yes, it's him."

"Well, we've got to get McNee in here then don't we, snatch him up if you need to."

It was agreed.

XXIII

Wednesday had been a beautiful day, Alec took a turn around the lake early in the morning. He considered getting out to the golf course, but decided that was not the ball he needed to be keeping an eye on. Instead, later in the afternoon, he took a second tour around the lake.

Afterward, he was staring out at the lake admiring the day when he glanced at the porch-cam in the kitchen and saw Roscoe coming up the drive.

He hurried to the front door and acted like he was leaving just as Roscoe approached. "Oh, what are you doing here, I was just leaving."

Roscoe looked askance. "Don't play games with me, jocko, I'm a detective you know."

Alec enjoyed the repartee, but didn't contest. "So, where's the beast. I didn't know you traveled without protection."

"Muscles, this was out of her way, it's on my way."

Alec smiled at the appellation, Roscoe reciprocated. "Well, come on in then."

Alec led Roscoe into the kitchen as he had done the first time, he was not ready to give Roscoe the full living room treatment. "Is this a social call, you want a beer?"

"No, not social, but I'll have a beer."

Alec grabbed a pair of Beck's from the refrigerator and delivered them to the kitchen table, they both sat.

"We got a call from your buddy Luftar today, he wants

to talk to you."

"Really. And what does he want to talk to me about?"

"We're dying to find out, he doesn't confide in us anymore. Noon sharp tomorrow, at our north end squad, your attendance is mandatory."

"Mandatory! You don't have to threaten me. I want to get to the bottom of this too."

"Good, because after the call we plan some entertainment. The update we failed to deliver on Sunday, with a lot more detail than we knew then. You should bring Dawes with you."

Roscoe got up and walked to the window, looking out at the lake. "This is a nice spot you got here, any fish in that lake?"

"Yeah, trout, perch, bass, and catfish, it's stocked every year, though only with perch, I believe. I've got a pole and a dinghy if you're ready to go now."

"Ah, next time, thanks. I used to like to fish, but it's been a while."

"So, how about a sneak preview."

"We need you tomorrow, with or without Mr. Dawes, I appreciate your cooperation."

Roscoe finished his beer and put the empty on the table, he handed Alec another of his cards, then headed for the door.

Alec called Spencer shortly after Roscoe left and told him about the visit. Spencer was suitably curious, so agreed to come in to Seattle and meet Alec at Sig's at 10:30, it was so arranged.

Later in the evening Alec was thinking about calling Angela when she beat him to the punch, she skyped him.

"Hi, good to see you. Were you reading my mind again, I was thinking of calling you."

"We got that visit yesterday from the Seattle Police, they came to see Corey and then me here in Puyallup."

"You look pretty cute when you're mad. Why do you seem so mad, I told you they were coming."

"Corey just called, someone called him, about a little blurb on The Olympian's website, here I'll read it for you. 'The Seattle Police Department has been in Olympia this week to investigate the disappearance of a Seattle man, Lukas Schmidt, missing since last week. A legal delegation led by William McNee, which included the missing man, visited various lawmakers, including Senator Corey Rasmusson, last week to advise them about legislation proposed for the next legislative session. There is no evidence that Mr. Schmidt had any subsequent meetings with persons in Olympia, the investigation was termed standard procedure by the officers.'"

"Oh, Christ, how did that happen?"

"I have no idea!"

"Who put that online, why would they even put that out, it's so .. William, where would they get William?"

"I looked at my notes, on your visit at our office you logged in as William, Patsy always gets everyone's name. She had William, Spencer and Lukas as coming that day."

"Ohhh, that's right, I did tell her William. I sometimes use my legal name for such things, William Alecsander. Who sees those notes?"

"No one, they're filed in the office … Wait I didn't go in yesterday as usual on Tuesday, but Patsy was there. She told me someone came in, who was that. Came in and wanted to meet with Corey. He sent her out to find him."

"Purser?"

"Yes, Walt Purser, that's it. You know him?"

"We met last week after you left me in that cafe, suffice it to say we did not see eye to eye."

"He's an asshole, Corey stays totally away from him."

"Do you know who runs that website, can you ask them why they put that on there?"

"Oh yes, he's easily intimidated, you won't see any more

from him after Corey has a word. But no matter, this kind of thing is never good, the airheads will talk it up."

"My god, you do get riled. What's going to happen if you get mad at me."

"I guess you better not let me."

Alec changed the subject. "Something's going on here too, I'm going in tomorrow to talk to one of the bridge guys who knows Lukas, at the police station. They tell me they're going to finally tell me what this is all about. Can I call you tomorrow?"

"Sure, yes, sure."

"Think hard about Saturday okay?"

"Okay, night now."

Thursday had the beginnings of another gorgeous day, the morning sun was working hard to lift the fog from lake. Cale Fazzio called Alec just after eight, getting feelers for a potential day on the course, Alec had to disappoint him. This seemed like another good morning to continue his habit of rowing around the lake. He put on boots, warm pants and his ski jacket, and made his way to the dock. As was his custom, he rowed vigorously for about five minutes, then coasted more slowly for the next twenty. He was now on speaking terms with an elderly couple, Pam and Harry Andrews, who were often on the lake in the morning, as they were today.

"Catch anything today, Harry?" This was his usual opening, he knew the couple didn't fish.

"Nope, Alec, not biting today."

"Hey, I was watching out yesterday and there was a guy who looked like he latched onto a marlin, his pole bent to the water until the line snapped, he almost went backward in the drink."

"You recognize the boat?"

"Silver rowboat, was wearing a blue vest."

"Sure, that would be Wiskers, lives two doors down

from us. Must have hooked ma or pa."

"Who's that?"

"They're two big old trout in the lake, three or four pounds they say, been around for years. Tony Noonan says he's caught 'em both and let 'em go, could tell they were different fish, he calls 'em ma and pa."

By this time Alec was in their wake.

Roscoe called Alec's car phone at 10:30 to make sure he was coming, minutes before Alec arrived at Sig's place. Alec confirmed, then mentioned that Roscoe might find something interesting on Thurston County's newspaper, The Olympian's, website.

When he arrived at the door, he was blindsided by a tantrum from Sig. "We try to keep a low profile and there you are, splattered all over the internet."

Alec was momentarily speechless as he followed Sig inside. "Umm, I .. we didn't .."

"No, you didn't. Why don't you go out and find the little bugger for Christ sake."

"Jesus, Sig, thanks for the nice welcome — let's get out of here, Spencer."

"So, you're going to be a cop now?"

"I'm outta here. I'll be in the car, Spence."

Alec didn't bother to check routes, they had plenty of time and he just wanted to beat it out of there. He took Denny east to Westlake, north to Mercer, and east again onto I-5 north. They didn't say anything until he was getting off the freeway at Northgate.

"He's human Alec, he's a little nervous about what's going on."

"Bully for him — like we're having a picnic."

There was another silence until they reached the North Precinct at 100th and Meridian.

"What's the schedule here, Alec?"

"In twenty-five minutes, noon, there will be a call to me

from Luftar Koleka, presumably from Last Chance, Montana. What it will be about I don't know. But whatever, after that the SPD are supposed to enlighten us about what the fuck is going on. That's all I know."

The squad room was buzzing when they walked in, the word was out, every cop not working a case was milling around. Alec and Spencer were being introduced to a few of them before Graham Martin put an end to it, directing them into his office and shutting the door, Roscoe and Beverly were in there waiting.

Graham was miffed. "How did that website get that stuff, who gave them your name?"

"I should be asking you that, you're the ones snooping around."

"None of our guys mentioned you or Rasmusson. So, you don't know."

"It was a guy named Walt Purser, he copped the agenda for the meeting we had down there two weeks ago."

"So who's he, why would he do that?"

"I don't know. Look, the person who put that out has been silenced, you won't see any more on that."

"Well, I hope not. It's tough enough to keep a lid on it here, I hope no one picks it up."

For the next ten minutes Graham gave pretty much the same instructions in different words over and over, keep him on the line as long as possible. For the last five minutes they all waited anxiously, the phone rang at exactly 12:00.

"Hello, Alec McNee here."

"How do I know that?"

"Aren't you skyping me?"

"We can't skype from here, but okay, I'm good with it now. I'm only talking to you, anyone else breaks in and I'll break off. I'll bet they told you to keep me on the line, isn't that cop 1-0-1? It won't matter a whit, I can talk all day, it won't matter." Luftar was enjoying himself.

"So, what do you want with me?"

"Just shut up and listen. I assume this is taped so don't ask me to repeat myself. The guy you'll be visiting is Vincent Swing."

"What, what are you talking about?"

"Didn't they tell you?"

Alec looked at Roscoe, who shook his head no, as did Beverly.

"Bullshit, Koleka, that's .."

Luftar was outright laughing now, "Ha ha ha, just my little joke, but that is what this is all about, in case you're wondering. You take I-90 through Montana and then switch to I-94, then take Exit 126. Go into the gas station, the only building there, ask to see Desiree, tell the person there that you are Napoleon. I've sent all the forms you need to the North Precinct, they should already be there. Send them to Desiree, PO Box 735, Miles City, Montana, 59301, that address will be on the forms you get. As the purpose for the visit, write, 'Visiting my brother-in-law, Vincent Swing.' The wheels are greased for next Tuesday, you should have no trouble. Just put your initials, not your full first name, just in case."

"Look, Mr. Koleka, this isn't going to happen, and someone else may be .."

"Haven't they briefed you yet, guess not? Well, no law enforcement person will be allowed here. If we did try to smuggle one in and are found out, which we almost surely would be, it would be deep-doo-da for us. Your guys desperately want to talk to us, I know. Hell, we'll show you where the body's buried, ha ha ha. That isn't funny either. What we told you last week is absolutely true, we are very concerned about Lukas, obviously even more so now. If you have any pictures or videos of Lukas, bring them with you," Luftar said.

Alec was about to say no about pictures, but saw Roscoe nodding yes, he paused for a bit. "I am very fond of Luke myself, but this is not my business, I .."

"Once you get in you'll meet Gracie, show him your copy of the entry forms and tell him you came to see Vincent. Don't make idle chit-chat with anyone, and avoid the warden at all cost. One more thing, no matter what they tell you, I can tell you positively that you will be perfectly safe here, you might even enjoy yourself. Do believe that." With that, he disconnected.

Alec breathed a sigh of relief, his end of conversation was very tense. "Well, did you get all of that?"

"It's about what I suspected he had in mind."

Alec looked at Roscoe incredulously. "Really?"

Before he could go on, Roscoe handed both him and Spencer a transcript of Earnest Bagnoll's presentation from the day before. Spencer read it in about half the time it took Alec, who then read it a second time.

After they finished, Roscoe took back the reports. "You understand that all this, obviously, is completely confidential, as in completely!"

Graham made a departmental statement of procedure. "The Seattle Police Department cannot encourage or even condone a lay person putting himself in the jeopardy required to fulfill the request stated by Luftar Koleka." He then removed himself from his chair with some effort and excused himself. "I need to go downstairs and update the Super, you are welcome to use the office," which seemed to double in space with his departure.

Alec turned to Spencer. "Do you believe all this, Spence?"

"Alec, as I have told you before, I have very little imagination, I believe what's in front of me until I can prove differently."

"Graham is correct about SPD policy. As I said, we are not surprised by Koleka, but we still have not fully developed our own plans about this situation. I suggest you both study the situation as well, Tuesday is just around the corner. The documents Mr. Koleka described did arrive today." Roscoe again handed each a manila envelope. "It is not appropriate for us to speculate at this time, so we are concluding this meeting, we will be in touch."

"If policy does not condone, why are you giving me this stuff?"

"It was addressed to you."

"Oh right. Well, I'm going to re-address it." He wrote, "fuck you" on the envelope, dropped it in Roscoe's lap and quickly got up and left.

Spencer had taken a Bubblebot in the morning, Alec gave him a ride home. Again, they had very little to say until almost to Issaquah.

"I admire your passion, but it often seems to be so misplaced."

"How's that?"

"When you left, it was such a childish tantrum, things just happen, deal with them."

"So you think what they want from me is just dandy. I suppose you'd jump at the chance to drop into a den full of sexual deviants."

"Me, not a chance. But you, I expect you'll go alright."

When Alec dropped him home Spencer asked him to wait for a second while he went in. When he returned, he dropped the manila envelope on the passenger seat.

Alec had turned off his phone early in the day, he checked for messages while riding the rail home. There was only one, from a woman. "Tomorrow, 7:00, on the phone, be there." It was Sandy.

Alec was scheduled to call Angela that evening, but he couldn't pull the trigger, he didn't see how he could keep from telling her the events of the day. Instead, he sent her a "record audio encrypted" with his phone's R-A-E app. "R-A-E Angela, start, I can't call you tonight, sorry. I'll pick you up Saturday 6:00 at your place, see you then, yours, Alec, R-

A-E stop."

An hour later Angela skyped him. "Hi Angie baby."

She grimaced. "I thought you called, but then I got a blank message."

"Oh, I left an R-A-E, obviously somebody tapped the line. Jesus!"

"Why'd you do that, anyway?"

"I can't talk about it, that's why. I guess I was right though, the phone lines are now out. Here's what I said on the R-A-E Can't talk, I'll pick you up at your place Saturday at 6:00, see you then."

"So, you're coming to Puyallup?"

"Yes, 6:00 pm, see you Saturday, bye for now."

XXIV

On Friday Alec spent the morning on the internet educating himself about all the various felonies considered to be sex crimes. About ten percent of all inmates in federal prisons are there for sexual offenses, the variety of their crimes is extensive. After reading a panoply of horrific case studies, Alec was more convinced than ever that he would never volunteer to visit Last Chance, Montana, he couldn't understand how Spencer could be so convinced he would.

At 1:00 he got a visit from Roscoe and Beverly. He invited them into the kitchen.

Roscoe began, "Yesterday, when Koleka asked about pictures, your buddy Max has some for you. He showed them when he was re-interviewed. We have copies, I suggest you get some for yourself."

"Why would I want to do that?"

"You'll want them whatever transpires, don't piss and moan, okay?"

"Anything you say Detective. By the way, you are number one on my list, or is it pissing and moaning to complain about being spied on?"

"What the hell are you talking about?"

"Someone tapped my phone, stole an encrypted message I sent. I suppose this is news to you hunh?"

Roscoe thought about this, "What was in the message, who was it to?"

"None of your goddamn business."

"Okay, okay, you're right, but can I ask if there was anything about your briefing from yesterday?"

"Sure, ask away. I am not in the habit of exposing secrets, that's all I'm going to say."

Roscoe paused again, Beverley volunteered, "Might be DOJ. Surely they found out Mr. McNee was briefed."

Roscoe nodded. "Very likely. We'll have to get Grumpy on it when we get back."

"Grumpty, as in Humpty Grumpty fell off the wall, that Grumpty?"

Beverly would occasionally smile, but this elicited an uncontrolled laugh, well, more like a giggle, the first Roscoe had seen from her in the three years they worked together. She quickly stifled it, but the dam had been broken.

"Uh, it wasn't us McNee, we'll look into it though. We have another problem to deal with. Joanne Arnold, reporter and webcaster for the Times, called me this morning. She read The Olympian's website article and wanted to know if the McNee identified was indeed Alec McNee."

"Shit! Did she find it herself or did someone else?"

"The later, she wouldn't tell me who that would be."

"Maybe that prick Purser again. Can't you just tell her to fuck off?"

Roscoe looked annoyed now. "I know you're not that dumb, why act so moronic. I stalled her, told her I hadn't seen the website, I'd get back to her. She won't let this slide, we need to work on a story that isn't too much of a lie. We can't have the press following you to Montana."

"To Montana?" He looked at Roscoe, then turned toward at Beverly. "How about you, you go to Montana?"

"No, I've been there, not much to see for a city girl."

"Muscles, I'm very glad to see you have a sense of humor after all, no matter how badly timed."

Beverly reacted mildly, flexing her shoulders.

Roscoe filled the lag. "Let's keep on target. We're going to tell Arnold that it was you in the article, but it's a dead story, we believe Mr. Schmidt has resurfaced, he had only been in Seattle a short time, he decided to pick up and go back east. She'll probably want to talk to you, so we'll have you call her since you want to keep your number private. You tell her that yes, he did go back, you got a call from him, he was traveling, and he didn't know there was a search out for him. He'll get back to you when he's resettled. Something like that anyway, you're welcome to improvise."

"So, you don't want to lie to her, you want me to lie for you, is that it?"

"See, I knew you weren't so dumb, yes, that is it. We can't get caught in a lie, we can't lose the trust of the media, you, as a private citizen, have the luxury that they won't demand the truth. We just have to hope they don't check Lukas out too thoroughly, they won't find any history, that might get them curious."

"When are you guys going to give me a salary for doing your job. I'm not sure I want any part of this charade."

"Fine, when she tracks you down tell her everything. That'll be a big hit with your friends and colleagues. Now, I want you to tell me that Lukas called you. Say it."

Alec paused for effect, then complied. "Lukas called and told me he was back east, he'll be calling me back. .. Are you happy now?"

"Just covering my ass, leaving yours exposed." Alec didn't appreciate the humor. "We're going. I'll call and tell you what she says."

Alec, of course, knew he couldn't go public, for the reason Roscoe gave and many others. He certainly didn't want to get on the wrong side of DOJ should their clandestine penitentiary operation be exposed. Then again, he didn't like the idea of having to tell an outright lie to a reporter. He had talked to many during the long litigation process. Some were jerks, but most were just trying to do their job, including local Joanne Arnold who he remembered had interviewed him well before the Supreme Court had decided to take up his case. She was in her forties and not unattractive considering the extra twenty pounds she carried in her ample rear end. She had been fair, she didn't accuse him of simply being a muckraker as many early articles by others in the media suggested. It was good that he remembered her because she skyped him an hour later. He now found any calls to be disconcerting, on this one he was going to have to lie to a reporter, knowing that someone may well be eavesdropping.

They went through the usual introductions, including the appropriate platitudes, before Joanne got to business and started asking questions. Alec wound up saying such things as "Yes, that was me, my legal first name is William," "I didn't know him well or for very long," "He's a lawyer working for the same client I lobby for," "He saw the article online where I was referenced, he called me to apologize," "I'm not sure where he's going, he said he'd let me know when he settled down," "Yes, I'll be glad to get back to you and let you know." A few more platitudes and the call was ended. Alec was an old poker player, good at bluffing, he thought she bought what he sold.

Roscoe and Beverly returned to the squad at just before 2:00. They went in to see Grumpy, he was reading a report with an elbow on the desk and one of his many chins resting on his left arm. Graham looked up and sat back in his chair. "Did you visit McNee then?"

"Yeah, he'll uh play ball with Arnold even though uh he complains a lot."

"He say anything about Montana, he going?"

"That's mostly what uh he complains about. He'll go though .. He said he's being uh spied, someone tapped into an R-A-E he sent, Bev thinks uh it's Justice."

"Hmm, maybe, don't know though."

"We told him uh you'll check it out, will you?"

"Sure, course. Did you have him call J-A, we gotta snip this. To tell you the truth, I'm surprised the press hasn't got wind of this yet, all the brass jumping around."

"I'm gonna uh call her back, then have him call her, like he wants privacy."

"Okay, take care of it."

When he got back to his desk he could hear Steffi Sanchez two desks down chucking while talking to someone on the phone, she put the phone down. "Special, it's J-A for you, I picked up your line while you were in with Grumpy."

Roscoe cut in, "Joanne, back so soon."

"Hey Roscoe, I just got off with McNee. Did you already talk to him?"

Roscoe had to quickly decide whether she knew the answer. "No, haven't got to it yet, Joanne, it's not at the top of my list."

"He says he got a call from, what's his name, uh Schmidt. That he left town, told you that?"

"Yeah, I told you it wasn't a .."

"Why didn't you tell me that then, is this one closed?"

"No, not yet, we need to talk to Schmidt first. He's traveling, I hear, though I don't know why that stops him from calling."

"Now I'm told there are big doings up north, Beardsley and Golanski up there for meetings, this Schmidt guy have anything to do with that?"

"Sure, an m-i-a nobody's ever heard of, sure, got everybody working it."

"Well, what's this about then?"

"Like I'm going to talk for the Commissioner, come on Jo."

"Okay, okay, Rosc, but I smell a .."

"You hacks are the rat."

Sandy called on the phone at 7:00 as advertised. "Hi, Sandman."

"Hi Alec. I have a quick message for you."

"You may want to keep it, I'm pretty sure I'm being bugged."

"Of course you are, you're nuclear babe, don't you know? It doesn't matter anyway, they might want to hear this too. Beware of Sig."

"That's it, beware of Sig — who's this from?"

"I'm simply a messenger."

"Just this dull message, you aren't interest in a visit?"

"Come on babe, I know you've moved on. I hear she's too good for you."

"Who isn't. I feel like the Truman Show, everybody watching, how the hell do you know?"

"Got to go, take care, and good luck on your trip."

XXV

This Saturday was cleaning day. Alec had hired a lady once but lost her number and never took the effort to find another. He had supplied her with all the necessary cleansers, mops, towels, he pulled them all out of the laundry room and put them to work. The first order of business was towels, sheets and pillowcases into the wash. The condo had oak hardwood floors throughout most of the unit, with thick pile carpet in the two bedrooms and vinyl in the bathrooms. He was not a complete slob but neither was he a neatnik. He started by sweeping all the hardwood and vacuuming the carpets, including the large throw rug covering most of the living room. He damp mopped the hardwood, then damp mopped a second time with protective Murphy's Oil Soap. By this time it was out of the washer and into the dryer. He scoured the bathroom toilets and shower with Lysol, the entirety of which was unpleasant, but this was the worst of it.

This wasn't a constant process, he took three breaks between different tasks, after the third he remade the beds and dusted in the living room. In the whole time he had lived there he had spent about one hour total in the living room, no one else had spent any. It was nicely furnished, although with little embellishment, only two paintings which were rather bland. The alder stacked next to fireplace had not been touched all year. There was no television, when he did watch t-v it was news and some sports in his office and old movies in the bedroom. He had never seen an episode of current hit sitcom Brothers of Mothers nor any of the endless stream of detective shows.

He took a plastic bag of garbage to the dumpster, when he came back into the condo the smell of detergents was overpowering. He found some air freshener but it smelled like over-ripe raspberries. He was pretty sure he didn't suffer from halitosis, but he knew his shit stinked even though he seldom focused on it — something about one's own. He did worry about smells. He hot-footed it to and back from the store where he purchased two orange blossom scented candles along with mango scented air freshener. He lit the candles and doused the air with freshener.

After all this it was now mid-afternoon. He showered and shaved and dressed up in his number three, a grey cardigan sweater over a light green, printed, dress shirt, jeans and his leather jacket. Now he did sit in the living room, relaxing and meditating for about twenty minutes. He went back to his office to select a music channel which would be pleasant but not conspicuous, he selected soft rock even though he considered it irritating pap, he was hoping he'd be able to ignore. It was now 5:00, he snuffed out the candles and headed out.

He took the same route as before, and arrived fifteen minutes early, as before. He idled away some time, then drove the rest of the way to Angela's house. She answered quickly, opening the front door as he opened the screen door. "Hi, come on in."

"No, thanks, I'll wait out here, grab your travel bag and come on out."

She looked at him as if she hadn't heard what he said, he repeated, "Yeah, grab your bag, I'll be in the car." He slowly walked back to the Tesla. She stared, a little stunned, while he leaned on the car, then eventually went back in. After at least a half-hour Alec was getting very antsy, he began to think his ploy was doomed to failure. As he was about to concede defeat and go back to the door she reappeared. She locked the door and slowly made her way down and into the passenger seat, throwing a bag over her shoulder, then glared at him. "You know I .."

He interrupted her by leaning over to give her a kiss, she backed off but he followed and made it to her lips for a quick but unresponsive kiss. He handed her one rose, then started the car and they were off.

Alec knew he had pushed the envelope, he would need to be very nice and tactful while she blew off a little steam. "I feel like I'm being hijacked. I thought I .. is this why you came to get me, so I wouldn't be able get away? where are we going anyway?"

"I made reservations at the Metropolitan, we may be a little late."

"Oh, nice. And what else have you planned?"

"I want you to come home with me, of course .. Look, if it's such a problem I'll take you home after dinner, okay?"

"You have to let me decide some things, we could have talked it over."

"You're right, I just wasn't in the mood to cajole, or beg, or whatever it might have taken to convince you to do what I think we both want."

"What you think I want, is that it, like I don't know what I want. Okay, why not just take me home now, that's what I want."

"Sorry, no can do, you are being hijacked for dinner."

She was at the tipping point now, fortunately she did not tip. They were silent the rest of the way to downtown Seattle.

They were only five minutes late, Alec had the valet park the Tesla. The Metropolitan was always packed during the week with working executives and clients, but often not so on the weekend. They were treated to a table in a private, very quiet part of the restaurant, sometimes chatter and clatter could be annoying at the Met. Alec had balked at picking a second steakhouse, but there were quite satisfactory seafood entrees available. They started with an appetizer, almond crusted scallops, and a bottle of Italian Red.

The conversation naturally was centered around all their recent activities. Alec let Angela lead with progress in Olympia. Corey had successfully cut the vocal cord of the website, using both outrage and persuasion, his name was printed in a matter in which he had no involvement. This slight blip had no effect on the progress being made with the legislation being devised. Corey wished the best in finding Lukas safe.

For entrees Angela ordered the Dungeness crab fettuccine, Alec prime rib. There was little conversation during dinner. Alec didn't take the floor until they were savoring the last vestige of wine. "That dinner wasn't so bad, was it, aren't you glad you came now?"

She was nicely lit, but still unwilling to completely forgive him. "Yes, dinner was superior, thanks."

"I have an amazing tale to tell, but I won't be able to finish it until I get home. Are you coming?"

"Why did you send me an R-A-E instead of calling, did you know you were being taped?"

"No I didn't. I was sworn to secrecy, I knew I wouldn't be able to keep my word once I started talking to you. I couldn't take the chance, good that I didn't."

"Ok, come on, give!"

"I'll give you a sample, but I told you, I'll need time to finish."

"Go!"

"Okay, Lukas Schmidt is a convicted felon, convicted of sexual assault on a seventeen-year-old girl, after a prior similar encounter with an eighteen-year-old. He spent ten years in federal prison."

She was surprised to say the least. "That little guy, really, he's so timid."

"That's the teaser, it's just a tasty tidbit to what's coming. But the waiter looks anxious, we'd better get going."

Alec got up and helped Angela out of her chair.

"Isn't he a lawyer, felons lose their license to practice, you must have something wrong."

"How about a presidential pardon?"

They made it outside. Alec gave the valet his number, then turned to Angela as she was going to question that and kissed her, she responded to the kiss.

"Am I forgiven. Can I go home now?"

"Mmm, yes, you can go home."

They talked very little on the way, Alec needed to concentrate on his driving. He turned left on Cherry to 4th, left again for six blocks to University, then right for four blocks to the freeway. The ride to the 130th took only nine minutes, and then another five to get to his condo. They walked arm in arm to and into the condo. Both of them needed relief, he escorted her to the guest bathroom and he went to the master. Out first, he turned on the music from in his office, then went to the kitchen and opened the bottle of cabernet waiting there. He brought it to a living room table beside the couch and turned on the lamp, he was starting a fire when she returned. He finished with the fire and came toward her.

"This is nice, Alec."

The living room had a large picture window. There were dark shadows looking out until he turned on a floodlight aimed over the lake. "That's Haller Lake, we can go swimming in the morning."

She looked at him, wondering if he might be serious. He kissed her. He turned out the light and they both retired to the couch. Although it wasn't cold, he pulled a blanket over their legs and pulled her into his arms, they sat and snuggled while he began his narrative.

He started with the bridge tournament where he met Luftar and Calvin and continued for twenty minutes, through the events of yesterday when he lied to reporter

Joanne Arnold. Angela asked him many questions along the way.

He took a rest after finishing, then, "Well, did that live up to its billing?"

"Remarkable, it doesn't sound possible. What did they mean when they told you he could come back now, why did he leave in the first place then, and why would he want to go back anyway?"

"Good questions, one of many the SPD wants me to find out, even though their official policy says the opposite."

"They'll want to know for sure he's there, I guess you'll find that out anyway."

"I'll find out. How will I find out, you really think I'm going in there?"

"Don't be ridiculous, of course you're going."

"You too? Spencer, Roscoe Romar, Muscles, and now you. Of course, of course."

"You don't know yourself very well do you. Who's Muscles?"

"Roscoe's partner, Detective Koenig. Didn't I ever mention her, she's a natural wonder."

"Oh, a she is Muscles." She suppressed a yawn.

"Well, I guess it's time to get you to bed little lady. Did you forget your bag?"

"No, it's still in the car. There's nothing in it, I didn't think I'd need it." She smiled sheepishly.

He smiled back, then kissed her deeply. On the way down the hall to the bedrooms, he stopped in the laundry room and grabbed a freshly washed pair of pajamas which he gave her, then led her back to the guest bedroom and guided her to the bed. "There should be a toothbrush in the bathroom, here's your room, my bedroom's right down the hall."

He gave her a brief kiss and then walked toward the door. She watched him go and appeared bewildered. He turned and walked back to her, she embraced him and they kissed again. He picked her up and carried her down the hall to his bedroom, the first across the threshold he could remember.

First time sex in a new and probably ongoing relationship is extremely impassioned. Unlike a one-timer where it's a slam bang event, every touch by him here or by her there is significant, revealing and very personal. If she worried to herself about being out of practice, she need not have been, they melded together like they were one. She wasn't animalistic as was Sandy, but their lovemaking was every bit as prolonged and intense. At a point he relaxed and held still while still in her, she was right that he wasn't spent, the pause was temporary, his spirit returned with even more fervor and fierceness until the eventual frenzied climax.

XXVI

They made love again in the morning. Not as fanatical as the night before, much more casual and playful and verbal, comments such as "Do you like it on top?" "You're really going to do that," "No, I never have," and, of course, "No no, not there." Afterward they lay in each other's arms, perfectly content. But reality always returns, he started with "The Seahawks play at home against Tennessee at one today, I'm going to watch at Max's. Want to come?"

"I thought it was a men's club, can I?"

"No, just thought I'd ask."

"You jerk!"

"Your breakfast choices are sausage and eggs, Raisin Bran with muffin, or sausage and eggs."

"Raisin Bran. I'd like to shower first, wish I'd brought some clothes now."

He told her she was welcome to any of his clothes. When she left for the shower Alec searched his wardrobe for clothes that she might be able to wear, he came up with a pair of too tight briefs, an undershirt, some sweatpants with a string belt, and a sweatshirt that had shrunk in the wash.

She was wearing the sweatpants and sweatshirt when she came back into the kitchen, he was finishing his bowl of cereal. They laughed at her outfit, it may have been small for Alec but she was swimming in it. She had more of a country girl look, sans the makeup of a city girl, but natural suited her well, she was every bit as attractive. She leaned on him as she looked out the large window, admiring the view. It wasn't raining but the clouds were wet and very low over the water, houses across the lake were not visible. After she had eaten he invited her for a boat ride, she accepted.

They cruised by Pam and Harry as usual, with the expected repartee "Catch anything today, Harry?" and the not unexpected return of "Looks like you caught a big one." Alec said he needed to see Max and again invited Angela to the football game, this time seriously. He explained about the pictures that Roscoe had mentioned, that were requested for Montana, finally admitting that he was going. She declined the invitation and she resisted his push for her to stay in Seattle, she insisted that it was time to go home. She wanted to hire a Bubblebot to get her there but he nixed that idea with vehemence.

Unlike the ride away the previous evening, the ride back to Puyallup was tranquil in the extreme. They held hands and cooed like teenagers most of the way. She started to talk about the pictures but he stopped her, he used his hands as if to swat insects, she got the picture of bugs quickly, looking somewhat incredulous. When they arrived at her house and he walked her to the door she could no long restrain herself. "You really think the car is bugged?"

"I don't know, but I wouldn't doubt it. What were you going to say about pictures?"

"The conference Lukas attended was recorded. Corey would need to put in a request, I would expect no objection to acquiring a copy."

"Yes, good."

She opened the door with her palm print and invited him in. He knew he'd have a hard time leaving if he went in so he gave her a reluctant no.

"You know it'll be your fault if I'm not the same man when I get back, do they sell chastity belts for men?"

"Oh stop, that's disgusting!"

"But you're not." As they kissed she tried to drag him in, but he broke it off.

Alec didn't arrive at Max's until halfway through the first quarter, traffic going to Angela's hadn't been bad, but going back north again the Seahawk traffic cost him. Everyone was relieved when he did get there, although that consisted of only Max, Rick and Porter. Porter was sweating out a seven point Seahawk deficit, Max and Rick seemed more concerned about Alec. By halftime the Seahawks, ten point favorites, had tied the score at ten.

When Max went into the kitchen to get some more beers, Alec joined him. "Max, you know anyone who's an electronics expert, surveillance?"

"Surveillance, ha ha ha ha ha ha, what the hell, you a spy now?" Alec waited him out. "Well, yeah. Remember Randy Korn, played some ball with us?"

"Yeah, yeah, I remember Randy. Got a job at what, Sunstrand?"

"He left there, started his own business, I think — I've probably still got his number."

"Can you give him a call for me?"

"Now, ha ha ha ha ha ha, like an emergency."

"Sort of, looks like I'll be going out of town Tuesday."

"Where you going?"

"East."

"East, you prick, that's it, east. What, a state secret, Mr. Spy."

"I'm not sure yet Max. I'm looking for Lukas."

"Really. Okay then."

Max went to his desk and found a number, which he called. Randy Korn was watching the game too, but had some time to talk, so Max gave the phone to Alec. "Randy, Alec McNee, remember me?"

"Sure, hard to forget you Alec. What's up?"

"Just a shot, but I'm wondering if you know anything about electronic surveillance?"

"That's my business Alec, like what in particular?"

"I'm afraid my house may be bugged, my car may be

bugged, hell, I might even have a bug up my ass. Anything you got to identify and destroy?"

"Sure, sure, but who's doing the bugging. If it's government or some spook, unfortunately, they stay ahead of the curve, you can't be sure you'll detect it."

"Is there anything that's safe then, like if I'm talking from my car. Nothing I can do to be sure?"

"There is one new piece of equipment that guarantees security, never been breached I don't think, it's called a Yakback. Each pack can be two to eight units I believe, is unique. It converts a voice to a garbled noise from one unit, which can then be interpreted perfectly by another unit of that pack. Basically just a sending phone and a receiving speaker with software encoded using a prime number, you know what I mean by prime?"

"Please."

"Sorry. Each unit needs to be encrypted with the same prime. The beauty is that no other Yakback can interpret even if they know the prime, so you use it to call someone and tell them to set the prime to say three, never been breached."

"Does it work over the phone?"

"It is a phone, number one usage. Another feature is that it is not traceable, it scrambles its location, no one can identify where you're located."

"Perfect, exactly what I want. Can I simply buy one, a three unit Yakback."

"Yeah, they're expensive, I'll have to get you a price."

"No problem, I need it right away, like tomorrow."

"I can do that. I don't have an office though, working from home. Is Max still up there on the hill, I can bring it by tomorrow afternoon?"

"Good, excellent. I'll have Max pay you for it."

"Doesn't have to be tomorrow. Hey, got to get back to the game."

"We're at Max's watching right now, you remember

Porter Nash, and Rick Kirby. Come on over and watch with us sometime."

"Porter, sure, he kicked my butt on the court, don't know Rick I don't think. Anyway, thanks for the invite .. If that Yakback has a problem let me know, it's new tech, sometimes quirky. See ya."

The second half was back and forth, until the Seahawks finally took a six point lead with less than two minutes left. But then Tennessee marched down for the winning touchdown as time ran out. Porter was in shock, Max tried to console him. It was late in the afternoon by this time, but Porter had done the family thing before the game so had some time before getting home to Sunday dinner.

Alec grilled him about Lukas, wanting to know if he actually remembered him when growing up. Porter did not. The Schmidts lived three blocks away, he remembered that but nothing more, not even if they had kids. Porter complained about Alec using the same tactics as the Gestapo police. He left in a huff, still irritated by Alec.

Rick then took over the questioning, he grilled Alec about the secret trip Max mentioned. Alec had been laid back the prior few weeks, he wasn't this week and Rick asked him if there was a new focus, a new mountain to climb as he put it. Alec acknowledged that there was indeed. Then, Rick inquired about Angela. Alec didn't hedge, he told of the previous night of bliss. This topic evoked a series of guffaws from Max, they finished the day on a high note.

Alec skyped Angela that evening, she received even though she was again naked, that is, dressed in a towel after her bath. Alec began with "Oh my god, you look hot." She did not object this time, but smiled. He told her that his bed was now a lonely place, and other such felicitations. She thanked him and encouraged him. He finished with the serious reason for the call, he would meet her Monday night at the same Puyallup restaurant of their prior meal, he had a present for her.

XXVII

Roscoe arrived at work at his usual 8:01 am. At 8:02 he got a call from Joanne Arnold. "You lied to me, Roscoe, Schmidt isn't back east, nobody knows where he's at, and he's a convicted sexual predator. Why didn't you tell me that?"

"You didn't ask."

"Goddamnit, do I have to treat you like the enemy all the time, why?"

"Look, McNee did tell me he got a call from Schmidt who said he was out of town. I didn't necessarily believe him. I told you the case is still open."

"Bullshit! This is what all the hoopla is about up there, isn't it, you lost some sex fiend. Is he out raping young women, is that it?"

"No, that is not it, but what it is is not for me to say — sounds like a Johnny Mathis song, doesn't it?"

"Very cute. I guess you aren't worth my time anymore Rosc, sorry to say that. I'll be prodding that fat ass Martin from now on."

Roscoe wanted to say something about a pot and a kettle, but restrained himself.

Alec was skyped by Roscoe at 8:10. "Oh my god, what a terrible way to meet the day."

"It will get worse. I just got a call from Joanne Arnold, she's hopping mad. She knows you lied to me about Lukas."

"I lied to you, that's a good one!"

"And she knows Lukas has a record, she thinks he's out

there at large raping women."

"Super ."

"You can expect her or someone else anytime, they'll want to rake you over the coals."

"Yeah, you made sure of that. Did you get any paperwork from the pen?"

Beverly was listening in, she nodded and opened an envelope for him. "Yeah, we got it, you're expected there by 3:00 tomorrow."

"I'll want that, I'll come and get it."

"Come now is my advice."

He realized from Roscoe that his house would not be habitable for the rest of today at a minimum, so he might as well plan the trip now. Alec was a quick packer, he did not fuss over what to bring. Montana in October, he thought cold and therefore packed warm clothing. He hoped for a two day trip but packed for a week. Seven undershirts, seven pair of socks, three pair of boxer shorts, three pair of pants, five shirts, three sweaters, a sport coat, and one extra pair of shoes. From the bathroom, it was waterpik, toothbrush, floss, toothpaste, razor with fresh blades, shaving cream, ibuprofen, omeprazole, soap and shampoo. It took him one large suitcase and one small one, and about five minutes.

He took another five minutes in his office, checking mail and messages, and shutting down everything. He grabbed his leather coat and put on a ski cap to take the luggage to his car. He was planning to go back for a second sweep, but he saw a t-v van slowly looking at houses as it approached, it was time to go now.

His place was on a dead-end street, there was no city street available to circumvent the van, but Hugh Sparkman below him had advised that a neighbor three houses down on the other side of the street had a driveway through his property to an outside road. There was a gate with a combination lock that locals could open in an emergency, this seemed like that. He had been told the simple combination, it was .... 1234, no, 1248. He found the gate and the combination worked. He opened, drove through, and closed, then drove down the through driveway to the far street, looking for the neighbor to acknowledge as he went, he didn't see him.

Roscoe was taking a sip from his still warm first cup of coffee. The sip turned into a gulp when he saw Alec, he hustled him into a private interview room. "She's here, talking to Grumpy, best not confront her now."

Beverly brought in the paperwork which Alec perused. The plan was pretty simple.

"When are you leaving?"

"Tomorrow morning early, I guess."

"Taking the bubble?"

"Yeah, it's almost a thousand miles, the bubble estimates a little less than nine hours, eta 5:00 pm."

"Here, I have something for you." Roscoe presented Alec with a pair of shoelaces, "These will match your shoes, snip off the left aglet if you get in trouble, it .."

"Thanks, but no, don't want it."

"Well, I was told to give this to you. I think you're right though, I suspect it would be detected and that might not be good. You have good instincts my lad."

"Got any more good bad advice?"

"Yes, lots, but I'll save it for when you get back, you're on your own. We will anticipate your return."

"I know I'm a smart ass, but you'll have to admit that I've been pretty cooperative on the whole."

Alec put his hand out to Muscles, and she took it. He then put it out to Roscoe who did likewise.

"There's something I want you to do for me .."

Alec hopped on the rail to Issaquah, then drove up to Spencer's house unannounced. When he knocked Martha answered and invited him in, but he declined, he asked if Spencer might come out. A few minutes later they were walking through the neighborhood.

"I know you and Sig are tight, but I need to ask if you told Sig about where I'm going in Montana."

"You continue to not understand me, Alec. I was given that information with the caveat that it was private and not to be disseminated. I am a simple man, I honor my commitments."

"So, that's a no then?"

Spencer chuckled, "I take it you no longer trust Sig."

"Everyone seems to know what I'm doing, I can't figure out how, Sig came to mind."

"Not an injudicious conjecture. Of course, I have no personal knowledge. This is important enough for you to come all the way out here?"

"Yes, it is. I don't like to think it .." Alec hesitated.

"Sig is not a simple man. He is generous in order to get what he wants, but Sig looks out for Sig and what he wants is not always obvious. So, you're going then?"

"Yes, tomorrow morning."

"I envy you. Good luck."

Alec's next move was to take a breather at Max's, he wanted to be there when Randy Korn delivered the Yakback. He took I-90 to I-5 through town to the Roanoke exit, from there he looped back over I-5 and took Boston west three blocks to Eastlake, then north four blocks to Daley's Drive-In, he was glad to see it was still in operation. Daley's roasted a prime beef every morning, the French dips he remembered were perfection, along with sweet potato fries.

While waiting, he scanned one of the free rag-mags distributed out front in old newspaper bins. Ninety percent of it was ads for various indie entertainers Alec had never heard of. Of the few articles most were radical rants from the underbelly, but occasionally a tidbit of interest could be found. The dip was every bit as good as he remembered, he mentally thanked god for that.

He arrived at Max's house at 1:15. The front door was locked, but the key he had left years before under a certain rock was still there and still opened the back door. He went to the living room and sat, then laid, on the couch, resting and planning at the same time. Resting won out, he napped for a good hour before he heard the knock at the front door.

Randy Korn was let in, along with the new gizmo. It was good that Alec was there, setting up the Yakback was not as simple as Randy intimated. It needed assembling, even Randy had to scour the manual to complete the job. Once it was put together using the device was as simple as advertised. It was an antique in that it was not voice activated, there was a key pad for entering a number, along with a "new prime" button to allow recoding the unit after entering a prime number and hitting the "send" button. They activated the other two units and then tested them out. There was no actual garbled noise, there was no noise at all, but the system worked as designed, messages could be left and numbers recalled as with any phone. Alec paid and thanked Randy, and again invited him over for Sunday football should he be so inclined.

At 5:00 Alec hit the streets again, heading to Puyallup. He didn't feel like driving so he took a different route, onto the I-5 rail south past Fife just short of Tacoma, and then Highway 167 heading ese to Puyallup. Traffic was bad, he arrived only five minutes early, Angela was already there waiting at a table. She looked every bit the executive, well-groomed in her fashionable woman's suit. There was an empty booth across the aisle, Alec moved them to the booth so they could sit close, she had to work to keep his hands off of her.

Neither was ready for a full dinner, she had a dinner salad and he the soup of the day, bistro French onion. He told her about being dislodged from his house by the press and the reasons for it. She sympathized, then asked if he wanted to spend the night at her house. As much as he wanted to be with her, he would feel awkward staying at her family home with her mother wandering around. He needed to get back to talk to Max in any event.

She handed him a stick with the recording of Lukas at the Olympia conference, he slipped it into his handheld and skipped to the middle to briefly watch a segment. She told him she found a website, which she identified as justice.gov/pardon, that listed all presidential pardons over the last ten years, Lukas Schmidt was not among them. Alec mulled this over.

In the back seat of his Tesla after the light meal, Alec showed Angela how to operate the Yakback. They tested it out, and she got the gist without difficulty. They necked for a bit, but she not too intensely. She repeated her offer to have him stay the night.

"I'd like to, but, have you ever been shagged in the bedroom you grew up in?"

"Shagged, I don't know that word but I can guess."

"You know, like laid-waste-to, or the shorter version, laid."

"Do you have ..?"

"You're so sophisto, what are you doing with a brute like me?"

"I'm beginning to wonder!"

He kissed her again, she resisted a little, but he persisted until she finally relented, relaxed and enjoyed.

"Sorry, you're just such a class act, makes me want to shake you up. I'll try harder."

"Please do."

He kissed her again.

On the rail going back Alec punched "justice.gov/pardon" into the Tesla's display, a couple more clicks and he found the list Angela mentioned. He too couldn't find Lukas's name. He then looked for Luftar Koleka and did find him, pardoned four years earlier for assault and attempted rape. He looked for others on that same date and found one of interest, Marshall Dixon, pardoned for sexual assault of a juvenile in Missoula, Montana. He re-routed his Tesla itinerary and drove to Porter Nash's house, he parked in front, and called Porter.

"Does the name Marshall Dixon ring a bell?"

"Dixon, sure, they lived two doors down from us. Marshall was about three years younger, so we didn't hang."

"So, you remember him then."

"Yeah, he was a strange one, smart, very smart. He was a homebody, didn't play sports or socialize. I didn't see him a lot, but I remember one winter we had a cold spell, Bonney Lake froze solid for about thirty feet out. Kids were skating and sliding around, and there was Marshall, way out on the thin ice, testing it. His mother was going ape, yelling at him to come in, but he was oblivious, paid no attention, just drifted a little farther out, then you could hear the ice crack. He was a tiny kid, no one could go get him. Then, after awhile, his curiosity satisfied, he casually walked back in, paying no attention to his mother who fawned over him."

"Lukas is Marshall."

"No shit, really. No way I'd recognize him. I remember my mother always fed up how Mrs. Dixon bragged about how smart he was, how he got a scholarship to, some big school. But something must have happened, she stopped bragging, then they moved away. So that little sucker's Lukas, hmm."

That evening, back with Max, Alec showed him how to use the Yakback. Max was beyond curious as to what the hell Alec was up to, he was damn pissed when Alec gave him no satisfaction with an answer. Alec told him that if he ever yakked a 911 message he was to get a hold of Detective Roscoe Romar and show him the Yakback. He also asked him to return the Tesla to his house after a few days. The bedroom upstairs was still vacant, Alec retired to it early.

XXVIII

The Bubblebot picked Alec up at 4:45, exactly as requested. He had ordered a sleeper, the passenger side of the vehicle was a pre-made bed. Alec threw his bags on the bed and got in the driver's side, but as a passenger ready to be driven by the bot. Before hitting the "drive" button, he cut the bot's vocal cord by hitting the "sound off" button, he did not like the constant reminders pre-programmed into the system telling him a lot of stuff he didn't want to hear. Much of that was pure commercials, he could always read it on the bot's display screen if he wanted. He double-checked the itinerary and the eta to his destination nearly a thousand miles to the east in Miles City, Montana, he was due to arrive in eight hours and fifty minutes, well before the 3:00 deadline.

He was now ready to roll, he pushed the drive button, and the Bubblebot was off. It was slow going until he reached I-90 where the autobot connected to the Bubblerail, then it zipped along quickly. He stayed awake and took in the scenery until he was well over Snoqualmie Pass, then rolled over onto the bed and slept for the trip across eastern Washington at speeds of a hundred and twenty, until he hit the border of Idaho. Once past Coeur d'Alene in the Idaho panhandle, the highway rises in elevation through the Lolo National Forest of the northern Rockies for the hundred and seventy miles to Missoula, Montana. A variety of conifers like the western hemlock, Douglas fir, and red cedar were intermixed with deciduous trees such as alder, birch, and aspen to enhance the majesty of the mountains.

From Missoula, the highway continues its jagged upward climb through the mountains to the near mile high elevation of Bozeman. Not far east of Bozeman the highway follows the course of the Yellowstone river as it descends toward Billings, the largest city in the state. Alec had been on the road for seven hours, he decided to stop just east of Billings in Lockwood for lunch, his Bubblebot suggested a few options. He settled for Blues BBQ where he expected he could get a good burger, he reprogrammed his autobot accordingly.

The restaurant had a rustic cowboy feel to it, so he instead opted for a half rack of baby back ribs with a side of baked beans and a pint of Yuengling, this turned out to be an excellent choice. The waitress was a saucy old gal with rawhide skin who recognized the city slicker in Alec and teased him accordingly. He wanted to stay for another pint, but thought better of it and was soon back on the road for the final leg.

Alec disconnected from the rail after arriving at Miles City at 2:15. The Bubblebot dropped him and his bags in front of the only building in sight at an otherwise desolate, cold spot. The gas station was your basic gas, smokes and snack store, there was a short native behind the counter, watching a sitcom on a tiny television, who paid him no attention even though she probably hadn't seen another human all day. Alec walked up and asked to see Desiree, she asked who he was, he told her Napoleon. She came out from behind the counter and led him to a back room, it was a warm lounge with several tables and comfortable chairs throughout. She told him to wait for Hicky and then went back to her t-v.

His choices of reading while waiting the interminable twenty minutes were gossip, sports or fashion magazines, all at least six months old. Eventually an s-u-v drove up, it was so dusty that the license plate was unreadable. A skinny kid dressed in jeans and a worn leather shirt came in a rear door and over to Alec.

"You are?"

"Napoleon."

The kid scoffed, "Paper."

Alec handed him the prepared documents. The kid studied it and tore out a copy, then said, "Okay, we're late." He grabbed the luggage and led Alec to the s-u-v.

It was actually warm and comfortable inside the vehicle. Alec was put in the back seat and the ride began. Alec never had any interest in the rodeo, but he imagined riding a bucking bronco was probably not unlike the ride from the gas station to the train station. The dirt road was replete with potholes and the kid hit every one before skidding to a stop fifteen minutes later beside a cargo train with two passenger cars behind the locomotive. The kid pulled Alec's two bags from the hatchback and dropped them in the dirt, pointing to the stairs of one of the cars.

"Gracie will meet you." He jumped back into the s-u-v and peeled out, leaving a cloud of dust for Alec to filter through.

Alec was the only passenger. He saw no one else on the slow train ride, first through bleak prairie and then up furrowed hills blown dry by swirling chinook winds. Fifty minutes later, the train pulled through some high cyclone fences and came to rest, a voice from a speaker not heard until that point said, "Please exit."

Alec grabbed his bags and climbed down the car's stairs to a covered platform, only one other person was visible down about twenty feet. On second thought Alec was not sure it was a person. It looked like a primate with thick shoulders rolled forward so that the arms dangled down to its knee, and it was gargantuan in size. Those adjectives seemed to fit, a gargantuan primate, it could have posed as Bigfoot without a disguise. Alec reluctantly approached and had a better look, he determined it was indeed a man. He had a large cowlick up the whole left side of his forehead, as if someone had buried a hatchet in his head and his black hair had grown back in random directions over the resulting scar. The eyebrow over his left eye drooped badly, so much so that it appeared to block sight. His entire face was severely pockmarked.

"Are you Gracie?"

Despite his appearance, his voice was clear and sure of itself, with an accent Alec couldn't identify.

"Yes, I'm Gracie. When I was a teenager I was wild. I got mad at everyone that looked at me strange, beat the hell out of a lot of kids for no reason, I was thrown in juvie jail six times. When I was twenty I decided it was time to have a woman, I had never been with a girl, they were mostly scared just looking at me. But there was one girl in town who actually smiled at me once, I picked her. When I went to see her she seemed to know what I was thinking, she ran into her house and locked the door. I knocked the door off its hinges and followed her to the bedroom. She was scared to death, cringing on her bed as I went to her.

"Her dad was in the garage and heard the ruckus, before I even touched her he was behind me with a shotgun. He didn't waste any time, he unloaded and left his mark, but didn't kill me. I got to him and tore his head off, then I staggered back and fell unconscious on the bed, on top of that cute young girl. She couldn't get me off her, she suffocated. I was charged with murder of the father and attempted rape and murder of her, I surely would have raped her. Before I came to Last Chance I spent fourteen years in Hazelton Federal in West Virginia. I've never had a woman to this day, probably never will, I don't deserve one."

Alec was taken aback by the diatribe, but he put his hand out with a simple "Alec McNee." His had disappeared into Gracie's.

"It says William."

"Oh, it's actually William Alecsander McNee, but I've

been Alec since I was a kid."

"Okay, Alec, let's go into town."

Gracie carried the larger bag and led Alec down the platform through a thick steel door which clanged and locked behind them. Halfway down the twenty foot hallway there was a bag scanner, Gracie put the bags through it. He stopped to look at the Yakback.

"What's that thing?"

"A new fancy phone."

Gracie opened the bag to look at the Yakback, it was not obvious how it worked, but it did look like a phone. "Well, it won't work in here."

They walked down to another large door, Gracie pushed a button and waited, the door unlocked, and they went through, it too clanged shut behind them. They walked down a set of stairs to a golf cart. Gracie threw the bag he was carrying in the back bin, Alec did likewise with the smaller bag. Gracie pulled the golf cart tarp over the bags and they both got in the cart, he with difficulty considering his large frame.

They drove for about five minutes down a nondescript street, vacant on both sides, then turned a corner into what looked like a modern-day strip mall. There were small businesses of all kinds including a cafe, veterinary clinic, coffee shops on either side of the street, hair salon, clothing store, pizza parlor, bank, jewelry store, and dry cleaner, to name those that jumped out. The street was peppered with other golf carts, parking spaces in front of the stores were sized for them. Unlike most small towns, everything was clean and new looking. There were some, but not a lot of people walking around, almost all men, but Alec noticed a few women. Gracie pulled in front of Trudy's Cafe, they got out and headed in, Alec looked back at the golf cart, Gracie noticed.

"Don't worry about your stuff."

Trudy's had a counter that seated about ten, another ten

tables that seated four, and four booths down the left side. There were six customers in all, four at the counter and two in the first booth. Gracie said hi as he walked by them and wedged into the last booth where a large impression on the seat fit his butt perfectly.

A cute waitress came over to wait on them, Alec looked up before she reached them. "Hi, I'm a little surprised to see you here."

The waiter had a soft voice, he made no attempt to conceal it as being male. "Hi, I'm Rob. I started trying on women's clothes when I was about ten. By the time I was sixteen I had a closetful, that's all I wore. It's not that I want to be a woman or anything, I like my body, I used to beat off every day, but I like dressing and acting female. When I was twenty-two I had my first boyfriend, he didn't realize I was a man, I have always been small. I worked in a bakery, he worked across the street, he eventually asked me out. I liked him a lot, we actually fell in love, but he still didn't know. By our third date he was becoming more physical, I finally had to open up. He was shocked, disappointed, he left me flat, I was distraught.

"But about a month later he asked me out again. We went to his place and had sex. I fell asleep, he got up and got a gun and shot himself in the head, killed himself. I heard the shot and saw him fall. I took the gun out of his hand. When the cops showed up I was in a stupor, still with the gun. I told them I shot him, they were glad to believe me. It turns out he had manic problems I didn't know about, I should have known, he was very sensitive and unstable."

"S'nuf, Rob, thanks. You want something to drink, no alcohol?"

"Ice tea?"

"And water."

"So you know, the first time you ask someone about themself they'll tell you the circumstances that brought them here. Rob's boyfriend was Robert Wills, the girl in my story was Gracie Markman, get the idea. If you want the person to stop their story, just say s'nuf. Sounds like snuff but it's short for that's enough. You won't offend anyone either way, we've all been s'nuffed many times. So, we eat first, and then no more touchy-feely. I know you aren't here to see Swing, so you're either going to tell me what you're doing here, no bullshit, or I take you straight to the warden."

Alec wasn't too hungry, he ordered a chicken salad sandwich anyway, Gracie a bowl of minestrone soup. They ate in silence, although Gracie went to the counter for a short time and had casual conversations with other patrons. They were all obviously curious about Alec, but none asked.

The sandwich was excellent, the conversation began in earnest not long after the last bite.

"Ready, set, go."

"Well, okay, you're right, I don't know anything about Vincent Swing, never met him. I'm here to meet with Luftar Koleka and Calvin Coors."

"Uh hunh, and why the phony story?"

"They thought the subterfuge might be exposed if I signed up to see them, I can't answer why that is."

"Just keep talking."

"Anyway, I came to talk to them about another, uh, resident, resident of Last Chance, Lukas Schmidt."

"Straw, Strawberry. Sorry, go on."

"I know Luke, we became friends and co-workers over the couple months, and now he's missing. He was taken from his apartment over a week ago, no one knows what happened to him. I came to see if those two gentlemen could help me find him."

"So, you're a cop, then." Gracie was smiling as best he could.

"No, no, not at all."

"I know who you are, Straw let everyone know, but how do you know Rachel and Tony?"

"I don't, oh, you mean, okay. Well, they came to see me

actually, out of the blue, before Luke disappeared. They wanted me to get him to come back here, said he could stay here now. I had no idea what the hell they were talking about."

"They shouldn't have done that, they'll get into a heap of shit if Warden Ben finds out."

"Luke disappeared right when they were in Seattle, so .."

"So, you're not a cop, but the cops sent you didn't they?"

"No, I came voluntarily, they know I've come but they didn't encourage it."

"Right. What do you expect out of Rachel and Tony?"

"I came mostly to see if Luke is here, or get help from them. They said they might."

"Well, I can tell you for a certainty that he ain't here. Hmm, okay, I'll keep this quiet for today. But I want to talk to you, Rachel and Tony tomorrow morning at nine. I'll bring you down to see Swing now, I expect he was talked into helping by those two, he's not a bad guy but — anyway, I'll pick you up in the morning just before nine. Be ready."

There were eight rambling private quarters well away from downtown spread out over ten acres for use by visitors to the city. These were mostly conjugal visits by wives, and in some rare cases, girlfriends, but never any children. The women were not barred from going into town, but they were advised not to socialize with the locals, to date none had done so. Their patrons were able to rent cars and go for rides and hikes in the hills, there were many areas to explore. Alec and his two bags were deposited in front of bungalow number seven by Gracie, there were no locks on the doors so he went right in and wandered around.

There was a direct hallway to the right that led first to the guest bath on the left, to the spare bedroom on the right, and to the master bedroom straight ahead. The rooms were not large, but certainly adequate. Alec put his large bag on the master bed, then used the master bathroom for relief and to harbor his modest toiletry. Back to the entrance, the short hallway directly ahead led to the kitchen on the left and a large living-dining room with a high vaulted ceiling. There was a gas fireplace on the far left wall which Alec ignited. The kitchen was large, with a nook, table and chairs, the appliances were clean and modern.

Alec was going through the cabinets when Vincent Swing came in, they introduced themselves. It was after six, Swing was just off work in the auto parts plant. He was about to re-heat some teriyaki chicken he had brought from town, nuking it in the microwave, but Alec asked him to hold off and save it for later. Alec told Swing that the jig was up, Gracie had quickly smoked out the situation, Swing was very dismayed even after he was told of Gracie's comments. They stumbled in creating a personal relationship, Alec s'nuffed him immediately, but Alec did get him to answer some questions about the overall workings of the city.

There were no restrictions of movement throughout the city and in the rural areas to the north. Everyone paid their own way, residences such as apartments or houses were rented or bought, food, medicine, all amenities were paid for by individuals, not subsidized by the government. Cable television was available but regulated, the internet was available but also regulated. Contact with the outside by phone or email was available, but only upon request and only through the city center's downtown equipment, it was closely monitored. Montana had no sales tax, federal and state income taxes were deducted from pay as with all businesses in the state. Personal wealth, Swing had virtually none, was able to be put to use. Stock market investing was very big, there were numerous groups that shared advice and pooled resources. There were three banks in town, all had brokers who offered monetary counseling.

Alec quizzed Vincent about his job at the auto parts plant. Most of the work was performed by robotics.

Vincent's current task was preventive maintenance on those machines. Workers rotated positions, his most common jobs were supplying materials for the robots, keeping up inventory, and shipping and receiving to and from the train depot. He had applied for the more advanced and lucrative position of repairing and installing the robotics, but that required training for which he had yet to get approval.

When Alec started asking about individuals Swing became much more cautious. Rachel and Tony were the upper crust, Vincent wanted to curry their favor because they were the foremost advisors to the mayor. There were two primary counselors, new recruits were required to see Betsy at least once a week for the first three months, then once a month through the first year, in order to assure they were properly integrated into the city. If Betsy had concerns they were reported up the chain to either Tony or Rachel and, if need be, to Mayor Ben. Roger T was available by appointment to discuss more personal problems, these conversations were private and confidential.

Vincent had met Strawberry, but never had any dealings with him, although he knew he was highly regarded in helping others with legal advice. He would not talk at all about the mayor, and when asked a second time would still not elaborate. Soon after, he said that he had to get going. Before going he did make one thing clear. Last Chance was probably the safest city in the country, the main goal of everyone was to make sure they did nothing that would get them sent back to the main prison population, which was at the absolute discretion of the warden Ben.

Before nodding off in bed Alec got out the Yakback and dialed up Angela, curious to see if the unit would get through the obstacles it would face. She didn't answer, but it appeared the Yak on her end did answer. He left a brief message, "All okay here, no security problems, very interesting place, love, A."

XXIX

Gracie arrived in his golf cart at exactly 8:45 as promised. It was a gray day, Alec had to fight the winds to open and get in the cart. He had not eaten, other than about three bites of leftover teriyaki, the cabinets had a few canned goods but nothing suitable for breakfast. They drove into town and parked in front of the City Hall building, it looked architecturally like a miniature courthouse. Inside, past the courtroom, they entered a door marked judge chambers, and Koleka and Coors were sitting on either side of the judge's desk when they entered. Gracie introduced them as if they were strangers, Alec went up to shake hands.

"This is Judge Rachel Koleka."

Koleka shook Alec's hand and then began, "Hi, when I was in my .."

Alec interrupted with "S'nuf," and he then turned to Coors. "So, you must be Tony Coors."

"Yes, I am. When I was in my late teens, I became obsessed with young boys, I can't explain why since I myself was never abused. I didn't wish them any harm, but as twisted as I am I did so nevertheless. I wanted to give them pleasure, I wanted to be the first to see them sexually satisfied. I did this both manually and orally, for some it took two or three sessions to achieve. Then the even more sinister happened, once they were pleased, once I had stolen their innocence, I wanted to be pleased and corrupted them into performing on me. I got away with my despicable acts for about six years before a mother of my next door neighbor caught us as her son was doing this. She .."

"S'nuf, sorry, I .."

"Not a problem."

Alec had intended to dish out a little humiliation, but in fact it was he who was humiliated, none of the other three seemed to think anything of it.

Gracie got back to the point, he grilled Rachel. "Okay, now, tell me what the hell's going on. Alec McNee here says he's here looking for Straw, that you guys came to him, is that right Rachel?"

"Yes, we found out Alec and Straw were connected, we want Straw back. We all know he can't survive for long, something will happen, he's still so unprepared for reality."

"What's different now from when he was sent out?"

"Well, it was clear to all of us that he was hiding something, something he still refuses to face. We didn't think he had confided in anyone so there was no hope for help. But, you know Terry D, they lived together for the last year, Terry says Straw told him something, then swore him to secrecy. We think we might crack Terry if we get him together with Alec, convince him that Straw is in danger."

"Hmm, maybe I should have a talk with Terry D?"

Rachel shook his head. "I don't think that works, Terry idolizes Straw, but not physically as some have thought, he sees Straw as a victim. We already tried to strong-arm him, he wouldn't budge, he has to be persuaded somehow."

"Alec says Straw was kidnapped. You know anything about that?"

"No, nothing."

"Tony, anything to add?"

"Alec brought some pictures of Straw socializing while watching football, it could make Terry D see that Alec and he are friends. We might get through to him using Alec here."

"Alec, you .."

"No clue what's going on, but apparently we all want to help Lu .. Straw."

"You know, I never keep things from Mayor B, not sure I want to start, but he left for a couple of days this morning. Keep me posted."

With that, Gracie left them.

"I met a female the other day who looks like an Amazon, very incredible. But this guy, Gracie, I mean, is that a human being in there, and where did such a monster come from?"

"The hills of West Virginia, maybe Mayor B knows more, but no one else does. The facial pockmarks are from buckshot, the forehead was from a prison fight with a couple of guards, they didn't try real hard to fix him."

Tony lightened it up. "You hungry Alec, we're thinking golf after breakfast, you're a golfer right?"

"You have a golf course! I can't believe the feds would build you a golf course."

"They didn't, we do. A number of years ago it was fashionable for billionaires to build their own executive courses. We had a rich rancher here who built his own, fifteen miles up in the mountains, a fantastic layout. Well, he died six years ago, his widow wanted no part of the course, just the upkeep was more than she wanted to spend. She gave it to the state of Montana, got some kind of huge tax write off. We arranged to get access, we've cleaned it up, it's in pretty good shape now. Sun's supposed to come out later this afternoon, that'll make it playable."

"Sounds good, but I'd rather get this business taken care of."

"We have a date with Terry D at 8:00 tonight. The golf course is a great place to talk business. You in, Rach?"

Trudy's was more active in the morning, the place was about half full. The booths were taken, so they sat with the folks at one of the center tables. Everyone knew everyone, as would be expected, except for Alec, of course. He was

introduced to a couple of the customers, immediately
s'nuffing before carrying on light conversations, no one
probed Alec about what he was doing there. Other than Rob,
who was back at work, there were two other ladies sitting
together who appeared to be a couple, one was petite and
the other very butch in appearance, they kept to themselves
but nodded to Rachel and Tony cordially.

They took two golf carts, the carts were public
transportation, anyone was welcome to take a vacant one.
Tony and Alec followed Rachel north about a half mile to the
edge of town. There was a lot in which about a dozen cars
were parked, they were all semi-antique autobots. These too
were public in the sense that any vacant car could be rented.
They rented a Ford s-u-v and headed north for the thirty
minute trip.

A half mile up the gorge going north, Alec gawked at a
huge mansion on a hill on the left. "What is that?"

"Oh, that's Jessie Tiggers' place, you remember him?"

"Uh .."

"Seven years ago in Texas, the textile magnate, it was a
huge story."

"Ah, Vernon Tiggers. Oh yeah, raped and pillaged
young women and then killed one. He was a devil, what's
he doing here?"

"Don't believe all you read. He spent four years in the
pen, finally got an interview with Ben. Cynics think he
bribed him, they don't know Ben, not a chance, apparently
he saw something. Ben turned out to be right, as usual. Jessie
has been great here, spends lots of money, like building that
place."

"It's impressive, what are they doing on the roof?"

"Decorating, Saturday is Halloween. Two big parties
each year, alcohol allowed, one on the Fourth the other on
Halloween. You should stick around for it."

"Halloween seems like an odd day to pick, why not,
Christmas?"

"Too many depressed people around here on Christmas."

On the way to the course, most of the exchange with Gracie that morning was explained to Alec. Ben Whitlock personally interviewed all applicants to Last Chance, with advice from wardens of mostly federal institutions. Virtually all of these felons had served a significant amount of time, they were thoroughly vetted, Ben could read them better than any lie detector, he would not be fooled.

Marshall Dixon was the exception. He had somehow heard that Ben was recruiting offenders for his penitentiary, and, although he didn't know the particulars, he managed to set up an appointment in Missoula when Ben was traveling through after a recruitment trip. Marshall was out on bail awaiting sentencing after his conviction. He convinced Ben that he was a good candidate, and even though he had served no time Ben signed him up, he had been looking for a lawyer.

When Marshall reached Last Chance the specifics of his court case had been sealed, the victim's name was not published, she was referred to as a juvenile with light strawberry blond hair in the press report, thus Marshall became Strawberry. Straw quickly became the number one resource for anyone in the city who needed legal advice, which was about half the population. What he didn't know outright he found out, he had no restrictions on internet access. It wasn't only other residents who he advised, Ben and his staff relied on his expertise as well.

The dirt road to the golf course was bumpy but passable, mostly up through winding windy hills. The course's clubhouse was originally the rancher's second home, a high-arched, two level, four bedroom, rustic log house. The lower level was now the Pro Shop, payment for a round was on the honors method using a public credit card reader, loaner clubs and shoes were available at no charge. Golf carts were required, the course was virtually unwalkable, long climbs from green to tee through the hills made it so.

A second lower structure that was originally secondary housing for up to twenty guests had been redesigned to hold thirty golf carts in the front, and four livable units in the rear where the course manager and greenskeeper resided. An irrigation system had been installed, fueled by a trickle offshoot of the Missouri river to the north, but many of the sprinkler units were clogged or otherwise in disrepair, some of the fairways and greens were splotchy and baked out.

The course layout, on the other hand, was spectacular, with elevated tees and carries over the top of hills down to the fairways beneath. Swirling winds made playing conditions particularly difficult on many holes, others were protected by the cleverness of the course's design. On the whole Alec was thoroughly impressed. Rachel and Tony turned out to be typical hacks, Rachel had a grooved slice with a maximum distance of about a hundred and eighty yards, Tony a pull hook that went a little farther but had much less control. The two were normally on opposite sides of the fairway, it was good that they drove in separate carts, Alec shared the front nine with Rachel and the back with Tony.

In dribs and drabs he got a more complete history of Luke's final days from them. Over the years Straw began to show signs of anguish, after "The Goddamn Paroxysm" these signs turned into cracks, they became more obvious. Straw had been holding something back and Ben had been fooled. When he served out his sentence a few months ago, he and Ben had an intense consultation where Straw refused to admit or come clean about what was bothering him. Ben was very fond of him, nonetheless he reluctantly expelled him from Last Chance. One of the conditions when transferring here is acceptance that there are no paroles, all sentences are served in full. Most citizens are given the opportunity to stay in the city after their time, they could stay immediately or leave and come back anytime within three months, about half returned. Straw was not given that option. Now, Terry D admits he knows Straw's deep dark secret, they needed to get that out of him, both for Straw and for all who want him back.

The word paroxysm was a new one to Alec, but neither of them would expand on it, apparently, they had decided that it should wait until after the evening conversation with Terry D, the D initial distinguished Terry from two others, Terry the first and Terry S.

It was a good round and a good experience. Alec was the better golfer which was little solace, but he made a few good pars on difficult holes which was gratifying. They all got along well, Alec learned to like them both, it became difficult to realize that they were extremely flawed individuals. Rachel and Tony told a little of their personal history, but it all revolved around their bridge game, a passion for both.

They had already been introduced to the game when younger, but began playing more seriously online nine years earlier. Both had completed their sentences, Rachel six years and Tony five years prior. They had time and permission to travel to some local and most national tournaments, and had good success. They always roomed together, and, for protection, were virtually inseparable on the road, although both thought they had a handle on their predilections. Tony had acquired a master's in business but had not secured a position, he was still working as a bartender when he was arrested. Rachel was a lawyer by profession, family law. As an early settler and the first lawyer in the city, Ben installed him as preliminary judge, he became an official Montana state judge a result of the paroxysm.

Tony dropped Alec off at his residence once they returned to the city, it was now 6:30. He suggested Alec try Maurice's for dinner, in particular the seafood. They were to meet again in Rachel's chambers at 8:00, so he had a half-hour to relax a little, and take a shower and change clothes before heading back out. Prior to going, he checked the Yakback, he had been sent a message but it was unreadable, apparently the city's blocking software thwarted the Yak. There were two golf carts out in front of the bungalow, Alec took the closest, he got a little thrill out of the simplicity. Maurice's was a block north of the courthouse, Alec had seen it when passing that morning.

He added his cart to the numerous collection in front of the restaurant and entered, the place was packed, all of the approximately fourteen tables. He was about to go elsewhere when a couple, one old with gray hair and a goatee, the other younger who looked like his grandkid, waved him over and offered him a seat at their table. Alec was obliged and sat. He quickly s'nuffed both Ms, Mindy and Marsha. Apparently, the two felt privileged to have snared Alec, he was a natural celebrity simply by being an outsider, but he was also known by all, Straw had educated the masses. Mindy recommended the scallops fettuccine, Alec so ordered, along with a cup of chowder and some ice tea.

There was no doubt that the pair was mostly interested in why Alec was there, it was a small town so everyone had an idea, but they were tactful enough to not ask directly. Instead they flattered and asked about his courtroom hijinks. Alec was able to regale them satisfactorily on that topic, after much experience, until dinner came and he was able to eat in relative peace. The dinner was superb, he told the waiter to thank the chef, after which the chef came to the table and was thanked in person, accepting with great humility. When Alec inquired, the chef told that Mr. Jessie owned the restaurant, Maurice was his father's name. Before he left Alec did drop a scrap of news to the clientele, he was there for Strawberry and needed to talk to Rachel and Tony.

Terry D was with Rachel in his quarters along with Tony when Alec arrived. Terry looked like he'd already been through the ringer by those two. As agreed, Alec played the good guy, he showed Terry a video taken by Sy with Max's handheld of the crew watching one of the Seahawk games, Straw was quiet but looked comfortable. He then showed some clips of the Olympia conference, the highlight was Straw vanquishing Shabat Odbayo when going toe-to-toe on a matter of law, they were all amused by that. The formula seemed to be having the desired effect, Terry was more relaxed after seeing his old friend. Alec then got into the reason for his being there, Straw was missing, they were all worried. They implored Terry to offer any help as to what might have happened to Straw, Terry was then given the floor.

"Straw's and me's really good fren's. We ain't fags or nuthin as some's people think's. We's both has the same pra'lem is all with girls, can't fig'er 'em out. Both's us dyin for comp'ny, when's a girl's jus a li'l nice we think's it all love, get's all jack'd up ya know's, like hardon's jus like that. When they's goes ape I goes ape back, I's want 'em and I take 'em, think's they d'serve it fer gettin' me all riled. Thas' how I gets in so mush tru'ble. Straw ain't likes that, he's gets hardon's jus likes me, but he's jus all embers'd 'bout it, would'n never hurt's 'em, tries ta hides it. Gets him in tru'ble anyhows. Those twos in M'sula, theys was fren's. Af'er da pra'lem with da fir's, the sec'on jus mad cuz Straw does da other fir's, thas why shes makes such a ruk'us, Straw ne'er tush'd ne'ther'em."

Terry took a break. Then Rachel asked to see the letter Straw had sent Terry just after meeting Alec. In the letter Straw had told Terry to say hi to Rachel and Tony for him, so Terry was okay with showing the letter. The only real thing of interest was what had scared Straw the most since leaving was tracking down Porter at the middle school where he taught, he was petrified that some young girl might flirt with him. Alec then asked Terry about the secret Straw shared with him, he was worried for Straw, the secret might be a clue as to who took him and why. Terry wouldn't open up, he had promised Straw to not tell. Alec let it go, they talked about what might have happened to Straw for a while, but the meeting seemed to be winding down.

Alec tried some misdirection. "Whatever he told you, I'll bet it wasn't Straw's fault, some young lady probably just didn't understand, young girls can be so stupid."

Terry felt the need to correct Alec, this started the ball rolling. "Wer'nt like that, shes wer'nt stupid, shes was mean."

"Mean, how do you know she was mean?"

"Shes saw Straw's peck'r and shes laughs at 'em, call'd 'em som'in nasy like dweeb I's thinks. Tole 'em shes wan's a good fuck, ev'n from a dweeb likes Straw. Straw try's get 'way, shes grabs em, goes down an suc's 'em off. Gets 'em good an hard then sits on it, pumps up'n'down. He cums, fir's time ever with a girl. He's gets her off 'em, but shes wan's more, calls 'em more names, tries suc him off ag'in. He clim's over da couch to gets'way, she follers but slips on cush'n, back, smacks head on table, dead."

XXX

After Terry D's startling revelation the previous night, they left it like that, they would get together in the morning to discuss ramifications. Gracie showed up at Alec's door shortly before he was going to head out to breakfast. Gracie said he told them to keep him posted, it was time for a post. All three who listened last night had recorded the conversation. Alec invited Gracie in and played him the tape of Terry's statement from his handheld. It was somewhat hard to interpret Terry, Gracie listened a second time. Alec invited him to breakfast but he had to pick someone up at the station.

"Well, did that satisfy you?"

"Hmm, yes, very interesting. What are you going to do about this?"

"I'll keep you posted."

Trudy's was about half full, as it was the day before. The two ladies were sitting at the same table, Alec went over and asked if he could join them, they were happy to accommodate. He s'nuffed them quickly and then asked what they did in town.

"We both work at the bistro, Drake is the tits, I'm Roxy, the bad ass."

"Are they real?" Drake flashed him. "Yes, very nice. I'm surprised they let you tease the men like that, doesn't it cause problems?"

"Nah, plenty of porn at the library for them. Anyway, celibacy is not mandated. Why you sitting with us anyway?"

"I'm tired of talking to men."

Alec ordered bacon and eggs, they continued with double entendres as best they could, the girls remained until he finished eating. They invited him for a free tomato juice that evening.

He wandered back to the courthouse and Rachel's chambers. The door was unlocked, Tony was the only one there, sitting at the judge's desk reading a document. He handed it to Alec. "I found this in Rachel's file cabinet after he asked me to dig it out, it's marked confidential. Not sure who wrote it, maybe me since I was told to report on the events, or maybe it was Rachel. Here, take a look."

Alec read the report.

Zeke knew there was something wrong the minute he came in the door, he smelled alcohol. There were papers strewn all around the living room, and a chair overturned in the dining room. A letter was open on the dining room table, Zeke picked it up to read, then he heard noises from the bathroom and Percy came stumbling out. "Well, the fucking, fairy, fruiter, fucking faggot is home, hooray — wha' the hell are you lookin' at!"

Zeke was stunned, they had been lovers for over two years and Percy had never so much as raised his voice. "What's going on, what's wrong Perce?"

Percy was a big man, he stumble-rushed over and backhanded Zeke across the face sending him sprawling over the table. "Thas' a pers'nal letta, none or yer bisses, you fucking faggot."

Percy grabbed the letter. "Tha' shudda been me, I d'serve it, she was pure, inna'cnt, why not me, or him, he jus' like me, shudda been him."

The big man attacked Zeke now, he picked him up to knock him back down, over and over. He ripped off Zeke's jacket and shirt, pulled off his own belt and began whipping him with the belt ripping up his back, all the while wailing "shudda been him."

Percy bent a now unconscious Zeke over a chair and yanked down his pants, then pulled down his own pants. He penetrated Zeke mercilessly with vicious force repeatedly, all the while yelling and pounding on his head and back.

Later, after Percy was spent and tired he lay on the floor crying. Then Zeke made a moaning sound which reawakened Percy, "Oh, ya ain't dead yet, you fuck, we kin fix that faggot."

He repeated the assault and rape a second time with equal vigor. Gracie arrived as Percy was still at it, Percy went after Gracie with a wine bottle. He was big but no match for Gracie who soon had him cuffed to the kitchen table while he took Zeke off to the doctor. Zeke was as near death as a person can be, he needed more care than the locals could supply. An emergency medevac was sent from Billings, a hundred and fifty miles away, it lifted him off. He was in Advance Care Hospital for six days before he expired.

How to handle this paroxysm was a dilemma for Ben Whitlock. Other minor spats had resulted in expulsion of one or both of the participants, but this was the first serious criminal activity that had taken place in Last Chance. He eventually decided it would be best to send Percy to the state detention facility in Deer Lodge, and have him put on trial there. He knew the warden well and was hopeful that the incident would not draw undue attention. This hope was dashed however. Percy had been crazy on cooking wine, stolen from the Mandarin restaurant where he was a chef, and a half-full bottle of antibiotics, left over after a respiratory infection, when he went ballistic on Zeke. Imbibed while depressed over a letter received describing the rape and murder of his nineteen-year-old daughter, the apple of his eye.

Percy was now ballistic and suicidal about his abysmal

behavior toward his good friend and lover. He wanted to die, he demanded death, he would shout and scream and attack until he got it, and he knew that wouldn't happen in a state penitentiary. Ben believed him, he was concerned this would expose Last Chance in the worst possible light. He sought advice from the DOJ, they could see the potential embarrassment as well. What they eventually concocted was a seminal event in the history of the city, more accurately the beginning of the city. Last Chance was to become an incorporated city of Montana, the trial of Francis, aka Percy, Castle would take place there. Judge Luftar Koleka and attorney Marshall Dixon were pardoned by the President, their licenses to practice law were renewed, and Koleka was appointed a state judge of District 16 by the governor.

All of this took time to accomplish, a little more than fourteen months. Percy sat in a Last Chance cell all of that time, until that time no one had ever spent more than one night. At no time did he lose his desire, he attempted suicide a couple of times at the beginning, but once the date was set for a trial he settled down, he thought a legal hanging was what he had earned. The point of the trial was not about guilt or innocence, Percy had pled guilty at the pretrial motions, it was all about sentencing. No one in Last Chance wanted to be a juror, a random drawing was held, the civil rights of the twelve losers were restored by the DOJ in order to allow them to sit in the box. Percy had waived his right to a lawyer, he would defend himself, and he was the most ardent witness for capital punishment. The only witness other than Percy, Gracie testified about the brutal nature of what he saw and heard, including Percy's stated intent to kill Zeke.

Marshall wanted no part of being the prosecutor, he knew the sentiment of the jurors was against the death penalty, and he himself was against capital punishment for any reason, he didn't want his name associated with it. He petitioned and was granted a sealed motion to legally change his name, he would be Lukas Schmidt as the prosecuting attorney. Nevertheless, his final arguments were persuasive, and he went through the legal history of capital punishment with precision, connecting it to the rape of the victim as the most egregious of crimes, and those most deserving a death sentence. The jury was out one hour, they came back with the death sentence Percy demanded, Judge Luftar Koleka determined that the decision of the jury was reasoned and appropriate. As was the verdict, carrying out of the sentence was also swift, no appeals were requested, Percy died of a lethal injection one week later.

Rachel had come in while Alec was reading, he let him finish at his leisure. "Straw was never the same after the trial. Conflict and hardship were second nature to most of us, he was really still a neophyte in many ways, at least we all thought so. That tale by Terry D last night was a real shocker to me."

There was a noticeable pause until Alec inquired of Rachel, "My handheld doesn't work in here, I haven't been able to get online. I'd like to check out the article you mentioned on Straw's Missoula conviction, any way I can do that?"

"Ah, sure, I guess so. Look, Tony and I are headed up to see Jessie Tiggers, he has some ideas about the party tomorrow he wants to talk about. You could go to the library and get online, but the restrictions there might block a lot of what you'd be looking for. I have total access, you can use my desk. Tony, show him."

Alec walked around as Tony got up and let Alec sit. He pulled the screen out from under a panel of the desk. "Be careful if you look at email, they can have attachments you wouldn't notice at home that ring an alarm here, and don't send out any, nothing can be sent."

Alec played with the computer for a bit. "Okay, thanks, Rachel."

Rachel and Tony then took their leave.

Alec was anxious to find Lukas's trail to Missoula, he began by searching the Missoulian newspaper website starting twelve years earlier. Within five minutes, he found the article with the strawberry blonde reference. It contained what he was looking to find, "The defendant has been a Missoula public defender for the last three years."

He went back an extra five years and scoured the northwest newspapers for unsolved murders, after another five minutes he found this headline on the Tacoma Tribune website. "Young Woman Found Raped and Murdered." An audible "Oh no" slipped out as he read. He found a few more related articles and printed them out to read in full, after which he sat silently pondering for about five minutes. He then woke up and checked his email, then current events.

XXXI

Roscoe had known Joanne Arnold for twenty years while they each became successful in their respective fields, they had shared many stories and not shared just as many, but they were cordial most of the time. There were other times like the current one where they did not get along, however Joanne's threat to ignore Roscoe was idle, it didn't last a day.

She strode into the squad room just before 9:00 on Tuesday and approached Roscoe. "Well, did you read it?"

"And what uh would that be stranger."

She dropped a copy of her morning article on his desk, he read it casually, the gist contained in this blurb " .. Lukas Schmidt is still missing, but he may be in hiding as he is a confirmed sexual predator. His associate, the well-known activist Alec McNee, is now also in hiding after giving false testimony to both the authorities and this reporter."

Roscoe pushed the article aside and went back to the report that he was typing when she came in.

"What, nothing to say, don't you want to comment?"

"Uh, me?" He pointed to Grumpy's office and looked away.

"Come on, Rosc, talk to me."

"Why, looks like you've got it uh all figured out."

She gave him an exasperated look. "Okay, Jojo, here's uh some advice. You were right about uh the brass being up here about this, but that's all you're uh right about. This may uh indeed become a big story, but if you continue uh to write trash like this you'll be on the uh wrong side of it."

"What's the right side then, where did McNee run off to?"

"You uh interviewed McNee before, didn't you. You think he's uh a liar? If you'll wait, I'll give uh you what I can, otherwise .." He again pointed to Grumpy.

Joanne returned to see Roscoe later that afternoon. She showed him her paper's link to The Olympian website where Senator Walt Purser was quoted saying Alec McNee assaulted him in an Olympia restroom when he questioned Mr. McNee about his relationship with Lukas Schmidt, the now known serial rapist, who was representing Mr. McNee in his lobbying activities. Alec's picture was included in the article.

"So, what, you uh now think he's a psychopath too?"

"Come on, Rosc, give me something to work with. I don't believe that bull, but .."

There was more the next day. The stories had spread to other northwest newspaper websites, including the Billings Gazette. A waitress in Blue's BBQ near Billings was friends with a local reporter who was a regular. She told the reporter that Alec had been in the BBQ two days before. The waitress was able to prove her point by showing a clip of Alec getting into a Bubblebot, taken from the restaurant's outside surveillance camera, both Alec and the license number of the autobot were clearly visible. This began a flurry of activity in eastern Montana, an enterprising student identified that Bubblebot vacant in a Bubblelot in Miles City, a hundred and fifty miles east of Billings.

Joanne was back in Roscoe's face on Thursday, showing her paper's link to the Billings Gazette website which was more than glad to print the story. "Well, surely you're going to check this out, Roscoe."

"Why's that, Jo, as far as I uh know McNee's not a suspect in anything?"

"Because the boy's in Montana now, he's surely on Schmidt's tail."

"I uh know where his is." She gaped at him. "Let me uh ask you, Jo, how do you uh know Schmidt is a sexual predator, and uh confirmed to boot, who confirmed?"

"I have a reliable source, Roscoe."

"Bullshit! But I will uh be a source for you on this point. Mr. uh Schmidt was found guilty of a sexual indiscretion, but uh that does not make him a predator. Now, I don't need uh these daily rants of yours, I told you to uh wait it out, that's it. Bye, Joanne."

Joanne Arnold did listen to Roscoe, she did hold off. However, others did not, the story was beginning to go viral. Alec already had made enemies of many, now that he was consorting with a sexual predator people started listening to them. Drones looking for him were disappearing throughout Montana, since Alec was a known enemy of drone surveillance he was suspected of creating his own cult with a base in eastern Montana. Conspiracy theories of all kinds materialized.

XXXII

Alec scanned the internet for another hour, then found a golf cart and drove the half-hour up to Jessie Tiggers' mansion. There were three cars and ten other carts in the looped driveway, he could see at least six people decorating the house on this chilly windy day. The roof already sported two witches on brooms, most of the windows were covered with cobwebs, carved pumpkins were scattered all over the porch, and skeletons hanging here and there. A heavily tattooed man on the porch waved Alec to the back, he walked around expecting to see a massive swimming pool, there wasn't one, but there was a sculptured Greek goddess pouring water from a pitcher over the head and back of a cherubic infant, the water cascading into a three-tiered fountain. Workmen were building a dais on the massive hardwood patio which surrounded the entire back of the house.

From the patio Alec looked up, Rachel and Tony were sitting one floor above in front of a large picture window, when they noticed him they waved him up. Alec found the back door and negotiated his way through the huge house until he found an open stairway, by the time he climbed the stairs he had lost his direction and another worker had to show him the way.

Rachel introduced Alec to the third person sitting there, not seen from below, Jessie Tiggers. Jessie was a few years older than Alec, mid-forties, with a full head of light brown hair, sideburns most of the way down his checks which met his bushy mustache at its tips, and sharp green eyes with a prominent jutting chin. He wasn't large but had a large personality, mentally very quick.

"I was born with a silver spoon, my father left me a small fortune when he died, I was only twenty-two. With sublime luck, I converted the small fortune into an immense one, everything I did turned to gold. I owned professional teams in baseball and hockey, they nicknamed me Malachi. I felt like a god, and acted like an anti-god, particularly with women. They gave themselves to me and I gave them gifts, I raped them with their consent. The daughter of one of my hockey team's coaches had the misfortune to make my acquaintance when I was partying one evening, she was adorable and innocent, I a narcissistic beast. I raped her, she was not one I raped with consent, she pleaded with me to stop, to no avail. After I was satisfied, I discarded her like she was trash, threw her into my swimming pool from the upstairs deck, I had done this many times. Only this time I slipped and she fell short, her head smashed onto the edge, she died from the fall.

"Even though I was completely guilty, I fought the accusation and conviction with appeals for over two years before I was finally incarcerated with a sentence of twenty-five years for manslaughter and rape. Prison was the hell I deserved for about six months, but by greasing as many wheels as I could it eventually became bearable. The warden could see that I was being pampered, so he transferred me to another prison, and again for about six months it was hell. I managed to get an appointment with Ben Whitlock, I had heard about him through the grapevine. I tried to bullshit my way through, a colossal mistake. He told me if I ever wasted his time again he would have me sent to the armpit of the world. Two years later I managed a second appointment. This time I passed the test, I didn't deserve it, but at least I was as honest as I know how to be."

"S'nuf."

"Thank you for listening, most people don't, maybe my

money still gives me the perks I don't deserve. Alec, I no longer bullshit anyone, I believe in admitting weaknesses and trying to overcome them."

"Ah, yeah."

"Okay, sorry, I'll get off the soapbox now. I want you to know that I admire you greatly, Straw kept me up .."

"Jesus, he got to you too."

"Straw and I are buddies, he gave me some excellent legal advice, I would have rewarded him but, not allowed here. I see you're back in the news, it seems you're now a villain."

This was news to Rachel and Tony, they were brought up to speed, and were not liking it.

Ben Whitlock never fraternized with his minions at the yearly parties. Rachel, Tony and Jessie had been plotting how to get Ben to tomorrow's Halloween party, they wanted to pay tribute. Alec's latest attention in the news was giving Rachel and Tony cold feet, Ben was going to be furious about it, and furious with them for their complicity. Jessie decided to put a temporary halt to that discussion, he invited them all up the canyon to his ranch for a prime Angus steak dinner, they had butchered four steers about a month ago, they should now be dry-aged perfectly. He had a mount for each in his stable, he suggested they ride the ten miles on horseback, all three declined that idea. They did agree to dinner though, at the mansion, so Jessie called the ranch and ordered four porterhouse steaks to be delivered.

The DOJ had leased a large mostly unpopulated piece of property from the State of Montana fifteen years earlier when Last Chance was first proposed, Jessie had managed to sublease a big block of property that was not in use for the cattle ranch. He owned his own massive ranch in Texas, he imported a hundred head of his finest to the Last Chance Ranch. He was negotiating with the state of Montana to acquire the rights for acreage four times what he currently controlled, although the legalities were a potential fatal encumbrance. Jessie was ever the entrepreneur, he was expounding on his plan to build a leather tanning plant in the town, not only for processing his hides, but for those in all of eastern Montana. It is a dirty and pollutive process, but modern technology had solved most of the environmental problems.

He was starting in on his beef jerky plans when Alec interrupted, "Sounds like you're still building your empire."

"Oh no, no. I'm a simple employee now, just making wages. An LLC has been created which actually owns everything, it's a special arrangement. When things go well, like with Maurice's, they are happy to take over, when they don't go well they were gambling with my money, I lose." Jessie laughed jovially at this.

The steaks had arrived from the ranch, it was cooked up by Jessie's personal valet, Alec enjoyed the finest steak he had ever eaten, a one-course twenty-four ounce meal. After a needed respite, they began the next day's plotting once again.

Friday morning, Halloween, was Alec's fourth day in Last Chance. He decided to take a closer look at the place. He took a cart into town and walked up and down the two blocks that constituted most of the business section. He found that there was a second breakfast cafe where he stopped for his normal breakfast from home, three sausage, three scrambled eggs, and an English muffin. He had no trouble striking up a conversation with the locals, it was sort of fun to be treated like a celebrity. He had run out of cash, in the real world it was used rarely, but here it was still normal. Only credit cards from the US Bank of Last Chance were honored in the town, no bonus miles or other perks were offered with them, the residents preferred money.

He stopped in the bank not long after it open at nine. The one teller was able to give him cash from his private card, the first he had seen in two years, he also offered Alec a fifty dollar bonus if he would open a new account, not everyone recognized him at least. The library was next door to the courthouse, although Alec had not until then been inside. It was modest in size, about one third displayed books, another third movie and t-v videos, and the other third pornography. The only other two patrons were unabashedly perusing that third third.

At just before eleven, he once again entered the judge's chambers, Rachel was there browsing the internet.

"Anything new?"

"Oh yeah, all over, security says they set a record for downed drones."

"Good there aren't any manned ones."

"There's plenty of manned drones, mostly news, but they pay attention to the warnings, the ones who don't are quickly scared off. It won't go on forever though, one will go down pretty soon, then more publicity. What a mess you've started."

That was worth a look but no comment from Alec. "Where's Tony?"

"Don't know, probably up with Jessie, the party's already started up there."

"Really, they're drinking already?"

"Nope, bar opens at four."

Not everyone was allowed to drink, those who were each had a designated chaperone. When the chaperone cut them off, that was it for the drinking, many a verbal disagreement ensued but no one had dared break the rules.

"So, everything still a go?"

"Guess so, Ben's coming in at 4:30. Gracie's sheriff car will be there waiting. Nervous? You should be."

Alec went back to his bungalow, he packed his bags, planning to leave early the next morning. He tried the Yakback one more time, but received and sent the same garbled messages.

At 4:40, Mayor Ben Whitlock was carrying one suitcase as he descended the stairs at the train station. He looked as Alec expected, purposeful, driven, not tall but stocky like a fireplug, short reddish hair and rugged face, ready for battle at any time. He tried the passenger door of Gracie's car but there were two bags in the front, the driver waved him to the back seat, which he entered.

"What's that shit up there, where the hell is Gracie?"

"Marshalling the Halloween party."

"Oh, I forgot, that fucking party, I shoulda nixed that idea years ago." He looked more closely at the driver. "Who the hell are you?"

Alec turned and looked back at Ben through the protective window, then he locked the back doors.

"Hey, what the fuck you doing douchebag, open that goddamn door." He looked a little closer at Alec. "Who the fuck are you? I don't know you. Hey, you're that fucking asshole, the dipshit causing all the goddamn trouble. What the fuck, how'd you — you better let me outta here buddy, I'll fucking castrate you, you sonofabitch."

Alec rolled down the window slightly and slipped the article about Lukas's conviction in Missoula back to Ben, who glanced at it. "Yeah, I've seen this before, dipshit, now open that goddamn door, I can't wait to get .."

Alec had started the end of Terry D's audio statement, Ben was still shouting obscenities but eventually began to listen.

Alec slipped back the two documents he had copied off the internet the previous day, he then re-played Terry's statement from the beginning as Ben read. Ben eventually sat back and absorbed what he had been given.

"You're right, I am the dipshit who's causing all the trouble, but you're the one who started it, when you sent Straw out of here without helping him."

Ben had settled down by now. "Okay, dipshit, okay. Now, let me out of here, let's talk about this."

Alec started the car and began to drive off.

"What the hell you doing now asshole, where the hell you going?"

Alec drove up to Jessie's party while Ben started to get re-charged, yelling and threatening. But when they were within sight of the mansion and all the partying going on around it he became a little desperate. "Oh, no ... don't take me up there, buddy ... I can't go up there ... please son, don't do that."

Alec turned back to him. "They all know what you're all about, let them see it Ben."

"I can't do that, I can't."

To no avail, Alec drove to the back of the house and parked next to the patio. All the revelers had seen them coming, they started yelling and clapping in unison. "Big Ben, Big Ben .."

Alec unlocked the doors and waited. Ben eventually bit the bullet and got out. To the first person he saw, he yelled "Okay, get the fuck outta my way, Nelda." but Nelda didn't move, he laughed and yelled with all the rest, "Big Ben, tough love Ben, Big Ben, tough love Ben."

Ben tried to shove his way through, but they all got in his way, then someone poured a bottle of champagne over his head, he finally succumbed and fell down on the ground in submission, they stopped yelling then. Instead they took turns hugging and thanking him until he eventually started to sob, and couldn't stop. When he was given all the love the crowd could muster without getting too over the top, Gracie came over and pulled Ben to his feet, he ushered him back to the car, they drove off to a standing ovation.

The party continued until midnight, though they didn't run out of booze no one was drinking at the end, all had been cut off. Alec left at ten, even more of a celebrity than before. Prior to departing he got a look at the show Drake put on, he had talent, and he could twirl his tit-rings in both directions at the same time.

Roxy had just come out of the house and motioned him over. "Looks good, don't she?"

"Yes, she does, makes me want to check out her box to see if there's really something there. Doing some pretty good business tonight."

"There's somethin' there a'right, and you somethin' too, you look good enough to eat, come on back, let me do the bizness with you."

"Next time .."

XXXIII

As arranged the previous evening, Alec met Rachel and Tony at 8:00, once again in chambers, Gracie invited himself. They were all smiles, the bulk of those aimed at Alec, even from Mr. Stoic, Gracie. The highlights from the party were recapped with relish, Alec amused them in particular when describing meeting Ben and the drive to the mansion. They wanted Alec to stick around for another day and entertain and be entertained by the rest of the inhabitants, but Alec was steadfast that it was time to go. They checked and found Ben in his office, all four went to visit him.

"Well, I have a good mind to send you all packing. In particular that asshole renegade who has no business here in the first place. You three, leave me alone with the sonofabitch."

The words were right, but the emphasis was much weaker than typical. They were no longer reluctant to leave Alec alone with Ben Whitlock.

Alec took the lead. "You know that whole party thing was nothing to do with me, that .."

"I know that, they've been trying to roast me for years, it took a stranger to trap me though, none of them have the balls for it. I think I'm getting too old for this."

"Not too old, but perhaps less able to change than you need be. I think you can see that change is inevitable. This place is going to be exposed, one way or another."

"Yes, thanks to you."

"And to you."

"I suppose, that stuff you showed me was .."

"Straw is surely innocent, both in Missoula and before. You couldn't help Missoula, but if we can track down Straw you can help going forward. Don't you think it might be time to go public with this place, it's not like five years ago with that catastrophe."

"It's not my decision."

"Bullshit, your legacy is assured. The guys at DOJ are sheep, they need to be led, you've been doing that for fifteen years now."

"How do you get off talking to me like that, dipshit?"

"'Cause I'm leaving in about thirty minutes."

"Says who?" Ben cracked a delayed smile.

"If I get the name of a good reporter who will be fair, will you talk to him?"

"A reporter .."

"Yes, reporter. I keep telling you, no more hide and seek. You want to get your story out first, before all the distortions make the truth of this place more difficult. Will you at least think about it?" Did his silence imply consent, Alec wondered.

Alec asked if it was possible for him to communicate to the outside, he showed Ben the Yakback.

"Let me look at that. You've been using that in here, haven't you? Security has been going ape trying to stop it and figure out where it's coming from, what is that thing?"

Alec showed it to Ben and told him how it worked, but he was not allowed to use it. Ben did let him use his personal outside line, however, under supervision. Alec called Roscoe at SPD, it was Saturday and Roscoe wasn't there, but he did get Beverly on the line. He told her to get Roscoe to Max's house by 11:00, he would call there, they would want to answer.

He said his goodbyes to Rachel and Tony. Tony told him that they could play bridge in a team game sometime with Judd, "Judd said you're good player," but Alec didn't know what he was talking about.

Gracie took him to the train station at 10:00, he carried both bags to the departure platform, and shook his hand warmly as he left. Ben had been generous when they parted, he gave Alec access to his autobot parked near the train station exit, Alec could take it to Billings and then send it back, it would be easier to avoid detection that way. The train ride going took the same fifty minutes as coming. He felt strange when he disembarked, back in the real world, but somehow less secure. Alec found the autobot at 11:03 and immediately called Max, Roscoe was waiting.

"Great to hear from you, boy, we were really worried."

"I'm good, had no problems."

"Well, what was going on there, what's it like?"

"Roscoe, I'll be glad to tell you all about it when I get back, but we have some business right now."

"Okay, okay, shoot."

"Schmidt's real name was Marshall Dixon." Alec gave him all the details of Marshall's conviction in Missoula. "I'm about the same distance east as you are west of Missoula. Can we meet there? Schmidt was no doubt not guilty of the crime charged. I'd really like to have this behind us before .."

"I'm not going to Missoula, what are you talking about, before what?"

"Wait, is Muscles there, way better idea."

"Yes, but she .."

"Hey, hi Bev, you want to meet me in St. Louis, uh Missoula?"

"Alec, you .."

"Do you trust me, Roscoe, do you trust me. Roscoe, do you?"

"Go on, spit it out."

"I'll tell you, but you have to promise you won't move until I get back."

"I can't promise without .."

"This is fifteen years old, okay, there is no rush. I trust you, Roscoe, if you say you'll wait for me, I'll believe you."

"I'll wait if I can wait, that's the best I can do without knowing what the hell you're talking about."

"Okay, Roscoe, I trust you to do the right thing."

Alec played Terry D's statement. Then, he told Roscoe the specifics about the articles he had found.

"So, you know why I want you to wait, right?"

"This is great work, Alec, great. Yes, I know, I'll see what I can do."

"Are you coming to Missoula, Muscles?"

Alec heard talking in the background for about a minute, then Beverly answered, "Yes, if we can get a meet set up with Detective Brisbane."

"Great, can't wait to see your smiling face. One more thing, Roscoe, do you know a reporter you can trust?"

"Why would you want to talk to a report ..?"

"Who's conducting this interview! Are you able to answer a simple question?"

"Okay, a reporter. Uh, your buddy Joanne Arnold, I guess."

"Really. I don't think so, she started all this shit."

"Only because you, that is, we lied to her. She stopped when I asked her to."

"Okay, I trust you Roscoe, you are trusted. Give her this number, 406-396-0352, she will owe you big time. One more thing, will you call Angela Nelton and tell her to Yak me asap. Hey Max, go Seahawks, sorry, will miss the game tomorrow."

Angela called about five minutes later. "Hi, Angie."

"Alec, oh, I was so worried, nothing from you all week, are you okay?"

"We aren't skyping, but your face is lighting me up through your voice. Yes. I'm good, never had a problem."

"Where are you?"

"Eastern Montana, around Billings. I'll be home tomorrow afternoon."

"So late, come on home now, you can come over, I'll cook you dinner."

"If you want to cook dinner at my place, that would be perfect, sleeping in my own bed, with you. Are you up on etiquette in the use of the "L" word? I'd like to use it, but I want it to sound sincere, can I use it now or should I wait till I see you?"

"Oh, you can be so .."

"Hold that thought — I'll wait then. I have a meeting in Missoula late this afternoon, and I think I'd rather sleep there tonight, the reporters may still be around my place. I need to see you tomorrow, you promised I could see you getting out of the tub naked."

"Tomorrow, well .."

"I wasn't very clear. I need to, as in must, see you and your brother on Sunday, somewhere private, maybe his, no, your house. I need to see you and your brother, Sunday, 4:30, at your house."

"Need. And Corey. This sounds mysterious."

"A great word for it. A better word would be urgent, much better. I am quite serious."

"I don't like this at all."

"I don't either, and you are right, you won't like it."

"God, you're awful, I was so happy to hear from you, now .."

"See you tomorrow, participation is not an option."

The ride from Billings to Missoula was uneventful. Alec had seen numerous drones circling between Miles City and Billings, but Ben Whitlock's autobot was inconspicuous so it drew no attention. Roscoe had taken possession of Max's Yakback, Alec called to talk to Roscoe a couple of times, a meeting was scheduled with Alec, Beverly, and Detective Brisbane in the Missoula downtown PD at 4:30, Alec programmed his Bubblebot rented in Billings accordingly. Roscoe also reserved two rooms at the Missoula Radisson for the night.

Alec was napping when his autobot dinged the two-mile to destination bell, it was 3:57 so he had a few minutes to spare. He stopped at a takeout for a small chili and a cup of coffee. He arrived at Detective Brisbane's office at 4:27, Beverly was already there talking to the detective, she introduced Alec. Not atypically, Brisbane was impressed, Alec was notorious by now. And typically, when Beverly explained why they were there, he turned to Alec.

"What the fuck are you doing here?"

Alec was going to respond in kind, but Beverly knew when to take charge. "Mr. McNee has been assisting our investigation, he is the one who uncovered indirect testimony that leads us to believe Mr. Dixon may have been unduly prosecuted."

"Bull, indirect testimony from who. He looked about as guilty as a man can look. Both girls said he molested them."

Beverly contested, "Both. In their original statements they used the word molested?"

"Well, okay, I've pulled the charts. The first girl we interviewed, actually the second girl he molested, Victoria Walsh. No, she didn't say molested, flashed, she said flashed over and over. The second girl, Tandy Mitchell, she said flashed and molested. The first girl said molested at the second interview. Anyway, he never denied it, his lawyer pled him out. Unlucky for him the presiding judge was string-em-up Rupp, Myles Rupp gave him the max."

Beverly was forceful in stating that Marshall Dixon was now under investigation by the SPD, they wanted to pursue a revisit of this case immediately, they were hoping he could help them without going through all of the paperwork and review that a formal request would necessitate. All they wanted was to re-interview the two ladies. Brisbane agreed to help. One of the now women was still local, the other in Texas, but they had contact information for both. Even though the next day was a Sunday, he would see to it.

Alec and Beverly met for dinner at 7:00 in the hotel restaurant, after they had checked in and had a little time to relax, and they were both relaxed and congenial at dinner. Alec plied her with wine as he delighted her with tales from Last Chance. Taking their victim's name, the Fahrenheit 451 analogy of men reciting their sins, the meeting with Warden Ben, the dinner with Jessie Tiggers, and Drake and Roxy, all delighted Beverly through the telling. Toward the end of the evening, he took advantage of her good humor by getting personal.

"Beverly, I asked Roscoe earlier if he trusted me. Do you trust me, Bev?"

She didn't know where this came from or where it was going, she glared at him.

"I want you to do something for me, Bev, but you'll need to trust me. Do you?"

"With what?"

"It's scary. Probably the most scary thing you've ever done."

In bed at eleven, he yakked Angela, and she answered. "Hi, Angela, just called to tuck you in."

"You .."

"I'll sing you a lullaby. Rock a bye baby, in the tree .."

"What's this about tomorrow?"

" top, when the wind blows, the .."

"Is this about Walt?"

"Walt?" Alec blanked momentarily, then remember Walt Purser.

"Did you really punch him out?"

"Walt? Oh, you and Walt, and Corey intro'ed you, didn't he?"

"Alec, please."

"So you think I'm out beating up your old boyfriend? Is this before or after he was an asshole?"

"He's always been an asshole."

"Okay, then. Are you all tucked in yet? I just called to say goodnight and tuck you in. Rock a bye baby in the tree top, when the wind blows .."

"Goodnight." She hung up.

XXXIV

The Seahawks were playing the 49ers at home this Sunday morning, game time 10:00. That was the same time Alec left Missoula, he decided to take it slow and listen to the game going back to Seattle. He had originally planned to go home to Haller Lake, but instead accepted Roscoe's invitation to stop in Duvall, they would be traveling together to Puyallup later in the afternoon. The Hawks were beaten badly, their first bad loss and third loss on the season, they were dropping back in the pack in the standings.

Alec was dropped off in front of Roscoe's house at a little before 2:00. It was a rustic old rambler, very likely the residence of the original owners of the property, but very well-kept. It was a cool, gray overcast day, but the clouds were high so there was little chance of rain, the sun could be expected to peek through in about four months. When he knocked Roscoe's wife, Rosalie, opened the door. No doubt her race designation would be black, but very light-skinned who had taken the best physical assets out of whatever the mix, jet black hair with a thin face and round nose and lips that worked well together.

"Hi, I'm Alec McNee, you must be Roscoe's daughter Mahalia."

Rosalie smirked a smile, "Rosc said you had a bit of the devil in you. I'm Rosalie, come on in."

She led him into the kitchen where Mahalia was reading a computer screen at the kitchen table.

"Say hello to Alec, Hallie."

She looked up briefly. "Hi."

"Hi, Mahalia." Alec walked by her and noticed what she was reading. "Edgar Rice Burroughs, he's like ancient, is that a Tarzan book? Isn't there something a little newer than that around?"

"It's not Tarzan. Anyway, he's a real great writer, all you get now are stupid comic books."

"Hallie wants to be a writer. Roscoe's at the back plantation, I've made up a lunch for you guys, come on."

Alec said see ya to Mahalia, then followed Rosalie out the back of the house for a couple of hundred yards through a copse of alder and maple, to some new construction. The foundation, framing and roof were in place on the large two-story house, but no siding, doors or interior wallboard as yet. As they entered the open front doorway Alec could see Roscoe on the second floor tape-measuring walls.

"Alec's here, Rosc, come on down for lunch."

She put her bag down on a table fashioned from a pair of rough sawhorses and a sheet of plywood, there was a pitcher of ice tea on the table and three stools surrounding it, this was not the first meal in the new house. Rosalie laid out tuna sandwiches and coleslaw, then made an exit as she called to Roscoe, "I have to take Hallie to the Franklins, she's spending the night. Nice to meet you Alec."

Alec smiled a goodbye. Roscoe limped down the center stairs and into what would be the kitchen.

"Hi, uh Alec, made it okay then?"

"Hi, yeah. What you measuring up there?"

"Oh, they uh just put in electrical this week. Think uh they messed up the virtualart wiring."

"Whoa, virtualart, the latest and greatest."

"This place uh isn't for Rose and me, uh building it for Junior, and maybe Hallie later. Private driveway and uh all, he wants to stay uh around here after school."

"Jesus, you are not in your element at home, you look twenty years older, limping and stuttering around here."

"No, you're uh wrong, this is my uh element. Old

accident, they tried uh to eighty-six me couple times, I been hiding my uh ailments at work, but don't uh have to 'round here."

Roscoe went back to his house and changed clothes. Before leaving, they chatted for a half-hour, and another hour on the drive to Puyallup, mostly talking about strategy, and some about Alec's exploits during the past week. Beverly called to tell them that both young women had cracked and recanted, the first, Tandy Mitchell, when Brisbane and Beverly visited her in nearby Orchard Homes. Alec could only imagine the impression Muscles made when meeting face to face. They interviewed the second, Vickie Walsh, via skype, she stuck to her original statement briefly until told of Tandy's admission, then she too broke down, admitting that Marshall never actually touched her. Both cried outright, blaming the other vociferously.

They arrived at the Rasmusson residence right on time, extra was allotted for Seahawk game traffic, they had needed it. Roscoe dropped Alec off at the curb and waited while he walked up and was admitted into the house, then drove off. Alec and Corey had become friends, they shook hands amicably, he and Angela kissed lightly on the cheek. They led him to the living room, but Alec didn't want to sit back in comfort, so he steered them instead to the kitchen table where he sat across from them.

"I better start with you Angela, I had totally forgotten about Walt Purser's fiction in the newspaper, this has nothing to do with that prick."

Corey was surprised at this, "You mean this isn't about your fight with Purser?"

"No, it isn't. Nothing so frivolous as .."

"Frivolous, you were in Olympia as my guest, a physical confrontation is anything but that. You don't seem to .."

"Okay, Christ, do we need to talk about this now?"

"Yes, I think we do."

"Okay, quickly, I ran into the prick after Angela left me

in the cafe down there, he gave me some shit for no reason whatsoever, I followed him back to his office, but he went to the restroom. I got in his face, he got scared and threw a punch, he missed. I shoved him against the wall and told him what an asshole he was, something we all agree on. That was it, end of story, okay. Now, we need .."

"You never hit him, then?"

Alec was almost apoplectic by now. "Shit! I've got it on tape, okay, here I'll play it for you"

"You can't make tapes in a restroom, it's not legal."

"Yeah, but I got one anyway, I turned on my handheld when I followed him, didn't know .."

"You shouldn't even admit having that."

"You want to hear it or don't you!"

They did. It wasn't really clear what happened, but it was clear no blows were struck.

Alec was finally able to get to the point. He directed a question at Corey. "How well did you know your other sister, Crissy?"

They both looked at him in amazement, affronted. Alec waited on him.

"What in the hell's that to you!"

"The police have been courteous enough to allow me to talk to you first. If you don't want to talk to me, I'll call in Detective Roscoe Romar to talk to you, he's waiting outside with some of your locals, would you prefer that?"

Now they were downright stunned.

"Police .."

"Police, yes, police, okay, let's do this first, your sister died in the summer house in the back, isn't that right?"

He waited. "Wake up ... wake up ... you need to talk, there are no other options."

"Uh ... yes, in the back."

"Has the place been used much since then? Corey, speak."

"Ah, no, never, I don't think anyone's been in there in

fifteen years."

"Good, thanks, do you have the keys?"

"Uh, sure."

"Will you authorize the police to search your summer house? They can't if you don't authorize, otherwise they need to wait for a subpoena."

"Search it, why?

Alec took a few seconds. "I guess I'm not doing this right. Okay, I better call in Romar."

Angela broke in. "No, don't do that, I'll get the keys." She found them in a cabinet over the sink and brought them to Alec.

"Good, now, do you authorize the police to examine that summer house tonight?"

Angela said yes, Corey mumbled something, then also said yes. Alec hit a button on his handheld, and twenty seconds later there was a knock on the door from Roscoe.

Alec went down and handed him the keys. "It's a go."

He went back to the kitchen. "Are you guys still in shock? Are you ready to talk now? Okay, Angela, I'll ask you. How well did you know your sister Crissy?"

"Well, she was six years younger, you know. I loved my sister, but .."

"What was she like?"

"She was a daddy's girl, my father doted on her, she was a lot like him in many ways."

"Was she shy, or timid?"

"No, she wasn't that at all."

"Would you say she was experienced for her age?"

"Yes, I would. What's this?"

"Okay, I'm going to play something for you now, it will be confusing so I'll play it again, and then maybe we can talk about it. You too Corey."

Alec played Terry D's statement for them. Before he played it a second time someone called his cell, and he answered. "Okay, nothing." He emitted an extremely relieved exhale.

Angela asked, "What were you expecting?"

"I wasn't expecting anything, but I was afraid they'd find the dead body of Lukas Schmidt."

This gave all three something to think about. He played the tape two more times.

"The person you heard, you don't need to know who that is, was relating a confession made to him by Marshall Dixon, aka Lukas Schmidt, aka Straw. He was describing the events around your sister's death. Can you tell me if your sister is capable of that activity?"

Angela didn't hesitate. "Yes, she was, I loved my sister, but she was very brazen."

"Corey, what do you think?"

"I wouldn't think so, Angie knew her better. She was a bold girl, though."

"Corey, I love your sister, but I have to ask. Angie, you told me once that you thought Lukas reminded you of someone, did you tell anyone else that?"

"Ah, I don't think so."

"Yes, you did, you mentioned something like that at dinner here a few weeks ago. Didn't you?"

"Did I, well, maybe .."

"Who else was here that night?"

"Only the three — oh my god, oh."

"What?"

"She has dementia you know, it's getting worse Corey. Lately she's been saying things like "what would your father do?" She stopped me on the stairs yesterday and asked, "Where's Stanley, why doesn't he do something?" Stanley was my father."

Corey finally got the picture. "I was going to come here for dinner last week, but had to cancel. When I called her, she said, "You're the head of the house now, you've got to decide." I had no idea what she was talking about."

"Well, we have to talk to her, is she home now?"

"Let me go up, I'm the head now."

When Corey left them Alec went over to Angela, she looked at him and started to cry, he held her close.

Corey came down ten minutes later, he said little other than that she had been talking a lot to her brother, Brooks. Angela described Brooks as two years older and in worse shape than her mother. Alec got his address, he lived nearby.

Roscoe, Detective Ron Hershey of the Puyallup PD, and Alec knocked on Brooks Nelton's door ten minutes later, his wife, Vivian, answered and led them to Brooks watching t-v in the living room. Roscoe asked to see Lukas Schmidt. Books answered, "Sure, he's downstairs," and took them to a locked utility room in the basement, they found Lukas unconscious, weak, starving, but alive, he was taken to the emergency room of Good Samaritan Hospital.

XXXV

Stanley Rasmusson and Brooks Nelton were childhood friends, and juvenile delinquents, Stanley was the bold one of the two. His first real job was as a truck driver for a local brewery. He managed to buy a neighborhood bar when the owner died suddenly and his widow wanted a quick sale. He kept his connection with the brewery and eventually bought a distributorship, and then another, until he became a major distributor for all of greater Tacoma. Brooks was his second man all this time, he took over the alcohol business while Stan moved into food, he acquired contracts from major supermarket chains and the warehouses to supply them. Some of his tactics were challenged along the way, but he managed to avoid any major legal pitfalls. He married Brooks' sister, Miriam, and raised his family in nearby Puyallup.

One of the two newspaper articles Alec had printed out from the judge's chambers described the murder and rape of Crissy Rasmusson, the details and timing convinced Alec that this was Marshall's waterloo. The second article was about the same acts, but from the perspective of Stanley Rasmusson, he vowed that he would have vengeance for his darling daughter, no matter how long it took. He greased the hands of certain persons who would see that through. Marshall was almost snatched in Missoula a couple of years after the tragic event, he had been tracked there, but they lost his trail when he was suddenly waylaid by Ben Whitlock and taken to Last Chance.

Stanley had drilled into Miriam that she was to tell him

or Brooks about any new face that popped up, it was an obsession with him. Likewise, he drilled it into Brooks that if anyone looked suspicious he was to call Donnely at the union hall. So when Miriam heard about the quirky guy Angela described, she told Brooks, Brooks called the union hall. Donnely was long gone but whoever answered read the situation and got through to the right people. They checked out Lukas and recognized him. Their instructions were to package him up and deliver him to either Stanley or Brooks who would take care of him, they delivered Lukas to Brooks who couldn't even take care of himself by this time.

The authorities arrested Brooks for kidnapping, they took him into an interview room and grilled him for only about an hour. It became apparent early on that he wasn't attempting to hide anything, his memory was shot. He recalled talking to his sister, and calling the union hall, but not who he talked to there, and he didn't know the two gents who dropped Lukas in his lap nor why they had done so. It was they who locked him in the basement, Brooks had brought him food now and then, but didn't know what else to do. He was waiting for Miriam to get Stanley to tell him what to do but she wouldn't tell him. Brooks was arraigned and released on bail Monday afternoon.

They would interview Miriam at her home on Monday morning, she put up the same resistance, a lack of memory. She couldn't find Stanley, she wanted to get her son to tell her what to do, but he was always too busy. This interview was also quick and non-productive.

At 10:00 Sunday night, the hospital made it clear that Lukas wouldn't be available to anyone until sometime the next morning. Alec hitched a ride with Roscoe back to the Rasmusson residence to see Angela, and to let her know what had transpired at the Nelton residence. Corey and Angela were both still there dealing with their mother who had come downstairs to complain about all the people milling around in the back yard. Alec got them up-to-date on what happened after he left earlier, they had talked to Vivian but it was still another shock to realize that their uncle had been arrested. Corey managed to come back to life, and thanked Alec profusely for the way he handled the situation, to that point in time no one from the authorities had even talked to him, he was anxious to keep it that way. Alec managed to get Angela alone and asked her to come home with him, but that was not going to happen and he knew it. He decided it was time to go finally home himself, it had been a long time.

The Bubblebot dropped Alec at home at 11:30, the media were nowhere to be seen, perhaps they had given him up for dead. The house was cold when he got there, he jacked up the temperature in the bedroom to seventy-five. He took a bath about once a year, this was that once. He filled the tub with near scalding water, so hot he had to inch his way in, toes first, and slowly slide in the rest of him until his body got used to the heat, then he laid back and soaked for about half an hour, occasionally tapping in a little more hot water. He then toddled his overheated body into his overly warm bedroom and splayed himself out under the bedcovers, he was sleeping soundly within minutes.

It was a raisin breakfast and a rowing boat workout in the morning before Alec made his way back to Puyallup in his Tesla. He wanted to be there when Lukas came to. At the same time, the forensics unit scoured the summer house to try to determine the actual events of that fateful day fifteen years before. The reports from the original investigation did not reflect what the newspapers had written about it. That the girl had sexual intercourse was not in doubt, but there was no indication of a struggle or rape. Forensic study of sexual assault cases had become a near exact science. Marshall's fingerprints and DNA had been found in various places in the house, the door handle, a glass, the couch cushions and back of the couch, also on the back of her head and on her left shoulder. None were found on the victim or her clothes in places traditional for rape, her chest, waist or thighs, her blouse, pants or panties, other than the semen from her vagina. The conclusion at the time was that there was no rape, murder, however, was not ruled out. Nothing found this Monday morning contradicted that original opinion.

Lukas was fed intravenously as he slept through the night in the hospital. He woke up at 11:00 the next morning, he was groggy and confused. Alec was there by then, they let him visit but he was advised to keep it simple, not discuss the events that got him there. Lukas was unable to focus, in any event, he drifted in and out of awareness throughout the day. Alec decided to stick around Puyallup until Lukas was out of trouble, and until he could tell him what had transpired. He was deluged with mostly unaffiliated paparazzi whenever he was recognized, so he reserved a room at the local Marriott for two nights in order to have refuge. Angela managed to find time to visit that evening, although she left early to be home for her mother's bedtime.

The next day, Lukas was somewhat more aware, Roscoe and Detective Hershey interviewed him for a short time, they asked about his abduction. Lukas had little memory of it. He had bought a gun at a pawn shop, he had never held one before, because he was worried about his safety. He was eating a small bowl of cereal before going to bed and heard the intruders at his door, he got the gun from his computer desk. When they came in the door, he fired one shot into the ceiling to try to scare them away, they rushed him and the lights went out. He never looked at them, could not possibly recognize them. The next thing he knew he was lying on a cement floor and an old man was untying him. The man left him a bowl of soup and then locked him in a strange room full of mops and tools. He drifted in and out of consciousness for about a month, occasionally, there was a little food, but mostly he was hungry all the time. That was it for that day's interview.

Joanne Arnold was rewarded beyond her dreams for listening to Roscoe and biding her time. On Monday morning she called the number given to her of Warden Ben Whitlock. She had no idea what to expect from the call, what she got took some time to interpret. That first call was somewhat brief, but once she processed it she got very excited. She called him again the next day for more, and then set up an appointment to go to Billings to meet him in person. Ben had received the okay from DOJ to open up, they realized that the cork was out of the bottle and decided that Ben was as low key as they could go.

She also called Roscoe on Tuesday, in part to thank him for the number, and to get more background on Ben Whitlock. She was surprised to find him in Puyallup. When she found out why he was there, that Schmidt had been found and McNee had materialized to make the find, she immediately headed there to get some interviews.

Her first was with Roscoe that afternoon. He told her the basic facts as he knew them. Brooks Nelton had been arrested in connection with the kidnapping of Lukas Schmidt, or Marshall Dixon, his birth name. Schmidt had been involved in the death of Crissy Rasmusson fifteen years earlier. McNee had found this out after interviewing a federal inmate, and McNee had tracked down the kidnappers. This was plenty for Joanne to start with, but he cautioned her not to duplicate past mistakes and make assumptions about these facts, she would be very unlikely to get it right. He also told her that Alec McNee would be available for an interview the next day, which kept her juices flowing.

Lukas was much more lucid on the third day, the detectives questioned him at length beginning with the death of Crissy Rasmusson. Lukas didn't know how they found out he was involved, but he wasn't surprised, he knew someone would find out eventually.

He had met her at a bookstore, she said she knew who he was, how smart he was, she asked if he would help her with her math. She drove him home. It was a big house, there was a second smaller house behind it where they went. He was very excited, he had an erection even before they went in, she didn't notice. She got him a glass of coke, and they went over to the couch.

He didn't know what would happen, but he exposed himself, he wanted to show what her beauty and love did to him. She laughed, called him names like a dirty horndog or something, said she didn't think it would be that easy. This turned him off completely, he attempted to cover himself but she pushed him back on the couch and went down on him, sucking his unit. He was appalled at first, but not for long, he began enjoying the sensation without reservation. At one point she stopped and removed her clothes, then went back to it. After a bit she stopped again, got up and sat on him, she began gyrating and told him to work it, work it. It didn't take him long to orgasm, he shrunk down and slipped out of her, then laid back on the couch to relish the moment.

She would have none of that, that wasn't nearly enough for her, she started down on him again, but he wasn't ready for that. He squirmed away and tried to escape over the back of the couch. She climbed up to pursue and grabbed him, but he shook loose and fell over the back of the couch, he saw her lose her balance on the cushion and she fell backward at the same time. It took him a second to recover, then he headed for the door, but when he looked back he saw her still lying there. He went back to her, she was face down between the couch and a metal framed glass coffee table, there was a big gash on the back of her head, she had apparently hit it on the table. He turned her over. He had never seen unresponsive, rolling, dead eyes before. They have haunted him ever since.

He ran, looking over his shoulder, expecting the police at every turn, three miles to his parents' house where he filled a suitcase and told them he would be back in a couple of days. Then, he got a bus ticket to Spokane, then to Chicago, but he stopped in Missoula, Montana.

They went through three or four iterations, but the basic story stayed the same. Now he was in Missoula, so they pressed him on what happened there. He had passed the bar but he would need to be fingerprinted in order to get a license to practice law, he was afraid of doing that, his prints had been left at the scene. He rented an apartment, he lived cheaply, and put an ad in the local paper as a tutor for English and math. He decided early on to turn down most requests from young women, still he managed to eke out a living for a couple of years.

When two young ladies taking the same class came to him, he thought that safety in numbers would keep him from getting in trouble. On the third appointment, one of the girls showed up at his apartment at 1:00 instead of the 3:00 agreed upon time, Lukas was sure that it was intentional. He got an immediate erection and showed it to her, he was not averse to receiving the same treatment as happened at his first ill-fated encounter, but it was not to be, she shrieked and ran out of the building.

At 3:00 the other girl showed up and the episode repeated itself, only she went to the authorities and complained. The first girl joined in on the complaint, both said he molested them. He felt so embarrassed by their complaints, and by the fact that forcing himself on them had actually occurred to him, that he had trouble defending himself. He felt guilty so he would plead guilty at his arraignment.

While waiting to do so, he overheard another defendant talking to his lawyer about an interview that afternoon with a man who offered him entry to an alternative prison. Lukas asked his court appointed attorney about it, his attorney found out the man's name was Ben Whitlock. Research was Lukas's forte, he had little trouble finding Ben Whitlock at his hotel and introducing himself in the lobby. Ben took an interest, he was looking for a lawyer. When Lukas was sentenced to twelve years at Deer Lodge Penitentiary he was instead sent to Last Chance, Montana.

Media stories of all kinds with very little truth to them continued to hit the internet. After Joanne Arnold's article on Wednesday, the media went ballistic. Many didn't believe he was now in Puyallup, they were still looking in eastern Montana. They doubted the federal inmate fiction so they played up the rape and murder. Many more people seemed to want to believe in conspiracies than in the facts that Joanne presented, conspiracies were rampant.

Joanne met Alec on Wednesday in his hotel room. He allowed her to take his picture, but would not allow the interview to be videotaped. Alec began by apologizing for lying to her a few weeks before, he had been trying to downplay the kidnapping at that time, she pooh-poohed the apology. Alec asked her if she had contacted Ben Whitlock, she realized it had been Alec who sent her the phone number. He then explained events not unlike those Roscoe had given the day before, but with a little more human perspective.

He had gone to the federal penitentiary at Last Chance over a week ago to try to find information about Lukas Schmidt's disappearance, he thought it possible that Lukas was in fact at Last Chance, he did not reveal who had told him about the penitentiary. He spent four days in Last Chance, he declined to comment about the conditions there or the individuals he met. He eventually met the one person who knew about Lukas' past. According to this witness, the conviction of Marshall Dixon for molestation in Missoula twelve years earlier was based on fraudulent testimony.

Detective Brisbane of Missoula, who investigated the original complaint, had reopened that case, even though Marshall Dixon was pardoned by the President of the United States for that offense.

Marshall's past connection to the death of Crissy Rasmusson was able to be identified after the inmate's disclosures. Crissy's now deceased father, Stanley, consorted with certain individuals to pursue the person responsible for his daughter's death until he was found. Those individuals, still unknown, recognized Lukas after he visited Olympia with Alec over a month ago. They kidnapped Lukas some time later, and delivered him to Brooks Nelton, Stanley's partner and brother-in-law, per Stanley's request before he died.

Brooks is an old man with dementia, he was not a participant in the kidnapping and, in his condition, is not responsible for the poor treatment Lukas received at his hands.

As to the death of Crissy Rasmusson, after hearing the testimony of Mr. Lukas Schmidt, and re-analyzing the forensic evidence found on the site, everyone involved believes it will shortly be determined an accidental death. Lukas is not totally innocent, he did leave the scene of a fatal accident, but he was not complicit in the death of Crissy Rasmusson.

This was the basic story Alec wanted to give out. Joanne went on to question him at length about details, how he got around, where he stayed, dates, times and so forth.

Alec had visited Lukas numerous times throughout the week, he was finally given permission by the authorities to tell Lukas what he'd been up to for the last two weeks. Lukas went through the gamut of emotions as he listened. Amazement at how Alec had gotten into Last Chance, gladness at the things said by his fellows there, laughter at the meeting of Ben Whitlock, disappointment tapered with understanding for Terry D, eventual relief that all was apparently now behind him, and tears when thinking about all that Alec had done for him. He couldn't thank Alec enough. He steadfastly refused to testify against his abductors, even though his testimony didn't affect whether or not charges were brought.

After Joanne Arnold's Thursday article written about the interview the day before, Alec became even more of a cult figure. For some he was a hero, others didn't believe a word of it, to them he was the ultimate villain.

Joanne managed to keep her appointment with Ben Whitlock in Billings that Thursday. She tried to get in to see the place for herself, but he would have none of that. On Friday, she wrote an explosive expose about the secret penitentiary at Last Chance in Montana, and the purpose for its existence. It was a massive story, not only the fringe but every legitimate reporter in the country was all over it. The court records about the case of Percy Castle's murder of Zeke Jester, to date ignored, and Percy's subsequent execution were sensationalized. As expected, a great many people considered the prison barbaric and suggested the inmates were being dehumanized, despite DOJ's steadfast defense of the prison. It was a political nightmare for the President who was credited with being the driving force behind the penitentiary's implementation.

XXXVI

Alec made the call on Friday afternoon. "You get the package I sent?"

"Yup, delivered it to the bungalow myself two days ago."

"And?"

"Sent Gracie down to check it out, haven't seen them since."

Alec talked Angela into going home with him on Friday evening, he didn't have to talk too hard. Corey and Angela had hired an in-home nurse to take care of their mother. On Sunday morning Alec and Angela drove to Puyallup, he dropped her at her house then went to the hospital to check Lukas out. There were media types out front, but Alec had cased a rear entrance that was unwatched, he managed to get in and out with Lukas without detection. He went back and picked up Angela.

The three of them made it to Max's just in time for 1:00 kickoff of Seattle at Denver. Lukas was back, the Seahawks triumphed. It was the grandest of football parties, Lukas, Alec and Angela were all celebrated. Alec handed Sy a package put together by Roscoe, Alec hadn't opened it but was told it contained all data that could be found about Sy's father and all other family members. When Alec and Angela left late in the evening, they brought Lukas with them, he would spend one night at Haller Lake and then be off to Last Chance on Monday morning.

On Monday, Alec received a call from Spencer Dawes,

he asked Alec to join him at Sig's place the next day, it was agreed to meet at 10:30 on Tuesday. Alec was followed everywhere now. He parked a few blocks away in the Regrade and walked to Sig's, his followers would have to guess exactly where he was headed. Sig was remarkably gracious and apologetic, very unlike his nature.

"I need to apologize to you, my boy, I doubted and bet on the wrong horse."

"That would be the snake, Walt Purser."

"Ah, yes. He came to me and told me the two of you had met in Olympia. That you cursed me because I wouldn't give you the help you needed. He played me, and it worked for him. I knew you held something back, I thought this was it. I told him to plant that story on the web. What can I say .. Why didn't you tell me you met him in that restroom?"

"Which time?"

" Which, you mean .."

"I stopped in to see him last week. Did you know it is illegal to tape conversations in a public restroom? We had a nice chat, I think we came to a complete agreement." Alec was rubbing his knuckles as he talked.

"We've created a monster here, Spence. What are we going to do with him."

"Whatever he wants Sig."

Alec agreed to be interviewed on a national daytime syndicated news show, he appeared the following Thursday. The moderator's goal was to capitalize on Alec's notoriety, he diverted all of Alec's answers toward that goal, what Alec had intended to say never got said. It was a ratings success, but Alec considered it a complete waste of time. He negotiated another interview, this time in prime time Sunday night. He did so with the assurance that the interviewer would allow him freedom to talk about some specific topics.

"Sexual deviants are the scourge of society, the majority

relish in their depravity. Minimum sentences and parole are much too good for most of them, they deserve the harshest treatment allowable. None of these felons reside in Last Chance Penitentiary.

"There is a minority of sexual offenders who are ashamed of their behavior, they recognize that they are flawed and not fit for society. Every inmate or citizen of Last Chance admits their flaws, is as repulsed by them as are we all. The warden of Last Chance combs the prison system for inmates who can still contribute to the greater good, he deserves a Congressional Medal for his work, not the congressional witch hunt currently being espoused.

"The people he recruits are not evil, they are sick and they know it. Other than being isolated in this remote spot in Montana, these citizens of greater Last Chance, Montana are free. There don't live in cells, there are no bars, and they all have full-time employment. They pay their own room and board, they pay taxes, they function as normal citizens. There is no crime to speak of, although the one aberration that has grabbed the headlines did occur. No one so much as locks a door in the city. Victims of these citizen inmates have been compensated at five times the rate of other felons.

"I am the only non-inmate in its fifteen years of existence who has spent time in Last Chance. It is a splendid place and completely safe. That's because the citizens do not live in fear, as they do in normal society. Not fear of others, but fear of themselves. There are no temptations for them in Last Chance, no children to abuse, no women to rape, they don't need to be stressed out about their deviant tendencies. Half of the citizens prefer to remain in the city after their time is served, they know they're safe, and they don't know they won't relapse somewhere else. I implore you to not let the naysayers have their way. Do not undo what is a shining example of penal brilliance."

Ben Whitlock didn't retire as warden and mayor, but he

did scale back and quit his recruitment activities. He had lost the killer attitude necessary in dealing with the twisted characters he encountered. And he found an ample replacement for this burden. Beverly "Muscles" Koenig retired as an SPD detective, she is now the only female resident of Last Chance, Montana.

Epilogue

Alec and Angela had spent a couple of days snuggled away at Haller Lake, before the press got so thick they could no longer bear it. They quietly spirited away for a week's vacation to the Bavarian town of Leavenworth in central Washington, just across the Cascade Mountains. Alec was not a skier but Angela was, he took her to Stevens Pass in order to admire her form on the slopes, she looked her name, angelic, like an oread, ever the mountain nymph.

Shortly after returning from the mountains, Alec was whisked away to the east coast, where he spent a whirlwind few months. He was in great demand after his stint on the t-v talk shows. His notoriety made him a popular draw at political gatherings and universities. Lukas and Spencer had thoroughly prepped him in the legal history of the penal system, so he became a formidable opponent for the clever young law students he faced. Unlike his previous such endeavors after the court case, he was now the headliner. His purpose was not to cash in as before, although the money was nice, he was a true believer in the efficacy of the penal reform displayed by Last Chance.

Congress, originally in an uproar over the sensationalized headlines, eventually held hearings, as they are wont to do, which actually toned down the rhetoric. Ben Whitlock was grilled for two days, first before the House and then the Senate, but it was Alec who received the most ink in the press. The media couldn't get enough of the speculations about his mad dash across the west coast in pursuit of the sexual deviant, Lukas Schmidt. Lukas was also subpoenaed by Congress, but he was safely tucked away in Last Chance, Ben would not allow the subpoena to be served.

After pressure from Congress and the DOJ, Ben

eventually was forced to allow a small delegation of lawmakers to tour Last Chance. They arrived unannounced, the residents were not unduly disturbed. Private and confidential interviews were conducted with many of the citizens, including Lukas, Rachel, Tony, Jessie Tiggers, and others. Congress concluded that no course of action would take place immediately, they would study their findings and come up with recommendations in due course.

Lukas had settled back into life in Last Chance, after the initial tumultuous reception he received. He was soon hard at work catching up on the numerous legal matters pending for the inmates that had been neglected after his departure, no suitable replacement had been found. Rachel was supposed to take up the slack, but he was inherently lazy. Lukas also kept in contact with Spencer Dawes, plans for campaign finance legislation were still going on in Olympia, there was always more preparation needed for eventual litigation.

After the initial trial residence, Beverly Koenig realized that it did not work being a female living in Last Chance. Ben Whitlock knew this all the time, he only allowed it to cater to Gracie, his most trusted anchor. She did relish the role of recruiter, replacing Ben in that capacity, but she wound up renting an apartment in nearby Miles City. Gracie had not completed his sentence so could not join her there, but they did continue with conjugal visits.

Alec returned home a couple weeks before Christmas. He and Angela spent some quiet time at his Haller Lake condo, the press had finally abandoned it, before the parties started. He brought Angela to meet his sister and mother in Stanwood on Christmas Eve. On Christmas day they partied with her brother and family at his house in Puyallup. Four days later it was Seahawk playoff football at Max's, they had managed a winning record and squeaked into the playoffs as a wildcard team. They won the game against the Buffalo

Bills 23 to 17, they would play another day.

The biggest party, and the grandest time they had, was the New Year's Eve party at Rick Kirby's, Alec's best friend. All the football clan was invited and showed up, including Sy, along with Corey Rasmusson and a few other political personalities, including the larger than life Nigerian, Shabat Odbayo. The most surprising and appreciated guest arrived with Max, none other than Lukas Schmidt. Well no, no longer Lukas, another legal name change back to his original Marshall Dixon.

Great stories were told, and embellished. Almost everyone had a Lukas/Marshall story to tell, including Shabat. Shabat and Marshall somehow had become good and reciprocal friends. However, the story that got the most laughs was initiated by Angela when she related the tale of the naked nubile. She had called Alec in the evening at his hotel in Washington DC after an event at nearby Georgetown University. A young woman answered the phone .. Alec interrupted her, he was embarrassed, he had no idea Angela knew about this episode. He tried to end the story, but that wasn't going to happen, so he took over the telling. When he returned to his hotel room and went into the bedroom there was a young woman, naked, lying in his bed. He tried to usher her out, but she was having none of it. So, to avoid attention, he simply left her there, went to the lobby and checked into another room, that was all there was to it. This elicited disbelief by everyone, and endless queries about the young lady and her attributes. Ever tasteless, Max blurted out "he never passed up a piece of ass in his life", crude for this crowd, but it brought the house down.

The Washington State Legislature began work in the first week of January. Corey Rasmusson wasted no time in entering the proposed legislation "Constitution Amendment to Limit Public Financing of State Elections" on the Wednesday of that first week. He explained the purpose of the legislation in a ten minute speech, and encouraged the Legislature to fast-track debate on this important legislation. Some of the opposition party was privy to the proposal, but most were not. Over the next few days the ramifications of the bill gathered a great deal of attention, both statewide and nationally. The die was cast.

Sig had called a meeting for 10:00 Saturday. Alec picked up Marshall who had been staying in Alec's old room that week, Max's second bedroom. They arrived for the meeting just before 10:00. Spencer Dawes was there already. They exchanged greetings, praised one another appropriately, and then got down to business. The State Attorney General and Sig had been in close consultation for quite some time. The opposition would be fierce from the federal government, implementation of the proposed amendment would fly directly in the face of current law concerning federal elections. Both major political parties, the DNC and RNC, had now been put on alert and would also strongly contest. A showdown in the Supreme Court seemed inevitable and Sig wanted it to happen as quickly as possible. It was not yet clear whether these potential legal proceedings would happen directly after passing by the Legislature, they were all now convinced that this would be accomplished, or whether it would wait until later in the year, after the State Amendment was adopted by the citizens, not something that they were quite as sure would happen.

Sig was sending Marshall, from now on to be identified as Mars Dixon, to Olympia to monitor all the proceedings and report back anything of interest. He would stay with Shabat Odbayo at his Nisqually residence, only twenty minutes from Olympia. Shabat was duly aware of Mars' proclivities, he guaranteed that there would be no incidents. Mars normally wore contacts, he would trade these in for thick glasses and wear a baseball cap, it was unlikely that he would be recognized.

Spencer would wait for the events to unfold, and then be

available to confront the legal battles that brewed. For early stages this would probably be limited to assistance to the Attorney General. Mars would be brought back to assist Spencer.

Alec was also sent to Olympia. He would mingle and slap backs. But his main job would come later, he would be the face of the effort to convince the populace about the merits of the amendment, his baby. This is where Sig's war chest would be spent, it was projected to be the most expensive battle in the state's history.

Alec was once again the first to arrive at Max's for a football game. He sat outside in his Tesla for a few minutes, remembering how he had sat in that spot for the first game of the season, and marveling at the turn of event since then. The Seahawks would be playing the Super Bowl runner up from last year, the Miami Dolphins. After the game he would drive to Angela's new apartment in Olympia, he promised he would be there to see her disembark from the bathtub. He wondered which of the two events he was most looking forward to … No he didn't.

ACKNOWLEDGEMENTS

As the author, I feel a need to thank everyone who takes the time to read this novel. Thanks go to my editor, Theresa Wyne, who showed me many of the errors in my way of doing things, and put up with my obstinacy. My daughter, Little Heather, took care of all the details getting this thing published, I am most appreciative. My sister, Marian, designed the cover and graphic artist Brandon Garet at ZGFCCC put it all together.

W. T. O'Brien

.

ABOUT THE AUTHOR

W. T. O'Brien has written short stories and screenplays, *Strawberries Are Free* is his first novel. Prior to being a full time writer, he has worked at an extensive number of occupations from which to draw ideas. O'Brien is a lifelong resident of Greater Seattle, now living just north in Mountlake Terrace, WA. He enjoys his large family living in the surrounding area.

www.ingramcontent.com/pod-product-compliance
Lightning Source LLC
Chambersburg PA
CBHW071131170626
46809CB00002B/566